Memoirs of a Switch-hitter

A Novel

George Beatty

ISBN: Softcover   978-1-9845-7709-2
            eBook   978-1-9845-7708-5

Print information available on the last page.

Rev. date: 02/28/2019

To order additional copies of this book, contact:
Xlibris
1-888-795-4274
www.Xlibris.com
Orders@Xlibris.com
790329

Credits and Disclaimer

The Turing quotations on pp. 204-205 come from A. M. Turing, "Computing Machinery and Intelligence," *Mind,* Vol. LIX, Issue 236, pp. 433-460 (October 1, 1950). They appear here by permission of the Oxford University Press. The yin-yang image on the front cover is in the public domain, courtesy of pixibay.com.

Real people, institutions, works of art, books, theatrical works, and movies named or alluded to in this novel are ones I regard highly. The rest of the novel is pure fiction. In particular, everything that happens or is said here, the thoughts and opinions expressed here, and the institutions I have named Hanson Country Day, Devon Academy, and Salisbury College, are all products of my imagination, as are all references to real persons like Melinda Gates and real institutions like Harvard and MIT. Any similarity perceived by the reader between real events, statements, thoughts, opinions, or institutions and my fictitious ones is unintended and coincidental.

G.W.B.

Publications by the same author:

Skellig Michael, a novel.
Washington, DC 1944-2044, a novella.
Argentina Revisited: The White Gate, an essay.
Fishing at the End of the World, an essay.
The New Forest: Penn's Woods Revisited, a poem.

For Eric, Ned, and Julia

Preface

At 94 I feel old, almost beyond caring. No one here at Wildwood will miss me when I'm gone; deaths are an unremarkable, almost routine, occurrence in a retirement community like this. Since there's nothing I could do at this point that might make a lasting difference to anyone or anything I care about, I occasionally think about ending the charade of living. I see no reason why suicide at my age should be frowned on by society—or by God, if one exists. We're all bound to die sooner or later; why needlessly prolong life when there's nothing left to live for?

The temptation to cash out gets stronger as I lose interest in pastimes I used to enjoy. When I first came here about four years ago I read constantly, savoring classics, devouring current fiction. Now it takes me two weeks, rather than a day, to read the latest bestseller. Same thing with puzzles. I used to enjoy timing myself to see how long it took me to complete all the puzzles on the back pages of the Sunday *New York Times Magazine.* Now, I rarely do half of them. Worst of all, I seem unable to rouse myself to go fly-fishing. For many years my principal activity—some would say my preoccupation—has been fly-fishing, but it's

October now and I haven't opened a fly box since I came back from Iceland in early July.

I suppose that what's kept me going—made me resist the temptation to call it quits—has been my pervasive stubborn streak. As a child I was obnoxiously stubborn, constantly refusing to obey my parents, whom I neither liked nor respected. A few days after my 20th birthday, I turned down my first job offer—a lucrative one from a high-powered Silicon Valley firm challenging Google—because I was unwilling to work on a major programming initiative suggested by my prospective boss, an overbearing samurai. I was convinced that I was smarter than he was, and believed my proposal for approaching artificial general intelligence was much more promising than the one he was determined to take. That same stubbornness, just as strong now as it was then, tells me that I should hang in here instead of taking the easy way out by killing myself.

Instinct tells me that I need to get involved in something new and different. Writing my memoirs may be just the ticket.

I think I'll wear bifocals as I look back on my life, recording what I see from two perspectives. Chapters dated before 2095 will be the work of an omniscient narrator reporting what I and others said and did back then; chapters dated 2095 or later will reflect my current thoughts and recollections. Writing about certain events from different temporal points of view will, I hope, more than compensate for the occasional repetition that doing so entails.

1: Wildwood at Lenox, MA – 2095

My earliest childhood memory is nuzzling Ellen's neck. It was warm and smooth, what I'd describe today as a safe haven. I didn't realize it then, but she was both my nurse and my protector. I dimly remember that she'd pick me up whenever I was cranky, cradling my bottom with one arm, wrapping the other around my back, so that I nestled against her chest with my head resting on one of her shoulders. Sometimes she'd sing softly, sometimes it was just a quiet 'shush, Fran, shush.' She told me years later that she fell in love with me around the time I turned three.

I think I was four when she taught me to read. After listening to *Good Night, Moon* several times I discovered that I could recite most of it from memory, which made "reading" a simple process of connecting what I saw on the page with the sounds I already had in my head. And that was basically Ellen's method of teaching me. She never complained when I pestered her about odd spelling. Why isn't laugh spelled laf, I wanted to know; how can bow and bow sound different and have different meanings? It became a game we played, calling out to each other whenever either of us spotted a word or phrase that seemed contrary to normal rules or common sense.

The computer was next. I took to it immediately and spent hours exploring the web, teaching myself all kinds of things: how babies are made and born; why the sun rises and sets and sometimes gets blocked out completely; the way to do simple arithmetic and use the magic "x" of algebra; and how to play double-deck solitaire and other card games.

When I turned five and Ellen took me to get tested for kindergarten, they weren't sure where to put me because they'd never had anyone who knew what I did about computers, or had learned as much from them as I had. Ellen said the two of us would talk to my parents to see what they'd like to do. Weird as it sounds, that was going to be a first for me—my first real conversation with both my parents together.

I knew my father worked in advertising, at a place called Becker Dickson in New York City, but he never talked about it to me and I didn't ask. All I really knew about his job was that he rarely got home before I went to bed. On the few occasions when we were together he remained silent unless he thought I was misbehaving, in which case he would bark at me to finish my vegetables, or be quiet, or stop doing whatever else it was that displeased him. From what I could see, he treated my mother the same way. So she made her own life, going by herself or with friends to museums, the theater and opera, and various charitable events, some of which I think she helped to arrange. I thought she wasn't interested in me at all; I was surplus baggage to be handled by Ellen.

When the four of us finally met to discuss my schooling, my parents talked over my head for the first five minutes, as if I weren't in the room. I stood up and started to walk out in disgust. "Sit back down!" my father yelled at me. I did, scowling straight at him. For thirty seconds no one spoke. Then my mother proposed that Ellen tutor me for the coming year, at which point I'd be enrolled at Hanson Country Day in whatever grade the headmaster thought best, considering all aspects of my "development." My father said nothing, but nodded. I was thrilled by the prospect of being with Ellen for another year, and willing to take my chances after that. I smiled broadly at her, turned to my mother and said OK by me, and walked out of the room without looking at my father.

2: Darien, CT – 2007

"Sydney, I don't know what we're going to do about Fran."

"What you're going to do, you mean; I'm through, I've got enough problems at Becker, Dickson."

"Be reasonable."

"I've been reasonable for seven years now. I'm through with this whole goddamn mess."

"Sydney, that's not fair. I can't do it on my own; I need your help. We're in this together."

"The hell we are. Godammit, I married you, didn't I? That was my part of the bargain. Preserve your reputation—not raise the kid—that's what I agreed to do. Of course, I'll pay the bills. But everything else is up to you."

"You're sleeping with Arlene, aren't you?"

"Arlene has nothing to do with this."

"I think she does. Your hotshot younger partner at Becker, you're on the road together all the time; don't tell me you're not sleeping together."

"All right, we sleep together. This house could be a monastery. What am I supposed to do, be a monk for the rest of my life? No thank you, Barbara."

"Well, I'm sorry I no longer turn you on the way I did when we conceived Fran. But you don't even give me a chance. Every time I make a move toward your bed you turn your back on me. Regardless of all that, Fran is still our child and I need your help dealing with—"

"The kid's our child because you told me not to wear a condom. You decided that, Barbara, not me. This whole damn business—our marriage, the kid, everything since—is because you wanted my bare cock so badly you begged for it."

3: Wildwood at Lenox – 2095

Being tutored by Ellen before I started at Hanson Country Day was one of the happiest times of my life. She knew almost everything, it seemed. Geography; the stars we watched at night after the neighborhood lights went out; how to say hello, goodbye, please, and thank you in a dozen different languages; you name it, she knew it. My favorites were the Greek myths and stories we read out loud to each other, particularly the *Odyssey*. Odysseus was my all-time hero, the wily warrior who could fool the giant Cyclops in his cave, and not give in to the Sirens when he sailed past them, and then fend off all Penelope's suitors when he finally made it home.

One summer day when I was six, Ellen took me to New York City for the first time, and that single day opened up an entirely new world for me: skyscrapers, elevators and escalators (alligators and escagators, I called them), Central Park and the Natural History Museum, an Egyptian temple, and paintings unlike anything I'd ever seen. We had afternoon tea at the Plaza, and I pretended to be like Eloise on her best behavior, eating all the delicious sandwiches and scones with ripe strawberries and whipped cream, and talking like a grown-up with my favorite aunt about all we'd done that day.

I begged Ellen to stay in the city overnight, but she said she'd promised to get me home by 8:30 at the latest. I wondered if we would see my father on the train to Darien, maybe with his partner Arlene, because I'd overheard him fighting with my mother about her. But the 6:30 train that Ellen and I took was probably too early for him. Still, I wondered what Arlene looked like, and what was going to happen, because it was obvious that my father had grown to dislike my mother almost as much as he disliked me.

Halfway to Darien I asked Ellen if she thought my parents were going to split up. "I don't know," she said, "but whatever happens, wherever you are, wherever I am, I'm your friend for life, OK?" I started to cry, then reached around and hugged her, my face buried in her neck. She rubbed my back for a while and I slept the rest of the way to Darien.

4: Darien – 2010

"Headmaster, I met Fran Johnson yesterday. Really a remarkable youngster, unquestionably a child prodigy. I taped our interview so you could judge for yourself. Do you have time to listen now, or should—"

"Now's fine. I'm fascinated; I don't think Hanson's ever had a prodigy."

"Good morning, Fran, how are you?"

"I'm fine, sir. How are you today?"

"Well, thank you. I was hoping that our Headmaster could join us, but it turns out he has to meet with the school's trustees today. Would it be all right with you if I recorded our conversation so that he could hear it later?"

"Sure, that's fine."

"From the tests you took last week it's obvious that you already know a great deal about virtually everything we normally teach here in Lower and Middle School, and a good deal about Upper School subjects as well. How did you learn all that?"

"I've had a wonderful tutor, sir. An Irish woman named Ellen Riley who graduated from Trinity College in

Dublin. She knows practically everything. Except she says she's not a maths wiz. So she suggested that I look at the MOOC on-line courses in first-year algebra and geometry so I'd be ready for advanced algebra, solid geometry, and trig, and could move on to calculus and statistics in middle school."

"Math fascinates you?"

"Oh yes, sir!"

"Why, do you think?"

"Because it's so open ended, because it makes everything possible. We couldn't have computers or the internet or spaceships or a zillion other important things without advanced math. When we finally learn for sure how the universe was created, I'll bet anything that math will be a big part of getting the solution.

"And math can be beautiful, like Phi, the Golden Ratio the Greeks used to design the metopes at the top of the Parthenon and da Vinci used when he painted the Last Supper, or the Fibonacci numbers that spiral as they grow, exactly the way some plants do."

"Fran, you scored 100% on the math test you took last week, but could I ask you one more math question— and would you please think out loud as you answer it— because it would really help us to hear directly from you how your mind works when you're trying to solve a brand-new type of problem, one that you've probably never thought about before. Would that be OK?"

"Sure.   I mean, yes, sir."

"You know about the number pi, I suppose."

"Yes, sir."

"Well, let's assume that you and another person are seated at a flat circular table that has a diameter of pi feet. Each of you has an unlimited supply of identical CD discs that have a diameter of pi inches. The two of you will take turns placing one of your discs flat on the table, anywhere you want to. The rules of the game say that no disc may be moved after it's placed on the table, and the entire bottom surface of each disc must rest on the table. In other words, no part of any disc may extend beyond the edge of the table, and no disc may overlap any part of another disc. Assuming the other person is as smart as you are, which of you will succeed in placing the last disc on the table, the one who plays first or the one who plays next?"

"Interesting…   oh, sir!—that's exactly what I meant about math being beautiful! A perfect example!! The dimensions of the circles are irrelevant. The first person to play can win by putting a disc in the exact center of the table."

"And why is that, Fran?"

"Because there's only one center, sir; it's unique. Wherever else the second player puts down a disc, the first player can match that move by putting down a disc on the exact opposite side of the table, the same distance from the center. Sooner or later—depending on how fast they play—there'll be no place left on the table big enough for the second player to put down a disc."

"You get A+, Fran. I've seen college math majors spend all day doing arithmetic on that problem, trying to get the right result.

"We think you're truly exceptional and we're going to do our absolute best to find teachers, from here and also from nearby colleges, who can inspire you and help you learn about any subject you want to explore. That a deal?"

"That's terrific, sir."

5: Wildwood at Lenox – 2095

Because Ellen and I got on so well, and my mother had no reliable way of predicting how I'd behave when I was shipped off to school, my originally planned year with Ellen became two years, and then three. Finally, in August of 2010 when I was about to turn nine, everyone agreed that the time had come for me to start outside schooling. A week later, Ellen drove me to Hanson Country Day to take some tests so they'd know what classes I should take.

It was a relatively small school back then, maybe 350 students all told in grades 1 to 12, but I learned from the web that it was generally regarded as one of the best secondary schools in the state, and also that most of its graduates went on to good eastern colleges. Given what Ellen had taught me, and the courses I'd studied on the net, the math and reading comprehension tests they gave me were a breeze. Not many of the words on the vocabulary test stumped me, but one that did has been a favorite of mine ever since. The test asked whether "cleave" means:

(a) to cling together;

(b) to split apart;

(c) both of the above; or

(d) none of the above.

When I got home I used the dictionary Ellen had given me for Xmas to look up the answer, and thought how neat it was that a single word could have diametrically opposite meanings.

I liked Mr. Hudson, the man who interviewed me a week later, and hoped that he'd be one of my teachers. Unfortunately it didn't work out that way, but he was a big help in planning my classes and getting me assigned to some really outstanding teachers—except for the one who taught my history of art class. She was a real snob who put me off paintings, sculpture, and architecture until much later, when I went to England and had an art teacher who was truly inspiring. So much so that collecting prints and drawings became an interest, and ultimately a passion, of mine.

Because I started at Hanson when I was nine, I was officially a third grader in the Lower School, but I didn't see much of my classmates because I spent all my time in Upper School buildings, either sitting in on classes with juniors and seniors or working one-on-one with tutors who taught mainly at other schools or colleges.

Most of the upperclassmen took no notice of me. But there were a few decent ones who made a point of saying they'd been told at the start of the year that a much younger child prodigy would be joining them, and were glad to discover that I wasn't a weirdo or a conceited jerk, but just an exceptionally smart third grader. And, of course, there were a few other older students who got on my case right away: "Hey, dwarf-boy, how's it going today?" followed by, "no, Justin, it's not a dwarf-boy; it's a smart-ass little girl dressed in dwarf-boy drag." And so on. Because I couldn't possibly take them on physically, I outwardly ignored their taunts, but inside they made me boiling mad and I vowed that someday I'd track them down and get revenge.

If it hadn't been for the small number of hecklers, Hanson would have been an ideal place to grow up. I liked the campus; the facilities and teachers were excellent; and my academic horizon seemed limitless. In my last year in Lower School, when I was officially a sixth grader, I became intrigued by foreign languages that used different alphabets from ours. Hanson's regular classics teacher was fluent in ancient Greek and she asked me one day when we were passing in the hallway if I'd like to learn to speak it. I thought that sounded like a great idea, so I joined her first-year class and had one-on-one tutoring sessions with her three times a week after school. By the end of the school year she had me talking in Greek about what Xenophon's army had done lately, and she promised me that before I finished Middle School, I'd be ready to talk with Plato.

During my first year in Middle School, when I was 13, I started to grow at a faster clip than I had before, and by winter break I'd reached five feet. Strangely, though, the growth spurt seemed to increase the amount of hazing, rather than decrease it as I would have expected. My bête-noire was a ninth grader named Justin. He was a lanky, good-looking boy with blond hair. Probably gay, I thought, and certainly much subtler than any of my other hecklers. Most of his taunts had sly, sexual overtones, all suggesting that I, too, must be gay, a false insinuation that really got on my nerves. It was particularly hard to take when he taunted me in a stage whisper loud enough to be heard by bystanders.

Justin's constant baiting and innuendos became so annoying that I finally went to Mr. Hudson to complain. He listened patiently as I explained what was going on. Hearing myself talk, I realized for the first time how really angry I was about Justin. "How do you plan to handle it?" Mr. Hudson asked after I'd finished my tirade. I still remember how I answered him. "I'd like to beat the crap out of Justin, sir. In public. With some seniors as referees, to make sure it's a fair fight."

6: Darien – 2015

Memo dated: April 14, 2015
To: the Headmaster
From: J.L. Hudson
Re: Fran Johnson and Justin Blake

I'm afraid we have a real problem on our hands. Johnson came to my office yesterday, complaining that Blake is constantly hounding him by falsely insinuating in the presence of others that he is gay, and making veiled suggestions that they should have sex together. Even though he is two years younger and at least two inches shorter than Blake, Johnson wants to get his "tormenter" off his back by taking on Blake in a barehanded "public fight" monitored by several seniors.

I called Blake into my office this morning and confronted him with Johnson's story. Blake (who is openly gay) says Johnson "walks like a queer and talks like a queer," but categorically denies suggesting that they have sex. After listening to both of them, I tend to think that Johnson is telling the truth and Blake is lying on the latter point.

Johnson is unquestionably the brightest student I have encountered in my entire career. Many child prodigies flame out early because they are expert in only one area, and totally inept in many others, but Johnson shows every sign of becoming a true polymath, with wide ranging intellectual interests. He is obviously motivated, hard working, and highly creative, in addition to being well adjusted socially. I strongly suspect that he will one day become one of our most illustrious and respected alumni.

On the other hand, I regard Blake as one of our rare admissions mistakes. I think that, either consciously or subconsciously, committee members voted to admit him largely because he is the only openly gay male who has applied in recent years, and we wanted to maintain as much "diversity" in the student body as possible. He has turned out to be a mediocre student.

If it were my decision to make, I would call Blake into my office and say that we're not passing judgment on anything that may have happened in the past, but we want him to avoid all contact with Johnson in the future. And to make it clear that we mean it, I'd tell Blake point-blank that he will be expelled if he henceforth molests Johnson *in any way,* verbally or physically.

7: Wildwood at Lenox – 2095

The happiest day of my first year in Middle School was the day Mr. Hudson told me that Justin had been called into the Headmaster's office and told he'd be expelled if he ever hassled me again. The next best was the day I learned to play baseball. I had an eighth-grade friend named Eric Davis who was shortstop on the Middle School team, and one afternoon, when practice was over, he asked if I'd like to play catch. I said sure, I'd like to learn, because my father, who was a real jerk, never taught me. Eric tossed me his back-up fielder's glove.

We started about 10 feet from each other, with Eric lobbing easy underhand tosses to me, then we stepped back a few paces and tried throwing easy overhand tosses to each other. My throws were pretty erratic, and for a while I dropped most of the balls he tossed to me, but suddenly I got the hang of it and started catching nine out of ten. Eric moved us from the grass where we were playing catch to the dirt part of the infield between first and second base, and began tossing grounders to me. Some went through my legs, others bounced off my glove or shins, and a few I actually caught. Pop-ups were next. I lost track of more balls than I caught, but I got the general idea.

Finally, Eric picked up his bat and a couple of balls, and walked to the plate. "Get a good, level swing," he said, handing me the bat. He walked midway between the plate and the backstop and told me to take a couple of practice swings, which I did. Then he told me to get set for a real swing, and pitched an easy underhand toss over the plate. I whiffed. On the next pitch I whiffed again. On the third I hit a solid line drive that missed his left ear by about a foot. "Jeez, man!!" he yelled. "You almost killed me!"

That was the beginning of a real friendship. Every weekday for the rest of the term I went to the Middle School ball field around 4:30 to meet up with Eric after he'd finished practice or a real game with some other team. By May Day I could play a respectable game of catch, come up with a lot more grounders than I missed, and judge infield pop-ups well enough to catch most of them. But what I really enjoyed was batting. To this day I have no idea why I was good at it, but I was. Eric said I was a "natural" and that really pleased me.

For the first two weeks of May, Eric pitched to me at what he called "batting practice speed." By the third week he was pitching fastballs to me, fired almost as hard as his throws from short to first in a real game. During the last week of school, he got his team's best pitcher to stay after practice several times to throw curveballs, sliders, and changeups to me, mixed in with faster fastballs than Eric himself could throw. I did respectably well, I thought. I was hitting more foul balls than before, and whiffing slightly more often, but I rarely struck out. What pleased me most was discovering that I could hit to either field, pretty much at will.

On the last day of the term, with Eric pitching at batting practice speed, I hit the first pitch down the left-field line, the next to left center, the third to center, then fouled two off, got the next one to right center, whiffed once, fouled one by several feet in the right-field corner, and ended up with a clean double down the right-field line. Eric tipped his hat to me and said, "Now go backwards." I did, needing only seven pitches to get the five shots I wanted from the right-field foul line back to the left-field one.

"I've got a hunch," Eric said unexpectedly. "Switch sides of the plate and try batting left-handed." I switched over and took a couple of half-speed swings to get the feel of it. "Fire away," I told him, and promptly struck out on the first three pitches. "OK, new batter," I said. On the next pitch I took us back to the beginning of our joint venture by whistling a line drive two feet to his left. We both broke out laughing and took a break.

After five minutes I said I'd liked the feel of that last line drive and would like to try one more left-handed session before we finished spring training. It was pretty clear after 15 minutes that I was a natural lefty as well. And I quickly discovered that I could hit to all fields left-handed almost as well as I could do it batting right-handed.

Eric finally said we should pack up, and then walked up to me and put one arm around my shoulder. "My friend," he said, "from now on your nickname is 'Switch' and you're going to be our starting second baseman next season. If I hadn't seen it myself I wouldn't believe that anyone could pick up a bat for the first time in late April and become a starter by May 30."

Here was my best friend telling me I was an athlete as well as a scholar. I was on cloud nine.

8: Darien – 2015

June 10, 2015

Dear Meade,

I've just completed an extraordinary academic year, which I want to share with you because it seems like the culmination of everything you taught me. A lad named Johnson, age 13, stopped me in the hall last September to ask if I would be willing to teach him Greek. I knew from remarks our Headmaster had made at our opening faculty meeting that Johnson was a prodigy, so of course I offered to work with him.

It took him all of five minutes to master the alphabet and less than an hour to absorb everything in the first ten lessons of Chase & Phillips. He devoured the μι verbs in a single sitting. By the end of the fall term we'd finished the *Anabasis,* and were well into the *Odyssey*. And suddenly, for the first time in my life, I thought I was listening to the original Homer, because Johnson altered the pitch and cadence of the Greek to reflect in uncanny fashion the substance of the narrative, turning the words on the page back into poetry. When I asked how he managed to do that so well, he shrugged and said it was just "whatever felt right." When I pressed him, he confessed that he was trying to reverse-engineer Fagles' translation, following McKellan's direction on the delivery.

During the spring term we read the *Apology, Crito, Republic, and Phaedo*; selections from *On the Soul* and *Poetics*; the *Oedipus* cycle; and *Clouds.* He is now more fluent than I will ever be, and our Greek conversations push me to my very limit.

I'm afraid there is little chance of persuading him to join our cohort of classicists, for he seems to be fascinated by the sciences, but when he exhausts our resources here, as I suspect he will in another year or so, I will urge his family to think about Devon. You would greatly enjoy conversing with him.

Φιλανθρώπως,

Wadsworth

9: Wildwood at Lenox – 2095

The week after I learned to bat left-handed, my friend Eric left for summer camp in Maine, a place called Flying Moose that ran serious canoe trips up in Canada. I decided I'd spend summer vacation playing more ball, trying to improve. I persuaded my mother to foot the bills for baseball camp, and got her to drive me to some nearby places that had indoor cages and a staff of teachers, but all of them turned out to be larger, more structured, operations than what I wanted. Then I learned that Bobby Anderson, a former Mets third baseman, was just about to open a small indoor cage outside Stamford. We found his address on his website, drove there, and got into a conversation with him.

I could tell he didn't believe my story about how fast I'd learned to play, so I asked if I could hit a few. He very pleasantly said sure, and ten minutes later I signed on as his first pupil.

We really hit it off, right from the beginning of our first two-hour session, which we spent on improving my fielding. He hit wicked ground balls at me, and dribblers that I was supposed to scoop up on the run and then fire back to first with a sidearm throw while I was still running away from the bag. He turned up the overhead lights and showed me how to flip down my sun glasses so I wouldn't lose pop-ups or foul balls in the glare. He reckoned that I'd end up playing second base, so we worked hard on the mechanics of double plays. He also taught me Spanish matadors' tricks that he said would help me tag (or appear to tag) runners stealing second, and reduce my risk of being injured if they came in with spikes high.

During our next session I learned how to slide— both feet first and head first—and how to bunt down both lines. He also showed me how the Mets stole signs from the catcher and relayed them to the batter when they had a man on second. Finally, Bobby let me get into the batting cage, which I'd been longing to do from the word go.

To give him a better feel for what I could do, I started out by repeating what I'd done with Eric on our final day, hitting to all fields from both sides of the plate. I was thrilled when Bobby said he wasn't going to suggest any basic changes in my stance or swing, because I was "born to hit baseballs," and he wasn't about to "mess around with god-given gifts." I couldn't believe I was hearing all that from a former Major Leaguer.

His objective in the batting cage, Bobby said, was to show me all kinds of pitches so that I could develop what he called "batter's choice." He had an all-star on the mound—a mechanical pitcher that could throw everything in the book, including screwballs, at any speed and in any direction that he programmed into his i-phone. He called balls and strikes for me the same way an umpire would in a real game, except that his calls were always right because he could tell from looking at his i-phone whether the next pitch was programmed to be a ball or strike.

I collected a demerit in his log book every time I swung at a pitch that was outside the strike zone. I got two demerits if I struck out on a called third strike, because Bobby insisted that looking at third strikes was the surest, dumbest way to put yourself out. My final score each day was the ratio of my demerits to the number of pitches I'd received. We were both pleased that the percentage went down slightly almost every day. Over the entire summer we cut it in half.

Early on, we got into the habit of taking a couple of five-minute breaks during each of our two-hour sessions to quench our thirst and rest up. I looked forward to the breaks because Bobby had all kinds of interesting stories to tell about his days with the Mets, and he asked lots of questions about my school and what I was interested in. With Ellen back in Ireland, he became my best grown-up friend—my favorite one by a long shot.

10: Stamford, CT – 2015

Aug. 30, 2015

Dear Ms. Johnson,

As promised at the outset, I'm writing to give you my impressions of Fran after working with him one-on-one over the summer.

I believe he thoroughly enjoyed our time together. I certainly did. He is exceptionally bright and very quick to learn, which makes him a joy to teach. I was amazed to discover early on that he could hit pitched balls to any part of the field, even though he'd been playing for only six weeks. And now, just eleven weeks later, he's able to do anything a manager could ask for, except for hitting home runs and making long throws. He grew almost an inch during the summer, but still doesn't have the heft or power needed to hit homers or play in the outfield. I expect he'll fill out and have that power by the time he goes off to college.

What most impressed me about Fran this summer, apart from his natural baseball talent, was the studious way he analyzed every new action or idea I exposed him to. I believe strongly that the most common batting problem—one that many major league players continue to have—is swinging at "bad" pitches that are outside the strike zone. Over the course of the summer Fran steadily got better at recognizing those pitches and not swinging at them. I believe that was in large part the result of his careful study of my pitching machine tapes, which enabled him to identify the types of "bad" pitches he was most often fooled by.

My pitching machine can create an image of each batter's rectangular strike zone and throw pitches that are close—or very close—to one of the four sides or corners of that zone. In our final session I programmed the machine so that most of its pitches would fall into that category. Fran refrained from swinging at 94% of the pitches that were programmed to go outside the strike zone, and he swung at 89% of the ones that were inside the zone. I don't think anyone I played with on the Mets could have done that well.

Fran has so much inborn natural talent, and is such a quick study, that I believe he stands an outstanding chance of getting a total scholarship to a Division I university or college. From our conversations over the summer it's obvious that he's smarter than a whiz kid, and is already taking college level courses, so I imagine that he'll be able to write his own ticket to anyplace in the country.

If he plays on the Hanson varsity (as I really hope he will), you'll probably be besieged by college scouts, because the annual game between Hanson and New Canaan

Country School always attracts a number of them. Since I truly believe that Fran has Major League potential, I'm going to tell my good friend Tommy Thompson, the Mets' top scout, all about him. If at any point Fran decides that he'd like to take a crack at playing professionally, I would urge the two of you to contact Tommy before talking with anyone else. His private cell is (212) 074-1776.

Thank you again for affording me the opportunity to work with Fran. Doing so has been both a privilege and a great pleasure.

Sincerely,

Bobby Anderson

11: Wildwood at Lenox – 2095

Eric got back from Maine soon after my final session with Bobby, and came over to my house for dinner the next day. He was amazed at how much I'd grown over the summer and asked if it had affected my batting, wondering, I suppose, if I'd turned into a bean-stalk at the plate. No, I told him, everything was still fine, just as fluid as ever. I told him all about Bobby, of course, and I think he may have been a touch jealous that I was the first player at Hanson to latch onto a Major Leaguer for a coach.

School started a week later, and Eric promptly lined up an afternoon tryout with Mr. Williams, the long-time Head Coach of Middle School baseball. I had a great day at the plate, hitting to all fields from both sides of the plate, and scrupulously letting Bobby's "bad" pitches go by without swinging. Mr. Williams noticed that pretty quickly, and asked if I'd ever umpired pickup or Little League games. I explained about Bobby and the "batter's choice" training he'd given me that summer, and the films from his pitching machine that I'd studied. Mr. Williams vaguely remembered that Bobby Anderson had once played shortstop or third for the Mets, but didn't know a thing about Anderson Baseball Academy. I wondered if I'd get an extra point or two in my tryout for having gone there and told him about it.

The fielding part of the tryout, with me at second base, was so-so—no screaming errors, but a couple of bobbled grounders that forced me to hurry the throw to Eric at first, and later on, a throw that pulled him off the bag. When Mr. Williams moved Eric to short and took over first himself, I did manage to complete a pretty decent double play that Eric started. So I figured that I hadn't disgraced myself.

After half an hour on the field, Mr. Williams walked us over to the first-base bleachers and sat down on the second row, motioning to us to sit on the first. Looking me in the eye, he said, "Eric tells me your name is Switch Johnson. Is that what you'd like me to call you, Switch?"

My recollection at age 94 is not the best, but I think replied along the lines of whatever you like, sir, Switch or Fran, either one is fine with me. "Well, Switch," he said, "how would you like to be our starting second baseman next spring?"

I still remember jumping up from the bleachers and yelling, I'd like it a lot, sir! I'd been hoping to make the team ever since May.

12: Darien – 2017

Memo dated: May 25, 2017
To: the Headmaster
From: J.L. Hudson
Re: Fran Johnson and Justin Blake

Yesterday, while you were at the Alumni Council meeting in the City, I had to deal with a horrible situation—one involving Johnson and Blake again. Around 4:45 in the afternoon Johnson telephoned me saying that he had just called 911 to get an ambulance and stretcher sent ASAP to the Upper School boys' locker room at the gym. He urged me to come too, because Blake was sprawled on the floor, writhing in pain, maybe in shock.

When I got to the locker room, Johnson was standing next to Blake, clutching an i-phone and wearing nothing but a towel wrapped around his waist. Blake was wearing only his boxer shorts and sox. The rest of his clothes were scattered on the floor in the general direction of the locker room door. A baseball bat was also lying on the floor, next to an open locker that turned out to be Johnson's.

His first words to me, as best I can recall, were "it's all on my i-phone, sir. When he came in and started peeling off his shirt, I was pretty sure what he was after, so I reached into my locker with my back to him, and started recording. I'm really sorry about what I did to him, but I had no choice."

The ambulance crew arrived in less than five minutes and said they would be taking Blake to St. Elizabeth's. I called their emergency room to ask that a shock specialist and an orthopedic surgeon be there when the ambulance arrived. I then called my secretary and had her put me through to Blake's mother, who was fortunately at home. I explained that Justin was in an ambulance on his way to the emergency room at St. E's, and said we would immediately begin an investigation to determine what had happened and why.

Next I called through to Johnson's home, but there was no answer. I left a message asking his mother to call me on my cell phone as soon as possible. Johnson normally walks here in the morning and back home at the end of the day, but he seemed so distraught that I thought he should stay here until his mother could pick him up. He protested that he was OK, but I insisted that he lie down for a while on the couch in my anteroom. His mother called around 5:45, and was here ten minutes later to pick him up. I told her that I'd let Fran explain what had happened because I didn't want to put words in his mouth until I'd heard what he'd recorded on his i-phone, which I'd have to keep for the time being. I offered to get a replacement i-phone for him, but he said he'll use his old Samsung until everything gets sorted out.

Last night I transcribed the locker room dialogue between the two boys as I heard it on Johnson's i-phone, and made duplicate recordings of the dialogue. To establish that I've had sole custody of the i-phone since Johnson gave it to me, I locked it in my office safe when I left last night, along with one of the duplicate recordings; the other is now in the master safe in the Registrar's office.

The transcript reads:

JB: … playing for the varsity as a ninth grader, isn't it? And then to tie the NCCS game in the bottom of the ninth with a perfect hit-and-run single? Must feel great, scoring Williams that way and sending your friend, Eric, to third. Especially when Lopez flies out deep on the next pitch to score Eric and win the game. And then to cap it all off you get clapped on the back by this guy who's got a bunch of your classmates following him because it turns out he played third base for the Mets. All pretty exciting, eh? [Five-second pause] So how about celebrating? I've been watching outside for the last half hour, and we're all alone in here. Door's bolted, no one's going to bother us. [Shorter pause.] Hey, Fran, relax. The two of us, we're both gay, you and I both know that. And I know that deep down you want me. Give yourself a break, let yourself—

FJ: Go screw yourself, Blake. I'm not gay, and you're violating the deal you made with the Headmaster.

[Short pause.] Lay off and I'll say nothing about it; come much closer and I'll clobber you with my bat.

JB: Calm down, friend, I'm just talking about a friendly get-together. I'll bet you're a virgin, so I'll be very gentle. You'll love it. Get that prick of yours all aroused so it's big and hard and I'll suck it. Blow your mind.

FJ: You try to lay a hand on me, and so help me God, I'll—

JB: You're not going to do anything except enjoy it, Fran. Why do you think you just said you won't squeal on me if I lay off. Deep down you want me to be a friend. You're just not willing to admit it to yourself, because you think being queer is queer. It isn't. You're smart enough to see that. I'll bet there are at least twenty-five LGBTs here at Hanson who are still hiding in the closet because this is Darien and their folks would never understand it. Total crap. The world has changed; we can finally be who we want to be, and be open about it. [Short pause.] Come on, Fran, you switch-hit on the ball field; switch hit with me— you'll love it, I promise. Scout's honor.

FJ: Stop inching up on me that way, Blake; it gives me the creeps.

JB: How can it give you the creeps if you've never even tried it? Com'on, I'll put out my hand, you hold it, and we'll very, very slowly start to make love, OK?

FJ: No, godammit! No closer!!

JB: You don't seem to understand, Fran. You turn me on; if you don't want to come in my mouth, I'm going to fuck you in the ass.

FJ: Stop it and get out of here!! One more step and I swing, maybe maul you for life.

FJ[?]: [Mutters something barely audible with top amplification.] Legs—around the knees.**[?]**

[Loud thumping noise, then a wailing scream.]

[Another thumping noise, not as loud.]

JB[?]: [More screams, then loud moans.]

[End of recording.]

After making the transcript I called St. E's around 10:30 p.m. to see how Blake was faring. I finally got through to an ICU nurse who said he was out of shock and heavily sedated, scheduled for another MRI in the morning. The preliminary assessment was not optimistic. Both legs may have to be amputated above the knees, in which case the surgeon is afraid he'll never be able to walk again, even with the best high-tech artificial legs that have been designed for vets of the Iraq war.

Given his current status, I think it would be inappropriate to consider whether Blake should be expelled from the School at this time. Assuming he recovers, we obviously need to interview him in depth. Before doing so we should advise his parents that he has every right to be assisted by legal counsel during the interview if either he or they so wish. Similar advice should be given to Johnson's parents before he is interviewed.

I suggest that we do three things immediately:

In furtherance of the transparency policy adopted by the Trustees at their spring meeting four years ago, I believe that a copy of this memo should promptly be furnished to the Darien Chief of Police and the Chief State's Attorney.

I assume that you'll also want to inform our alumni about the incident, and would be happy to take a crack at drafting a letter to them if you'd like me to. My initial thought is that it should be quite brief, stating simply that an altercation in the Upper School locker room, which was recorded on an i-phone now in the School's possession, resulted in serious injuries to an 11th grader; the matter has been reported to outside authorities; and a further report to alumni will be forthcoming after the School completes its internal investigation.

My other disclosure recommendation relates to the Johnson family. Johnson recently told me that his parents are divorced, and added that he and his father no longer speak to each other. While his mother has total custody, his father still pays his tuition and incidental school expenses. All things considered, I think it might be advisable if you called his father this morning to let him know what has happened. He heads a NYC ad agency named S & A, LLC. His office phone number is (212) 898-9800.

JLH

13: Wildwood at Lenox – 2095

A few days after my confrontation with Blake, my ninth-grade class graduated from Middle School. Mom came, of course, and said afterwards that she was really proud of my three-minute speech as class valedictorian, because it didn't contain a single graduation cliché. Frankly, I don't remember a word of what I said.

That evening at the dinner table, Mom asked me what I'd think about taking on new educational challenges by going to one of the top New England prep schools. I was obviously ready for college academically, she said, but if I wanted to develop social skills, and experience all the joys and frustrations of growing up, it was important to be with classmates my own age during my teenage years.

She told me she'd spoken briefly with Mr. Hudson and the Headmaster, who were sad to hear that I might be leaving, but entirely willing to write letters that might help me get admitted on short notice to whatever school we chose, so that I could start that fall. Mom also mentioned that she'd talked with my Greek teacher, who said she had a good friend on the faculty of a school called Devon, and thought it might be the perfect place for me. Take a look at their website and tell me what you think, Mom said as were finishing desert.

So of course that's what I did as soon as I got back to my room. It was obvious right away that Devon was Hanson on steroids. Co-ed with some 1,200 students and a 7:1 student to faculty ratio. Founded in the countryside near Portland, Massachusetts in 1797 by Josiah Phillips, a noted minister. Now by far the largest prep school in Maine, and close enough to the eastern Massachusetts schools to play them in baseball and every other major sport. Easy access to Portland with its revitalized downtown. Good science labs, attractive classrooms and dorms, and a lovely campus. A zillion extra-curricular activities, including a student-run FM station. And most important of all, a vast array of college-level courses, including six in computer science, a field that I wanted to explore in depth.

I took a look at the Andover, Exeter, and Deerfield websites, which were similar in many respects, but there was something intangible—a feeling I couldn't verbalize— that said go with Devon. So I relayed that to Mom at breakfast the next day, and she promptly called the school, promising to deliver my application to the Admissions Office within a week.

Blake's lower legs were both amputated in late June, and from what I heard after that, he never did walk again. The other fall-out from our confrontation was that my ex-father said he was going to sue Hanson, claiming large damages for psychological injuries I'd incurred, and for the great mental distress and pain that he and my mother had suffered, as a result of the whole "traumatic episode." When I learned from Mr. Hudson that my asshole father was threatening all this, I was furious. Hanson had been really generous to me, giving me one-on-one special tutoring in courses they didn't offer, and creating a special curriculum for me that was off the charts. There was no way I was going to let my ex-father get away with making outrageous claims against a place I loved, simply because one bad apple had fallen into the student-body barrel.

But first I had to figure out how to confront him. In the end, it turned out to be simple. I get his secretary on the phone, and talking in my new deep voice I say I'm Jacob Heller and would like an appointment with Mr. Johnson to discuss an advertising program for a breakout electronic product I've designed, produced, and successfully tested in my basement workshop. Details to follow after he signs a a nondisclosure agreement that protects me if we don't end up working together. She believes me and says that he is free to meet with me at 11:00 the following Wednesday.

I took an early train to the City that day to ensure that I'd be able to enter the lobby of S&A at 11 o'clock sharp. The receptionist looked a little surprised when I said I was meeting Mr. Johnson, so I nodded and said something like, "I know, younger than you expected, but it's all right, I'm a child prodigy, here to talk about advertising my latest invention." When his drop-dead blonde secretary appeared minutes later, I repeated a variation of the child-prodigy spiel.

As the two of us walked into his office he looked up from his desk, then shouted, "What in hell are you—"

I cut him off with my memorized speech, which I can still recall almost verbatim because I had certainly practiced it enough.

"I know, I'm here under false pretenses, but you're going to listen to me for once. I won't let you get away with trumped-up claims against a school I love. If you file a law suit, everything becomes public and I will shit all over you and—"

"Get out. I'm through with you forever, you're a—"

"Good," I ad-libbed, "you've just dug a hole for your own coffin if you go to court, because your secretary here has heard everything, and we'll call her to testify if need be." I segued into my memorized argument, adding the new one he'd just given me. "What jury in the world is going to award you a nickel for injuries that you as a parent say you received because of what happened to a son you haven't talked to once—not once—since it all happened? Particularly when you add insult to your specious injury by renouncing him 'forever' when he seeks you out, asking to talk. You file suit, and I'll tell the court that I don't feel 'traumatized' at all by anything that happened. Sad, yes; more experienced because of it, yes; but nothing like what you're—"

"Shut up. You're being just as obstinate as you always were when—"

"Don't tell me to shut up until you hear what Mom's going to say—"

"Oh, it's 'Mom' now, is it?"

"Yes it is. We've become friends since you took off to shack up full-time with Arlene—I overheard you and Mom arguing about her one night, so I assume she's the A in S&A. Mom's another story, totally different from you. She comes to my games and we do lots of other things together, like going to one of the very first previews of *Hamilton*, and reading Chernow's book out loud to each other, the way Ellen and I used to do—stuff like that. You have no idea how enjoyable home has become since you left.

"You sidetracked me; if you file suit, Mom's also going to say that she doesn't feel injured in any way by what happened, and she's going to tell the world what a lousy, selfish, god-awful father you were because you couldn't stand your son from the get-go. You'll be fodder for the Darien cocktail party circuit when she gets through with you in court, and poison to your clients who sell their soap and cars to happy, All-American families.

"Listen to me just this once: drop the suit, and I promise that you will never see or hear from me again."

Without waiting for an answer I turned and headed out, nodding briefly at his secretary—Arlene's probable successor, I thought to myself—as I passed her office.

Two weeks later, I got an E-mail from Mr. Hudson saying that my father had called to notify the school that there would be no law suit after all. At last, after all those years, I was finally rid of him.

14: Wildwood at Lenox – 2095

It's a lovely New England fall day here in the Berkshires. Sun's warm and a gentle breeze is wafting through my open window—my visual access to a vista of meadow grass and a stand of trees beyond the local creek, where I sometimes walk when I think of The Woods at Devon. But I'm getting ahead of myself, which I suppose is not uncommon for someone as old as I am.

I entered Devon in the fall of 2017 as a 10th grader, or "Lower Middler" in the official campus lingo. Having just turned 16, I was the proud possessor of a newly minted Connecticut learner's permit, but it was of no immediate use because students weren't allowed to have cars at the school. I realized on day one that I was in for a lot of walking, because my dorm was on the south edge of the campus and all the classrooms were at the north end, about half a mile away.

When I met my academic advisor two days before classes started, he told me that he was amazed by my transcript, which he said entitled me to graduate from Devon without taking a single additional course, provided I passed the obligatory life-saving test. So he suggested that I look through the catalog and tell him what I wanted to take.

He said he'd approve anything I asked for unless my slate of courses looked completely crazy.

I told him I'd already studied the catalog and would like to immerse myself in computer science by taking five of the six courses that were offered, saving the artificial intelligence course for the following year—my "Upper Middler" year in campus lingo. My advisor said that sounded fine and sent me off to the Registrar's office to get signed up.

On my way there I stopped off at the main office of the Classics Department in Phillips Hall, a small brick building that I assumed—correctly as it turned out—was the oldest building on campus, and hence had been named for the founder. I asked if the department head was available, and met him moments later. In Ionian Greek I said, "Good morning, sir, it's a pleasure to meet you. My name is Fran Johnson; I'm a former student of your protégée, Miss Wadsworth, at Hanson Country Day. She was pleased when I told her last July that I would be going to Devon in the fall." Then I added—in Attic Greek—"And I hope that the two of us can talk about Aristophanes, Euripides, Plato, and other major figures during my three years here." We became friends on the spot (and closer still over that three-year time frame).

That fall, as I learned the syntax of major software development languages during the day and spoke Greek with a classical polymath at his apartment in the evening, I became intrigued by the notion that there might be a connection between the two—that in some significant, perhaps profound, manner, Greek thought and modern computing might be interrelated. Little did I realize then that my notion would lead me on a prolonged quest through the Greek world of ideas, searching for a key that might—if I could ever find it—open up limitless possibilities for programming the modern world.

Through my computer science classes I made an array of acquaintances, both male and female, from all over. About a third were Asian—from at least six different countries, I learned over the course of the year. Several were from Latin America and Europe, one was Russian, and the rest were scattered around the US and Canada. Two became good friends.

Charley Johnson (no relation), a Senior who played center field on the varsity team, became an immediate friend and we often worked out together, along with half a dozen others on the team. Although there had been no fall tryout, I think everybody assumed after several of our sessions that I'd make the varsity as a utility infielder and be our designated hitter against teams that used AL rules.

My other friend was Katherine French, an Upper who was in two of my classes. She was a lot smarter than Charley, and certainly much better looking—a quite tall, long-haired natural blonde, with an engaging smile and a wispy air about her, and lovely, lanky legs that I admired from my seat in the row behind her. We quickly discovered that we were neighbors at home; she lived in New Canaan, and had gone to NCCS, Hanson's arch rival. She had a fey, offbeat sense of humor that I'd never encountered before, and I found myself trying to adopt her style, but couldn't do it. Frankly, I couldn't figure out why she wanted to spend time with a five-nine, average looking Lower who had tousled, mud-colored hair and some acne scars still on his left cheek, but for whatever reason she seemed to enjoy eating together at Commons, studying side-by-side in the library, and going for long walks together around the campus.

During the winter term I took a chance and asked if she'd like to go into Portland with me on my two Saturday Day Passes. To my relief, she said yes, she'd like that. I can't remember now exactly what we did because I was in a pleasant haze most of that day, but I do remember saying several things that made her laugh, and when we got back to school just before curfew, she paused in a sheltered place where no one could see us and kissed me lightly, then invited me to go back to Portland with her when she used her remaining pair of Day Passes later in the year.

After I made the varsity as starting second baseman at the beginning of spring term she began showing up at practice, and I think she was in the stands for every game we played at home. Everyone on the team liked her, but some of the guys were jealous because they were just as mystified as I was about why a really good-looking Upper like Katherine would hang out with a scruffy Lower, even if he was a pretty decent ballplayer. When I doubled to win

the game against Andover, I could hear whistles and loud
catcalls when she came out of the stands and planted a loud
kiss on me, in clear violation of school rules on permissible
public conduct. She thought it was all a lark, even though
she knew she'd get two demerits and lose her remaining
Day Passes for doing it.

Proceedings of the Faculty Meeting
April 15, 2019

The Head of School: I've convened this meeting pursuant to Rule 29, which states that, notwithstanding any other rule, a student may be expelled from the Academy only by majority vote of the faculty members attending a meeting duly called for the purpose of considering the proposed expulsion of that student.

As stated in the notice sent to all of you, Katherine French and Fran Johnson were apprehended at 2:00 am on April 1 by the night watchman, who detected the smell of marijuana when he was in the vicinity of the library and traced it by walking across the Great Lawn to the statue of General Knox where he found French and Johnson sharing pot on the pedestal of the statue, underneath the General's horse.

As all of us well know, Rule 15 states that any student found drinking an alcoholic beverage, or smoking tobacco or marijuana, on campus while school is in session shall "forthwith be expelled" from the Academy. The issue posed by Rule 29 is whether a majority of you believe, for any reason, that some lesser punishment, or none at all, should be imposed here.

Dean?

The Dean of Students: Because this April Fools' escapade has become common knowledge throughout the school, I believe the credibility and integrity of our rules are now at stake. Like every other applicant, French and Johnson were told about Rule 15 early in the admissions process so they could look elsewhere if they were unwilling or unable to abide by the rule. They decided to come here, but now have chosen to violate the rule.

To me it is immaterial whether they did so in jest, for their personal pleasure, or to protest the rule. Assuming it was the latter, I have no sympathy for them because they surely must have realized that they had countless other ways of making their voices heard. We try hard to teach our students, by precept and example, how to exercise good judgment. If we don't abide by our own precepts, we undermine that effort severely. I will vote to expel both of them.

The Dean of the Faculty: I think Dean Russell's comments fail to reflect the fact that Rule 29 expressly overrides every other rule in the book relating to expulsion, including, of course, Rule 15. In reality, all those other rules are really only general principles or guidelines to be applied unless a majority of the faculty believe, in any particular case, that expulsion is not warranted because some other disposition of the matter in question is more appropriate. That's why we're here today. To repeat, we are *not* bound by any "precept" that we *must* enforce; we have total discretion to do what the majority of us think is most equitable and appropriate, considering all the facts and circumstances.

Mr. Sampson, Chair of the Computer Science Department: I totally agree with Dean Fulbright. And I start my consideration of all the facts and circumstances by looking at all aspects of who French and Johnson are as people, not simply what they did during a single, ill-considered "escapade," to use Dean Russell's own, very apt, characterization.

I know both of them well, having taught them in four computer science courses. French is an outstanding student who has contributed greatly to group projects and been generous in tutoring classmates less able than she. I have talked with all three of the housemasters she has had here at Devon, and all of them tell me that she has been a model citizen.

Her sole misdemeanor before the one we are considering now was rushing out of the stands to hug and kiss Johnson immediately after he drove in the winning run in the ninth inning of the Andover baseball game last year. Yes, what she did was impetuous. Yes, it was against the rules. But what she did was also completely human and understandable. I tend to put their April Fools' escapade in the same category. Certainly more serious because of the marijuana, but basically, I think, an impetuous, enthusiastic statement of adolescent rebellion against the rigidity and conformity of daily life at Devon.

Given all that she has accomplished academically in her three years here—eight straight terms on the High Honor Roll and a ninth in the offing—and her overall record as a model citizen of the school, I think it would be draconian to deny her the opportunity to take her final exams and graduate summa cum laude this June, especially when doing so would quite probably prevent her from going to Harvard, which accepted her last December.

I feel even more strongly about Johnson. Most of you have not yet had the privilege of teaching him because virtually all his work here has been in the field of computer science. When he arrived as a Lower he had already taken, with great distinction, enough liberal arts and science courses to qualify for an Ivy League college degree. Everyone who has ever taught him regards him a true prodigy, a brilliant, original thinker who is destined to do great things in whatever field he ultimately selects. At present, he is working on a new computer software language that he began to write last fall, a language designed to extend the horizons of artificial intelligence by creating an entirely new category of software programs. He is so far ahead of me that I can understand only the broad outlines of his AI language—just enough to recognize that it is the work of a genius.

I cannot conceive of it being in Devon's best interests to expel a genius who has the potential to change the world, as I believe Johnson may very well end up doing. I venture to predict that Devon will never have another chance to graduate a well-adjusted, polite, athletic, imaginative genius possessing even half the intellectual prowess of the young lad who is in the dock today. I believe we should cut him some slack by telling him to think twice next time and set a better example for classmates who look up to him.

If you disagree and believe that his adolescent indiscretion *must* be punished, then put him on probation for a while—over coach Fitzgerald's dead body, I assume, if you do it now, in mid season. But do not make the catastrophic mistake of expelling the young man who is likely to be our most illustrious and respected alumnus—if he graduates.

Mr. Meade, Chair of the Classics Department: I cannot comment about Miss French, because I have had no contact with her, but I second everything my distinguished colleague just said about young Johnson. When I first met him as a Lower he introduced himself in Ionic Greek and, when context made it appropriate, switched to Attic Greek. Since then he has come to my quarters in McGrath Hall on many occasions to discuss virtually every major aspect of

Greek civilization, all in idiomatic, grammatically correct, beautifully phrased Greek that Demosthenes would have admired. He is an imaginative thinker, with insights that have never occurred to me in my years of reading and teaching the philosophers and playwrights that he and I have discussed. He is constantly and seriously curious, posing probing questions and searching for links between classical and modern thought that others may have overlooked. Expelling him for smoking pot would be as barbarous as executing Augustine for stealing the pear.

Mr. Delaney, English Department: I haven't met either Miss French or Johnson, but I'd like to note my disagreement with Chairman Sampson's suggestion that a school like ours should protect students who may become illustrious alumni. I assume he'd apply the same reasoning to protect students who are likely to be major donors to the school in the future. I dislike the notion that rules of conduct apply in practice only to oi polloi—not to the rich, or the gifted, or star athletes.

This goes to Dean Russell's point that the integrity of our rules is what's really at stake here. We've got a very smart student body that has a very good institutional memory. If we give French and Johnson probation, but then expel a school nobody who's caught smoking pot next year, student opinion is justifiably going to turn against us. Probation for exceptional students and expulsion for rank-and-file ones is rank discrimination, pure and simple.

Precisely because Johnson is an exceptionally gifted student, I think it is important that he be expelled so that other students and the world understand that Devon is a truly democratic institution governed impartially and fairly, not a bastion of privilege where the elite can expect to receive favored treatment.

The Head of School: Does anyone else wish to comment?   Well then, we'll vote on expulsion for each of them separately. If either of them is not expelled, I will entertain proposals for some other punishment, or simply a cautionary warning, for that person.

Whereupon, by secret ballot, the faculty voted by a margin of 96-75 not to expel French, and further voted by a margin of 97-75 not to expel Johnson.

The Head of School: Do I have a motion for some other form of punishment for either or both of them?

The Dean of the Faculty: I propose that French be placed on probation until one hour before Commencement proceedings begin, and that Johnson be placed on probation until midnight on May 23, thereby rendering him ineligible to practice with any school team or play in any baseball games against outside teams during that period, but leaving him eligible to practice after that, and then play against Exeter in the final game of the season on May 30.

Mr. Sampson: I second that motion, and move that we adopt the Dean's proposal by unanimous consent.

Whereupon, Mr. Sampson's motion was seconded and the Dean's proposal was so adopted.

Albert Whitney, Registrar

16: Wildwood at Lenox – 2095

By the end of my Upper year at Devon, I knew that computer science would be the focus of my life, and that achieving AGI—artificial general intelligence—would be my goal. During the preceding decade great progress had been made in programming computers to perform specific tasks more efficiently than humans, but we were still years away from programming them to think and behave like humans. My ambition was to devise a new programming language that would enable me to write a new generation of algorithms for creating machines with AGI.

Mr. Sampson, my department head and mentor, had some useful suggestions, but I realized midway through the year that I had outstripped him and was basically on my own, unless I could persuade Katherine to team up with me. We took a long walk together one Sunday in late March, and discovered that we had more in common than either of us had realized. She told me her secret ambition was to program computers to become high school math teachers; I told her for the first time about my ambition to go even further than that by developing algorithms for replicating general human intelligence. By the time we got back to the campus at sundown, we'd agreed to work together on improving my new programming language so we could use it to work on both projects.

To celebrate our partnership and April Fools' Day, Katherine came up with the crazy idea of sneaking out of our dorms around 2:00 in the morning to smoke pot under the statute of General Knox, the Revolutionary War hero who came from the part of Massachusetts that's now Maine. We got caught by the night watchman and threatened with expulsion, but Sampson and several others on the faculty came to our rescue, and we were put on probation instead.

I couldn't play baseball with the team while I was serving out my probation sentence, so I sat in the old wooden bleachers to watch my teammates crush the Bates and Tufts freshmen teams, and then Andover. Fortunately, I was able to play in the season finale, and remember that we beat Exeter handily to finish the year with a 12-1 record, the best for over a decade. I went three for four, drove in several runs, and got an unassisted line-drive double play. It came within a split second of being the first triple play of my life when my throw to third was a blink too late to get the runner who was diving back to the bag.

The minute the game ended Katherine came bounding out of the stands and raced toward me, arms outstretched. Three feet short of me she slammed on the brakes, crossed her arms over her chest, and stood there grinning at me with the broadest smile I'd ever seen. Everyone on the team got it, and the whistles and catcalls from the stands were even louder than they'd been the year before.

As she and I were walking toward the gym together I asked if her parents were coming for graduation. No, she said, they were going to be in Kuala Lumpur on their three-month cruise around the world. I said I was sorry because I'd hoped to meet them. Not to worry, she replied. She stopped and turned to face me, her eyes glowing like car headlights turned on in daylight. I've got a better plan, she said, one that wouldn't work if they were here. What? I asked. I still remember her answer. "As soon as I get off the stage with a diploma, I want to go back to The Woods with you."

I was waiting for her at the bottom of the steps as she came off the graduation stage, diploma in hand. As soon as we got out of the auditorium she waved it toward the sky, put both arms around me and kissed me—not gently, but emphatically, with an extra squeeze from arms and lips before disengaging. "I'm a graduate!" she yelled, then added in a normal voice, "I talked to Dean Russell, and he said once a diploma is delivered you're on your own, Devon rules no longer apply."

Well, what about me, Miss French? I asked, smiling at her. "Oh, my God!" she cried out. "Fran, I'm so, so sorry; I got carried away. Did anyone see us, do you think?" Not sure, I said, I couldn't see a thing for a while there—but no, I didn't think so.

We walked in silence for several minutes. Then I blurted out what I'd been thinking to myself: You're so alive, it's one big adventure being with you! I never know what's coming next. I love it, love being with you. She reached out and squeezed my hand.

On the east side of the campus we came to a dirt road that took us through scrubland for several hundred yards to a large wooden sign reading 'Devon Park.' A bronze plaque embedded in the sign provided information about the park, but we continued on because Katherine had already filled me in on its history.

The property had been owned by the Phillips family for many generations, until it was given to Devon in 1959 by the last surviving member of one branch of the family. The Academy opened up a trail through the forested section, dredged the large pond on the south end of the property, mowed the overgrown meadows and planted wildflower seeds in some of them, and placed teak benches and a few picnic tables at strategic locations. Following the restoration work, the property was transferred by the Academy to a charitable land trust, and then opened to the public in 1961. Officially it was named Devon Park, but everyone in the Academy continued to refer to it as 'The Woods' because of the 40-acre forest that covered 75% of the property.

We walked to the head of the trail that led into the forest and followed it for 15 minutes. When she spotted a small boulder by the side of the trail Katherine said, "This is where it gets interesting, something I've never shown you before." She veered off the trail and slowly led me through a maze of trees, turning left, then right, then left again until we unexpectedly came to a small clearing in the woods. Just in front of us we saw remnants of an old stone foundation, and behind them a stone structure with walls five or six-feet high, open to the sky.

"It must have been the cold storage room for the house," Katherine said, "used for root vegetables, milk and butter, and probably beer and wine as well. The old wooden roof obviously rotted away decades ago; there're only traces of it left." The back and both sides of the structure were surrounded by forest; the front wall—the one facing the old house that no longer existed—had a door.

She reached under her graduation gown and extracted a large, black key that looked partially rusted. "This worked a year ago," she said, "here's hoping it still does." She spent 30 seconds coaxing the key into the lock. Finally, we heard the bolt slide back into its housing. She pushed on the door and it creaked open.

Looking around I had a welter of thoughts: hope, uncertainty, a premonition. I wasn't sure where this was going. A large portion of the old dirt floor was covered by thick, dark-green moss—moss as soft as the dove's breast in the impression of Picasso's fantastic lithograph that I gave to Harvard several years ago, now that I think back on it. The branches of the old maples and oaks surrounding the outside walls had grown together to create a leafy canopy that filtered the sunlight, blocking glare to leave only glow. Leaves that had fallen inside the structure were piled in one of the corners, presumably blown there by swirling winds. Katherine pushed the door shut and took off her graduation gown. She shook it once, turned to me and said, "welcome to Shangri-La, Fran." Still looking straight at me, not the gown, she shook it a second time and spread it on the mossy floor.

She sat down on the moss next to her gown and began to take off her shoes. I was pretty sure now where this was headed. But the major question still remained: could I do it right? Could I do justice to her, this beautiful creature with the long, lanky legs I'd dreamed about when jerking off, but never touched.

She never asked, but ten-to-one she knew I was a virgin. We undressed each other slowly, silently, savoring it. When we were both bare to the waist I leaned forward and kissed her gently. Amuse bouche? I asked. "Very good," she said. "Next course, please." She drew my hand to the belt she was wearing, then reached out to mine. "I'm on the pill and just over my down time, so I'm not for condoms unless you are," she said. I told her my mother had gotten pregnant that way and then had a shotgun wedding that she'd always regretted. "Fran, the best thing that could ever happen to me would be marrying you," she said. "Shotgun or no shotgun."

My spirits soared; the anxiety was blown away. Whatever happened was going to be all right because she honest-to-god loved me, for whatever reason I couldn't fathom, but she did!

After we were down to bare skin she gave me the most fantastic massage imaginable. She'd come very close to my genitals, but bypass them every time. I was aching to step it up, but smart enough to stay calm and let her teach me by example.

When I finally got a chance to reciprocate I wanted to use some of the maneuvers she'd just taught me, but couldn't remember a single one. So I freelanced and before I knew it she'd rolled on her back and was guiding my hands for me, one uptown, one downtown.

Over the next hour I got a graduate-level course in female sexual anatomy. Of all the things she taught me, my favorite was kissing her downtown with those sinuous legs of hers draped over my shoulders. I couldn't wait for our first chance to try it with her stretched across a bed and me standing beside it, instead of having to kneel or lie prone.

Eventually, long after the sun had passed beyond us, she stiffened me up again and asked me to come inside her. It went OK, but in my book it wasn't up to what we'd being doing before. Coming together seemed pretty good on the timing, but I had to explain to her that I really had come, because I never ejaculated at all. Much later, I learned that she'd faked her climax as part of her gift to me.

We roused ourselves late in the afternoon, locked up Shangri-La, and headed home, taking a different route back to the trail to avoid leaving a twice-traveled track through the woods that someone might spot. How do you remember the route if you do this only once a year? I asked when we were back on the trail. "It helps to be part Indian" she said, "and also to have the map I'm going to give you tomorrow with all the blazed trees marked on it." I didn't see any blazes, I said, feeling chagrined because I'd looked for one every time she'd changed direction.

We returned to Shangri-La the following day with backpacks containing two small pillows, a bed sheet, and picnic supplies that Katherine had bought at an upscale delicatessen just off campus. Using the map she gave me, and the hints she supplied about the location of blazes, I managed to get us there with only one mistake, and no evident damage to the forest that others could track. The lock posed no problems, and by noon I had our picnic fully laid out, in plenty of time to bask in the filtered mid-day sun.

Sated, we napped after our picnic, lying together, still fully clothed, with our legs intertwined, my left one between hers. At some point I vaguely woke up, brought back from indistinct dreams by her gentle rocking motion, and slowly, one pelvis against the other, we quietly coupled until we came together—indisputably, I thought. Forever, I hoped.

When we finally woke up for real she murmured to me, "That was lovely; you're a wonderful lover, Fran." Who's talking? I whispered in her ear. She leaned over and kissed me, briefly flicking her tongue against the roof of my mouth.

A moment later, she unexpectedly floored me. "I think you're a wonderful lover because you're both male and female," she said. After a long pause she added, "I'm bisexual, have been ever since I can remember, but I've never doubted that I'm a woman. With you I think it's more profound. I could sense it in the way you make love: you're innately a combination of both sexes. On the ball field, in the locker room, you're male, but the way you intuitively reacted to me—with me—you were like a loving lesbian. I originally fell for you because of your brains; now it's far more, far deeper than that, Fran. I've just slept with a kindred soul. I never thought I'd have a chance to do that."

After closing the door on our way out and locking it, Katherine handed me the key and said softly, "This is yours now; take good care of it. Pass it on next June to an Upper you trust and care about, someone special." She paused for a few seconds to look back at the door, then said, "Legend has it that the tradition started back in the late 1980s, so by now there must be at least 30, maybe 35,

Devon alumni who've slept with their successor here. And so far as I know, members of our secret society have never said a word about it to outsiders—not to anyone else, ever."

17: Wildwood at Lenox – 2095

I itched for much of my senior year at Devon—itched to be with Katherine instead of talking to her on the phone, itched to resolve the problems I was having with our new programming language, itched to get out of the indoor cage and back onto the diamond. In February, Katherine saved me from going stir crazy by suggesting that I use one of my Day Passes to meet her in Ogunquit so we could walk the winter beach together.

We walked for miles it seemed, sometimes with no one else in sight, listening to the shrill gulls and whistling wind, and the steady drumbeat of waves pounding the foreshore. As I looked at the beach receding into the gray winter day far ahead, I thought of Joyce's metaphor for eternity and said that if we counted all the grains of sand in the entire beach, the number we reached would be an unimaginably small fraction of infinity. Katherine turned and nodded at me. Joyce, she said, with just a trace of a smile. And Swift, too, in a famous letter to the Spectator. We didn't talk much as we were walking, because being with each other in those surroundings said it all.

When the snow finally melted in late March, and we could get out of the cage to begin spring training on Sloan's

Field, life finally got better. Luckily, Katherine had a spring break at Harvard that overlapped mine by several days, so we had a great time talking about exotic jaunts that we could theoretically take to the Caribbean, or maybe even Paris, before we finally settled on the more prosaic option of going down to my house in Darien for several days so that she could meet Mom and I could meet her parents. Everybody hit it off, which was a relief to both of us.

One day Mom inadvertently found us making love in the afternoon and used the occasion to tell us that she was currently sleeping with a wonderful widower, a partner in Cravath, Swaine & Moore, a major law firm in the City. "I'm beginning to think this could be a lifetime deal," she said to both of us, "but before I go all in, I want you to meet him, Fran, and tell me what you think." It really pleased me that we'd grown close enough for her to ask that.

Back at Devon, I had an unexpected encounter with the Head of School. I was walking to afternoon class along Founder's Way when he suddenly appeared, coming from nowhere it seemed. "Johnson," he said abruptly, "what would you think about spending a year at one of the top British public schools? On an exchange scholarship, with all costs covered except for your transportation."

I was taken aback, because this was coming from way out in left field. Well, I've been planning to go to MIT graduate school, I said. And thought to myself that I wasn't about to be separated from Katherine for another year. But you don't say that to the Head of School, so to be polite, I told him that I hadn't made any commitment yet to MIT, and a year in the UK sounded like an interesting possibility, one I'd like to consider. I asked what school he had in mind so I could do some on-line research. "It's Salisbury College," he said to me. "Since I'm chair of the selection committee that assigns each successful applicant to one of the public schools participating in the exchange program, I think I can assure you that if you'd like to apply, you will be assigned to Salisbury.

"You understand of, course, that the British public schools are private," he added, "somewhat like St. Paul's or Groton in nature." I said I'd heard of Eton and Harrow, but not Salisbury. "It's a latecomer to the scene," he replied, "founded in 1855 by Queen Victoria. She proclaimed that it should adopt all the best public school traditions and rigorously reject all the anachronistic ones. It's an excellent school, not as famous as the two you mentioned, but definitely in the top-ten tier." I said it sounded intriguing, and promised to get back to him promptly.

I did considerable research on the web that night and concluded that what I'd said out of politeness really was true; it *was* intriguing. I called Katherine, as I did almost every night, and we talked for at least an hour. Characteristically, she took the long view of it. We had already agreed that we shouldn't get married until we were self-supporting, and we both knew that the graduate-school stipend MIT was talking about wouldn't be enough to get us over that threshold. "It's a unique opportunity," she said finally, "you should go for it. I meant it that first day in Shangri-La when I told you that the day I marry you will be the happiest one of my life. Whether it's one year, five years, ten years from now—there's no rush, Fran. I really want you to do it; living among the Brits will be a whole new experience, maybe an eye-opening one. I'm sure you'll learn stuff there that you could never learn here.

"I truly, truly love you. And I know how much you love me. We can wait."

Ten days later the Head of School called me into his office to tell me that I'd been awarded a total scholarship to spend the coming academic year at Salisbury, which in turn would be sending one of its sixth formers to Andover on a similar scholarship awarded by it. I thanked him profusely for telling me about the exchange program and getting me into Salisbury. The thanks were genuine, because I'd done more research in the interim and was really hyped up by the prospect of spending a full year abroad.

The rest of spring whizzed by and we finished the baseball season 11 and 2 by clobbering Exeter again, this time by seven runs. I'd been debating myself for some time about what to do with the Shangri-La key. Rita McDowell, a statuesque 5'11" track star with a classical Greek profile and large, luminous bedroom eyes, was unquestionably the sexiest female on campus—good-looking faculty and knockout faculty wives included. But I was so totally committed to Katherine that the idea of sleeping with Rita had no appeal at all, meaning I'd surely screw it up if I tried to fake enthusiasm. So I settled on a teammate, our new center fielder and captain-elect for next year, Rob Thomas.

I made only one trip to Shangri-La with Rob, because he was an Eagle Scout when it came to reading maps and finding obscure blaze marks. When I unlocked and pushed the door open, the first thing I noticed was the old pile of leaves, still in the same corner, but bigger now. The mossy section of the floor was still as large—and just as soft—as it had been last year. Rob looked around, tested the moss with his fingers, and burst out, "Who gave you— it had to be Katherine, right? You were here with her last year! Oh, my God, dude, I can't believe this!!"

Hey, man, I said to him, giving him a fist bump on the chest. You've got a whole year to whack off, thinking about coming back here. When you do, choose well, as Katherine said to me when we left on the second day. And don't forget to bring a picnic.

"Rad, really rad!" Rob said as he looked around again. Then he grinned at me for several seconds, and gave me a hard high five.

Perhaps I should depart from my chronological account at this juncture to explain why I'm violating the de facto vow of secrecy that Katherine described to me when we were leaving Shangri-La on the second day. In 2025, about six years after we were there, the trustees of the charitable trust that owned the park decided to build a network of trails throughout the forest. The engineers who designed the network must have thought that the old stone walls of Shangri-La were unsafe, because the trustees decided to demolish the building and set up several large picnic tables in the clearing, with drinking fountains as well. Since all that happened about 70 years ago, I'm probably one of the few Shangri-La alumni still alive who knows the whole story—maybe the only one.

Given the history I've just described, it's obvious that my disclosure won't have any impact on current or future Devon students. Katherine and Rob Thomas are no longer alive, so I'm not identifying any living Shangri-La alumnus except for myself. And that brings me to my reasons for wanting to disclose the whole Shangri-La story before time runs out and it gets buried forever in an unmarked grave.

The day before I graduated from Devon I called on my Department Chair, Mr. Sampson, to thank him for all he'd taught me, and all the help he'd given me on my project to create a new AI programming language. He, in turn, thanked me for what I'd contributed both in classes and on the baseball field, then told me—in strict confidence until he retired—about the faculty expulsion debate the preceding year. I was amazed to learn that the Dean of

Students was ready to expel Katherine and me for smoking pot underneath General Knox's horse at 2:00 a.m. without even asking us why we did it. And also amazed that 44% of the faculty were willing to go along with that. Give us a break guys; we simply lost a bet.

I said earlier that we did it to celebrate April Fools' Day, but there was more to it than that. Katherine had just won the yearbook poll for most popular girl in the Senior Class. According to school custom, the runner-up was entitled to challenge her to see which of them could successfully pull off a stunt that was voted "more popular" than the other's by the Senior Class.

Her challenger got away with climbing the tower of Witherspoon Hall and ringing the bell twice at 2:00 a.m. on a Sunday morning, when it wasn't supposed to ring at all. But then we got caught doing our thing, so it was no contest. As her prize, the other girl got a magnum of champagne she could legally drink when she got home after graduation.

For years I've wanted to repay Devon in kind for putting Katherine and me through the wringer. So it pleases me enormously to disclose here and now that Devon Seniors and Uppers fornicated in a secret midsummer's ritual for more than 35 years without being caught. The final irony in all this—or maybe it's poetic justice—is that the Dean of Student's vaunted "Devon Rules" would not have applied even if the Academy had discovered what was

going on. I checked recently and "publicly kissing" on
"Academy grounds" is still forbidden. But there's nothing
in the Rules then or now to prohibit fornication next door
on property the Academy used to own. The Woods were a
true refuge, never to be forgotten.

18: At Sea – 2020

7.13.20

This has been some summer. On my way home from Devon, I stopped off in Cambridge to help Katherine find an apartment for her sophomore year, and with help from the internet we hit the first pitch, leasing a ground-floor, one-bedroom apartment on Chauncy Terrace just off Mass Avenue. The bedroom is large enough for a king-sized bed, the kitchen is serviceable, and there's another small room with a fireplace that will work as an office for both us after I get back from England next year.

After signing the lease we headed south to break the news to her parents that we're "unofficially" (but very definitely) engaged, and are planning to spend most of the summer traveling together in Britain. Two weeks later, they respond in kind with what they call an "unofficial" engagement present—a round-trip ticket for both of us on the Queen Mary, sailing from New York to Southampton in mid July, returning in late August for Katherine and open-ended in 2021 for me.

"Everybody flies these days, but they don't know what they're missing," her father says as he hands the ticket to me and puts his other arm around my shoulder. "We took the old Queen Mary on our first trip to Europe, and we've never forgotten it." He beckons to Katherine with a little nod that says 'come on over here' and puts his free arm around her shoulder.

"You can only take your first trip once," he tells us, "and we want you to share our experience." Pausing for a second, and glancing to his right at Katherine, he smiles and adds, "We briefly debated sleeping arrangements on the way over, but decided you'd want us to save money by booking you in a double-bedded cabin rather than two adjoining single ones. We hope that's OK with you." Katherine's so happy she starts to cry. I have to wipe away some tears.

Mom is even more generous. I know that Sydney—I refuse to refer to him as my father anymore—is paying her a handsome sum of alimony every month, but it's news to me that she also has income from a trust her father and his bachelor brother set up years ago. "It's sizable," she tells me, "far more than I'll ever need or want. Since everything that's in it when I die is going to you anyway, I want you to have some of it now so you and Katherine can eat well and stay in decent places instead of youth hostels." Turns out the sum she has in mind is $25,000, a king's ransom by our standards. That night I toss Lonely Planet aside and start leafing through my Rough guidebook, looking for new places to stay.

And now we're about a third of the way across the Atlantic, on a clear July evening, waiting for darkness so we can go out on deck to watch the stars before the waning moon comes up. When it does we're going to dance on deck, all by ourselves, to K's i-phone collection of Cole Porter and Benny Goodman.

7.14.20

This is my first diary. I decided to start it yesterday because I realized after a day at sea that K's dad is right: the first trip abroad *is* special. I want to keep track of ours so we can recall it years hence, when our memories start to disintegrate.

Tonight we're going to have dinner at the Captain's table. I have absolutely no idea why we've been invited, but when we got back to the cabin after breakfast this morning, there's the invitation on our bedside table, in an unsealed cream-colored envelope with the Captain's crest, addressed in fine italic, handwritten script to Ms. French and Mr. Johnson.

K has a summer dress in her cabin bag that will marginally pass muster at the Captain's table, but I have only a pair of gray slacks and a dress sweater, so I track down the steward who looks after our cabin to ask if he can help, and he immediately says, "Certainly, sir." When we return to our cabin after lunch, a dark blue blazer is laid out neatly on our bed, along with a crisply ironed white shirt and a striped tie colored silver, green, and navy blue. I try on the shirt and blazer, both of which fit as though they'd been custom made for me. Suddenly, an image I'd seen during my research on Salisbury College flashes through my brain. I get out my laptop to see if I can find it again. And five minutes later I have it—a photo of the College Chancellor wearing a tie exactly like the one on my bed. Coincidence, I wonder, or does it have something to do with why we've been invited to the Captain's table?

When we eventually sit down for dinner there, the woman on my left turns out to be an upper-crust Brit who's not at all bashful. I say very little myself, just enough to learn that she's Provost of Leeds—which she refers to as "one of the better red-brick" universities—author of several books on philosophy and education, and film critic for the *Sunday Times*.

After the Captain adroitly turns the conversational vector midway through dinner, I discover fairly quickly that the woman on my right is the wife of a famous, high-powered software expert, the CEO of Almega. While we converse about our respective travel plans, my brain works hard to figure out a subtle way of letting her know about the new AI language I'm working on. Minutes later she hands me the proverbial silver platter. "The Captain tells us that you're a software genius," she says. "My husband would very much like to have a drink with you after dinner."

After we finally finish the five-course banquet I have a chance to speak briefly with K before we get separated again. You learn about the man on your left? I ask her. CEO of Almega, the start–up with the fabulous IPO last year? She nods. His wife was on my right, I say. He wants to talk with me! They're already challenging Google and IBM for leadership on AI software—their Holmes just beat IBM's Watson badly in a three-game Go match in Japan. Good luck! she whispers, giving me a quick kiss before darting off to catch up with the other women who are on their way to the Captain's salon. We men get the smoking room to ourselves.

On our way there, I figure it out: as a result of the restructuring several years ago, Google is now owned by a holding company named Alphabet. So when the founders of the start-up decide to go public, they rename their company Almega, an obvious contraction of alpha and omega, and a shorthand reference to the whole Greek alphabet. The start-up founders are clearly challenging Google to a duel—one they think they can win by being leaner and quicker. Their streamlined Almega vs. Google's over-extended, more traditional Alphabet.

Their CEO appears beside me and we walk together the rest of the way to the smoking room. "I very much enjoyed talking with your charming Katherine," he says. "She told me you're one of the smartest people on the planet, and she clearly adores you. Am I right in assuming that she's been helping you on the new AI language you're working on? She obviously knows a great deal about programming."

She's been helpful, very helpful, I say, without elaborating. The truth is that Katherine's been doing most of the innovating lately.

"Here's my card. I don't know what your current plans are, but if you ever decide to leave the academic arena, I hope very much that you'll get in touch with me," their CEO tells me. "I'd like to show both of you our campus, and talk in some detail about where we're headed and the potential we see in our approach.

"Happy as we were with the IPO results, I frankly feel the market is undervaluing us by a third, perhaps even 40%. Which is fine for the long-term, because it enables us to attract top talent now, using relatively inexpensive stock options and other equity packages that will be worth millions in ten years if all goes as planned. We've gone from the basement where we started to the ground floor, and now, with the IPO, to the third or fourth floor maybe, but it's designed to be a 50-story skyscraper."

Sound adult and be as cool as possible, I say to myself. I greatly appreciate your offer, I say to him. Both your offer and your advice—your comments about the advantages of getting involved early on. As Katherine may have told you, she currently expects to be at Harvard for three more years and I'm planning to be at Salisbury College in England through early June of next year. When I get back to the States, I'll definitely call to let you know what our then current thinking is. From what I've read recently, I can well imagine that your work and ours might mesh to the benefit of all of us.

The ladies rejoin us shortly after that, we spend a few minutes being polite, then thank the Captain again and make our way through all the arrant opulence to our more modest quarters back in cabin class. I tell K that I think we can both bank on jobs at Almega if we ever decide to go that route.

She says she's going to write a note to the Captain thanking him yet again, because almost no one sends handwritten thank-you notes anymore, so they tend to get remembered by the recipient, and who knows when it might come in handy to be remembered by the Captain of the Queen Mary. I suggest that she also ask him how he learned of us, because we want to thank that person, too. She quickly writes the note, rings for our trusty steward, and asks him to deliver it.

When we get back from afternoon tea there's a note from the Captain awaiting us. "I greatly enjoyed meeting you," it says. "Our office in New York routinely identifies American passengers who should be invited to my table, and you and the Goddards were both listed in their cables. Sorry I can't tell you anything more than that."

Well, so much for that idea.

7.15.20

Stormy today. A pewter sky, strong winds out of the south-west, and long waves quartering on our stern. Good day to work at the computer, have high tea in our cabin, and make love.

7.16.20

Our last full day at sea. K woke up this morning with a new syntax idea for Artel, the name she recently coined for our AI language, and we worked on it together for most of the day. As I mentioned earlier, she's come up with most of the new ideas we've adopted since we teamed up in the spring, thereby adding greatly to my prior work. We can't quite read each other's minds yet, but we're getting close.

Our friend, the Captain, hosted a dinner dance tonight, but since we weren't dressed for it, we used the passes he'd given us to go to first class and watch the swells for a while, before retreating to our own deck where we could slow dance, unobserved, until we were ready to come standing up. I never ejaculate, but coming together the way we do is far better, far more intense. My god, I love you, she whispered in my ear moments after we'd peaked, and I came a second time, something I've never done before.

I write all this as I watch her undress, and I'm turned on again. Her legs, her thatch, I can't resist going back there for thirds, lips to lower lips this time. Already I can feel it: her quiver, my quivering tongue. Driving us both crazy.

19: England – 2019

Docked at Southampton in mid morning, picked up our rental car, stowed our bags in the back, and headed north. To give us more room in the car, I wanted to drop off my footlocker, containing the clothes and gear I'll need for the coming year, at Callahan's House—the place where I'll be living during my time at Salisbury College.

Drove through the historic New Forest, passing small hamlets with names like Netley Marsh, Cadnam, and Cherford. Finally reached the College grounds on the outskirts of Salisbury, in a place called Henderson Water Meadows on the River Avon (not Shakespeare's Avon to the west, which is a different river altogether).

Seconds after I rang the doorbell of Callahan's, a short, stocky, white-haired woman appeared at the door. Good afternoon, I said, I'm Fran Johns—"Well, from the sound of it, you must be our American sixth former," she said jovially, cutting me off in the middle of my own name. "I'm Miss Carrier, the House Matron. Please come in." May I bring in my trunk to stow it here until I return in the fall? I asked. And show my sister where I'll be living—

before we head off on our trip around England? Miss Carrier nodded and said, "Of course, dear."

This afternoon we strolled around the College grounds, taking in the mid-19th century brick and stone buildings, the Victorian chapel with stained glass windows neither of us could decipher, the playing fields that flanked the river, and the stream itself, a lovely meandering limestone spring creek filled with dark-green flora that trailed long tendrils in the undulating current. I was fascinated by the weaving strands of freshwater seaweed; they seemed seductive, almost hypnotic.

After a quick visit to the Salisbury Cathedral in the center of town—quick because it seemed overwrought to both of us—we headed for our inn here in the town of Avebury. We're not far from Stonehenge, and very close to an ancient circle of megaliths, said to be the largest stone circle on earth.

20: Wildwood at Lenox – 2095

After reading my diary entries for the days that Katherine and I spent on the Queen Mary and our first day in England, I'm sorely tempted to do some red-line editing. Boasting about three times in one night seems undignified from my current perspective. As does denigrating Salisbury Cathedral the way we did. After all, Constable was one of England's greatest painters and Salisbury was his favorite cathedral, the one he chose to paint more often than any other. How could a couple of young students like us call it 'overwrought?' And write it off without even mentioning the working 14th century clock we saw inside it?

Despite my misgivings I'm going to leave the diary as is, to ensure that it remains an accurate reflection of what I thought—or the thoughts I was willing to record—at that stage of my life. And to avoid having it influence what I say here, I'm going to defer reading any more of it until I've set down my independent recollections of our trip—the memories and impressions that have survived for some 75 years, with initial help, perhaps, from photos and other memorabilia that I packed away many, many years ago, but could not find after I moved here.

My earliest vivid recollection of the UK is of white horses carved into the hillsides north of Salisbury. Our guidebook said they were formed by digging a trench in the shape of a horse and stripping away the sod in the area enclosed by the trench to expose an underlying layer of chalk. I can also shut my eyes and see Stonehenge from a distance, as well as the prehistoric circle of huge stones at Avebury where we spent our first night in England. I know we saw numerous other prehistoric stone circles in the surrounding countryside, but I can't visualize any of them at this point.

Driving on small roads across the broad moors and downs of southern England, we got a good sense of how beautiful, and sometimes desolate, the unpopulated open spaces of the countryside were back then, and perhaps still are. We jested about having to drive on the wrong side of the road; the left side was wrong, we decided, because it was sinister, both literally and figuratively.

In the course of our travels we also acquired a new automotive vocabulary: the engine of our little Vauxhall Corsa was under the bonnet; our bags were luggage; our luggage was in the boot; the car ran on petrol; our stick shift was a gear lever; traffic circles were roundabouts; and traffic jams were called tailbacks. Katherine was the first to remember Churchill's quip about two peoples separated by a common language.

I remember eating ploughman's lunches in half-timbered pubs, and picnics in the countryside; an excursion to see the old Roman baths in the city of Bath; an impressive suspension bridge over a gorge in the outskirts of Bristol; and a series of charming small villages we encountered as we drove north through the verdant, gently rolling hills of the Cotswolds—villages with picaresque, unforgettable names like Lower Kilcott, Upper Slaughter, Hawkesbury Upton, and Chipping Campden.

We went to Wales next, and promptly stumbled onto an eisteddfod—a singing festival where old Welsh songs were being sung with abandon by a chorus of lusty, full-throated Welshmen, accompanied with precision and clarity by female altos and sopranos. For the next two days we hiked in the mountains of Snowdonia, where we encountered cold weather, patches of snow and slick ice underfoot, and a surprising number of other hikers, given the conditions. More than once, we asked ourselves if we were crazy to keep dogging it.

I remember getting deliberately lost on our way back to the English border, by turning onto progressively narrower roads until we were finally down to a two-track lane. It led us to a farmhouse where we met a sturdy Welsh woman who told us that we'd reached the end of the road and best turn around—but not until we had come inside for a bowl of her hard cider.

After we finally got back to real roads and crossed the border into England, we decided to stop for a while in the market town of Chester to soak up the feel of the place by walking along its main streets, all of which were lined with attractive half-timbered shops that must have been at least 200 years old. I had the feeling that life was imitating art: the street looked like the set for filming a Thomas Hardy or Henry Fielding novel.

I have no recollection of driving through the British midlands, but I certainly remember our next destination, which was a country house in the Lake District—the Watergate Inn, I think it was called—near the town of Ambleside.

Katherine, who had studied Romantic poetry in her freshman year at Harvard, was looking forward to visiting the Wordsworth Museum near Lake Grasmere, and Dove Cottage next door, where the poet lived for many years. We bicycled there the morning after we arrived, and in the days that followed we did a lot of walking along an extensive network of trails, some flat, some on the fairly steep hills that surrounded us. We carried our lunch and Katherine's anthology of Lake District poetry in my backpack, and read Coleridge and Wordsworth poems out loud to each other during our picnics.

When we stopped for lunch on our final day we quickly found a mossy bank in a small clearing, shaded by an overarching tree. We immediately broke out laughing, because the resemblance to Shangri-La was so obvious. We kissed, but were much too close to the trail to think about doing anything else. Instead, Katherine recited one of Wordsworth's Lucy ballads from memory:

She dwelt among the untrodden ways
Beside the springs of Dove,
A Maid whom there were none to praise
And very few to love:

A violet by a mossy stone
Half hidden from the eye!
—Fair as a star, when only one
Is shining in the sky.

She lived unknown, and few could know
When Lucy ceased to be;
But she is in her grave, and, oh,
The difference to me!

I weep now, as I write this, remembering our mossy spots.

21: England – 2020

7.28.20

    Fran hasn't written in his diary for days, and now he wants me to take his place because he's wrapped up in a new idea for improving Artel. I thought we had a pact that we were going to forget AI during our trip, but ever since we met the Goddards at the Captain's table on the ship, F has been unable to turn off the spigot completely. Thoughts drip out now and then, until they pool together to form a new idea that he has to explore if he wants to avoid the Chinese water torture of listening to still more drips.

    I've never read Pepys or Boswell and don't have a clue about writing diaries because I've never kept one. To boot, I suspect that most people who do keep them are unreliable narrators, F included at times. I've looked back at what he's written, and think he's given me far more credit than I deserve for recent improvements in Artel. He also has me sharing some of his own ideas when I haven't said (or even thought to myself) anything of the kind.

    For example, he says that neither of us could decipher the stained glass window in his College chapel. But had he asked, I could have told him that it must have been a late addition to the chapel, installed to celebrate

Kitchener's 1898 victory in the Sudan. And unlike F, I thought Salisbury Cathedral was pretty amazing, actually. (The Brits we've encountered so far seem to say 'actually' at least once in every five sentences.)

These are just quibbles, though. I'm going to use this opportunity to tell F on the record that I love him to pieces. I've told him before, but never in writing, so here it is, Mr. Johnson, official notification that I am absolutely smitten, because you are the smartest, nicest, most lovable (and loving) soul mate I could ever hope to meet.

That said, I guess it's up to me to describe what we've done in the last ten days. So, here goes: Prehistoric Stonehenge, large stone circles, and chalk horses in Wiltshire. The moors and downs we crossed on our way west. The American museum in Bath where F spotted the distinctive upholstered seat of his father's dining room Sheraton chair, along with a small card saying his mother had donated it in 2015 (the year they split up). Also, the well preserved Roman baths we saw nearby, and a famous crescent of well-preserved 18th-century townhouses. Then, outside Bristol, the dramatic Clifton Suspension Bridge, an 1864 engineering triumph spanning the Avon Gorge, high above the tidewater tail-out of several west-coast rivers, including Shakespeare's River Avon.

Next, the gentle, rolling hills and shallow valleys of the Cotswolds. And the "tyre puncture" we had to deal with in the middle of a market-day crowd in a place called Moreton-in-Marsh. More scenic countryside in the lovely

Wye River valley. A great Welsh songfest we happened
upon shortly after we crossed the river into Wales. Freezing
our butts off in Snowdonia. Barking dogs and the Welsh
woman who invited us in for hard cider when we got lost
(deliberately, F claimed when it happened, but I don't think
so).

After that, the quintessential, poster-perfect English
main street in Chester near the Welsh border. Our first
expressway trip, driving from there to the Lake District on
the M-6 "motorway." Our lakeside Edgewater Inn, which
reminded me of Bedford Lodge on Lake Cayuga, one of the
New York Finger Lakes, where I spent early childhood
summers with my grandparents. Wordsworth's cottage and
the excellent museum next door. Picnics and poetry on our
long walks. The love I saw in F's eyes as I was reciting
Untrodden Ways—an old favorite that popped into mind
when we picked our mossy picnic spot, I suppose.

That's my catch-up list. If I've missed other things
Fran would have included here, he can always scribble
additions in the margins when he eventually reads this.

We drove northeast today, walked along Hadrian's
Wall (the old Roman defensive barrier), and then visited
the remains of several Cistercian abbeys in Yorkshire. The
most impressive (and my favorite) was Fountains Abbey,
which was founded by a small band of Benedictine monks
in 1132. Tonight, at the nearby Water Garden Inn, we had
our best meal of the trip so far, rare roast beef au jus with
string beans straight from the inn's garden, together with

Yorkshire pudding that had risen in their old brick oven to peaks 4" high. Plus excellent apple crisp for dessert, with a piece of real Cheddar cheese—from the village of Cheddar in Somerset—on the side. A perfect example of my mom's axiom that simple done right is the absolute best.

7.29.20

In all candor, I have to say I was surprised to learn that K thinks I'm an unreliable narrator. I feel compelled to reply in kind. In her final paragraph she says "we had the best meal of the trip so far" at the Water Garden Inn. The truth is I never said that and she never asked me. Who does she think she is, using the royal "we" to describe her own opinions?

Well, she's my Queen of Hearts, that's who. How can I feel fed up because she puts words in my mouth? It's simply not possible. I must tell her here, when she reads this, that all is forgiven because I love her. Love her buckets!

BTW, Miss French, my favorite meal of the trip so far was actually the Captain's dinner on the QM. Or, if we're talking only about meals in the UK, the Welsh rarebit and pint of lager I had at the Shipman's pub in Llangollen on the River Dee.

Today, on our way south, we stopped in York to see the Yorkminster, a majestic Gothic cathedral built over a 250-year period beginning in 1220, and recently restored. Impressive as it was, both of us—having consulted together in order to restore peace and domestic tranquility—now agree that the cathedral we saw in Lincoln this afternoon is even more memorable. Some of the west front dates back to 1073, but an earthquake in 1185 destroyed everything else; apart from the original remnants, what we saw today dates back to the century following the quake. Opinions of its height vary, but it's indisputably one of the tallest cathedrals in the world, and the Romanesque carvings on the west front and around some of the doorways are superb, even to uninitiated viewers like us.

Off to dinner now at the Royal George next door to our hotel, and on to Cambridge tomorrow.

7.31.20

As we reached the outskirts of Cambridge around noon the glowering sky started to leak raindrops, prompting K to retrieve her poetry anthology from the back seat, and recite Wordsworth's recollection of coming to Cambridge as a young scholar. We parked in town, and in the drizzling rain retraced Wordsworth's path, disappointed to find that his "famous Inn," the Hoop, no longer existed, and his gowned "doctors [and] students" were all on vacation. After a very instructive guided tour of St. John's College, the one Wordsworth attended, we listened to a recording by the world-famous St. John's Choir, whose members were also away for the holidays.

In mid afternoon, the skies cleared and I played gondolier when we punted on the River Cam with K facing me, comfortably stretched out in the bow, supported by a back rest, as she shared more of Wordsworth's Cambridge recollections in Book Third of the *Prelude*. Both of us found it easy to imagine ourselves in his place—as American "striplings" we, too, would have been delighted to spend several years in this age-old center of academic excellence, with its storied history and impressive setting.

22: Wildwood at Lenox – 2095

I remember very little about traveling through the English countryside after we left the Lake District. I know that we walked along Hadrian's Wall and saw some ancient abbeys and cathedrals, and I dimly recall that after a dreary morning in Cambridge it finally cleared, enabling us to punt on the river. I think I told Katherine that we were really in Venice, and promised to be her gondolier for life.

London was not only civilized, but surprisingly easy to negotiate. We'd made advance reservations for our hotel, several evenings at the theater, and a cricket test match; the rest of it we simply made up as we went along. We certainly walked a lot, taking in parks, museums, and historic buildings like Westminster Abbey, and I remember eating well, particularly at a quiet place around the corner from our hotel that served the best pigeon I've ever had. Because their menu was very imaginative and au currant, I was amazed to discover afterwards that they'd been in business for almost 50 years. Named Greenfields, I think, but they're probably long gone by now.

I also remember a lunch that lasted two hours in one of the swank hotels. The Doncaster, maybe? Whatever, it had three Michelin stars, and we agreed that it merited them. The chef was French, the quenelles de brochet were ineffably good, and the grilled Dover sole was astounding. Our waiter said it had been swimming in the Channel the day before, which probably explains why in all the years since then I've never had Dover sole to match it.

I know we spent a whole afternoon walking through a crowded street market, because that's where we found the lovely Roman glass beakers that are on my mantle now. And I remember the first museum we went to, because of all the Cézanne paintings they had. My favorite was a foreshortened view of Lake Annecy in southern France, a lake so blue in Cézanne's rendering that I wanted to dive into his canvas. Well traveled friends have since told me that Annecy is one of the loveliest lakes in the world. I thank Cézanne for telling me that long before they did.

Of course, there was a lot we didn't see or do. When I eventually got home a year later, friends were amazed that we hadn't gone to the Tower, or the British Museum (which I eventually did see on my own), or even Piccadilly Circus. I shrugged them off because instead of all that tourist stuff, we'd had a better time in bed. I remember best the afternoon after we'd walked in Hyde Park and seen a test match at Lord's, when we went to bed and got really bound up in each other for all time. Katherine told me again that she admired me as a man, but loved me even more as a woman, and that touched off a long conversation about who we were and wanted to become. I can reconstruct it because it's burned in memory.

"You obviously want to be a male at Salisbury," she wound up telling me. "Showers in the locker room and all that." She paused for a moment. "And when you get home and eventually go to work, best to dress like a man, and tell the guys a few raunchy jokes, so you don't have to bang your head against the glass ceiling. But, please, don't ever forget who you truly are."

Tactfully, very gently, as she was arousing me again, she suggested that when I got home I should consult a top-flight endocrinologist to find out what was really going on inside me. I didn't tell her that I'd already made a provisional appointment to see a Boston specialist.

My final memory of our UK trip together was saying goodbye to Katherine just before she boarded the Queen Mary for her voyage home. It was getting maudlin until she remembered the first time she'd kissed me in public at Devon and did it all over again, surrounded by a big crowd. Did that ever make a splash!

23: London – 2020

8.2.20

In London for a whole week! We dropped off our car yesterday because no sane person drives in London unless he has to, and checked into the Berkeley Plaza, our boutique apartment hotel on a quiet residential street here in the West End. We've got far more space and are paying a whole lot less than we would in one of the nearby upscale hotels like the Dorchester.

Knowing that the famous Portobello Road Market operates at full tilt only on Saturdays, we decided to start off there yesterday afternoon. Learned to navigate the underground "tube," which got us to the Notting Hill Gate station, and walked from there to the top of Portobello Road, and then down a few blocks to the beginning of the antiques market. Not surprisingly, it was jammed with people—and undoubtedly a passel of pickpockets as well.

We decided to look for Roman glass and much to our amazement quite quickly found a shop with a small collection of pieces. They looked old and the shop owner had papers for all them, showing that he had purchased them from registered antique dealers in Israel, Jordan, and Syria. We wound up buying two lovely small beakers from Jordan, both with iridescent blue, silver, and beige deposits on the inner side of the thin, gray-green glass that some Roman Empire artisan must have shaped at least 1,500 years ago. The notion that a household glass object that old could survive unscathed for that long blew our minds.

After taking our beakers back to our apartment we headed to Brown's Hotel for high tea, which we'd been told was the best in London. At the price they charged, it should be. We gulped at the cost, but enjoyed sipping champagne with our cucumber sandwiches, and decided, on the spot, to add afternoon tea to our daily routine when we got back home.

Ended the day by crossing the Thames to the Globe Theater where we saw a superb production of *Hamlet*, with Oscar Isaac reprising his award-winning 2017 performance as Hamlet, and Ian McKellen personifying evil as Claudius. Then late evening supper at La Coupe d'Or, a small French bistro two blocks from our hotel. We could eat there every night and be happy, but I'm sure we'll end up exploring other places.

8.5.20

F has taken another break so I'm scrivener again. We've done so much, it's hard to sort out the days, but I think I can still recapitulate fairly accurately.

On Sunday, our first full day here, we went to the Courtauld where I introduced F to Cézanne. It was love at first sight, so after we'd toured the rest of the museum and had lunch, we came back to the Cézannes and spent the rest of the day there, focusing in the end on F's half-dozen favorites: *Montagne Sainte-Victoire with Large Pine, the Cardplayers, Man with a Pipe, Lac d'Annecy, Pot of Primroses and Fruit, and Route Tournante.*

Without knowing anything about art history, F picked up intuitively on Cézanne's genius: foreshortening perspective to bring distant landscape closer to objects in the foreground, deliberately distorting background shapes and perspective to emphasize the fruit in his still life, leaving different parts of the canvas unpainted to suggest a road winding through abstract fields and trees, and above all, using different shades of his intense colors to create shape, volume, and depth in his subject matter. The different blues in *Lac d'Annecy* so engaged F that he talked seriously about changing our plans and going to France so we could see it in real life.

We had tickets that night for *Pirates of Penzance*, our favorite of the four Gilbert & Sullivan operas being performed at Covent Garden over the next two weeks by a new, highly touted G&S troupe prosaically named the Gilvans. They lived up to their reviews, giving a spirited performance in which every word was delivered with the clarity and precision that committed G&S fans demand. Excellent tapas afterwards at Barrafina, where we lucked into the perfect table for watching a worldwide assortment of Covent Garden pedestrians stroll past us.

Monday morning we went to Greenwich to see the Observatory and straddle the prime meridian, then came back for a walking tour of the City that included St. Paul's Cathedral, lunch in a Fleet Street pub where at least a dozen print journalists were swapping current rumors about the upcoming British election, a look inside one of the Inns of Court, and ten minutes at an Old Bailey trial that was impressive visually, but otherwise boring—nothing even remotely resembling the trials we'd read about, like Oscar Wilde's.

Excellent high tea in the late afternoon—at Fortnum & Mason this time—then on to the Victoria Palace Theater for an outstanding performance of *Hamilton*. Near the end of Act I King George makes his first appearance, drawing a few tentative laughs from the audience because he is dressed in a foppish, almost prissy, send-up of royal garb. In witty, bemused rap verse—which draws more laughs, because it's genuinely clever and his rap delivery quickly adds another dimension to the send-up—he asks the leaders of his former colonies what comes next, now that they're on their own. Lots of trouble, he predicts, before dismissing them with royal disdain. At which point he breaks into his now-famous 19-syllable "Da da da Dat" rap refrain, and starts mincing across the stage, beaming gleefully to tell us how important and self-satisfied he is. Immediately, the whole audience erupts with the loudest sustained laughter I can remember in a theater.

Fran told me afterwards that having seen a preview performance in the U.S. he knew what was coming and wondered whether a British audience would be offended by the send-up of one of their monarchs. He was pleased to discover that they could laugh heartily at themselves, aided, perhaps, by the great temporal distance between the rap-loving American archers and their royal British target.

Late evening supper at Tamarind, a highly regarded Indian restaurant several blocks from our hotel. Our grilled shrimp—"prawns" on the menu—were good, but I don't think I'd travel all the way to New Delhi to eat Indian food.

On Tuesday we decided to start at Westminster Abbey and walk our way home. The Abbey was full of buried British history, some of which we overheard from tour guides as we walked slowly past the groups they were leading. Parliament wasn't in session and Big Ben was still being restored, but we did get to see all the maps and communication equipment in Churchill's War Rooms, Britain's underground command center during WW II.

Glimpsed the famous door at Number 10 Downing Street and then crossed over to St. James's Park for a pleasant walk along a lake to Buckingham Palace, where we luckily caught the daily 11:30 changing of the guard, just as we reached the palace gates. The Union Jack, rather than the Royal Standard, was flying over the palace, meaning that the Queen was not in residence and tours could be conducted, but we opted for moving on, because F had other things in mind.

He'd never worn a piece of custom-made clothing in his life, he told me, but this was London, and he wanted to get a pair of "bespoke" shoes that would last him a lifetime. So i-phone in hand he led us across the park to St. James's Street, where we found the venerable shop of John Lobb, Bootmaker. I wish I had a tape of the conversation that took place over the next hour and a half; listening to F and the impeccably dressed Englishman who counseled him was surely worth the price of the shoes.

First, they talked about his last. Each Lobb client has one of his own, an exact replica of his foot that will be sculpted from wood, and used to shape his shoes as the leather is cut, stitched, and sewn, thereby ensuring that they fit him perfectly. After much discussion of Lobb's styles, leathers, trees, and polishes, F settled on their "Becketts" shoe, with the addition of a single "brogueing row" across the "vamp." He will receive a trial pair of his shoes that he can wear for several months and then return to the shop so that any slight pressure points can be detected and the last can be corrected to make his final pair a perfect fit. I hope they're ready for delivery by the time he sails for home next year.

Walked through Green Park on our way back to the Berkeley, then had tea and muffins ("crumpets") in our apartment and napped for a while because we knew we had a big evening coming up. First, a West End revival of *Wit,* a debut play by an American named Margaret Edson that won the 1999 Pulitzer Prize. We thought the all-English cast did a good job, particularly the lead woman who portrays a testy, but very savvy, English professor confined to a hospital bed; she spends most of her time reciting John Dunne sonnets to her doctors, knowing that she is dying of cancer. After the play, dinner at Greenwood, an attractive two-star Michelin restaurant that is literally just around the corner from our apartment. F has tender wood pigeon and I have delicious veal sweetbreads, we splurge on a bottle of 2006 Chateau Talbot, and share a marvelous Gran Marnier soufflé for dessert. And then we walk home hand-in-hand, two very happy campers.

Today is Wednesday, the 5th, and F's diary is now up to date. We're going to walk in Hyde Park this morning, and then watch crickct at Lord's.

Well, it's been a good day. The speaker at Hyde Park Corner this morning was obviously an educated, very fluent firebrand who tore into President Trump's foreign policy. When he switched to domestic issues, he really went on the warpath, berating the current government and calling for reforms way to the left of anything proposed back home by Bernie Saunders or Elizabeth Warren.

After half an hour of English oratory we hailed our first London cab at Marble Arch for a short hop to Lord's cricket ground, where we had seats to watch the opening innings of the test match between England and Sri Lanka, beginning at 11:00 sharp. F had bought our tickets before leaving the States, because both of us wanted to find out first-hand how cricket differs from baseball.

We ended up sitting next to a burly, florid-faced man with beer on his breath, a heavy cockney accent that made it hard for us to understand him, and the proverbial heart of gold. The minute he heard us speak, he adopted us. We were obviously clueless Americans who would have to be patiently instructed if we were going to have any glimmer of what was going on. In actual fact, F had done some Google research and already knew a lot, but he held back, because listening to our friend speak his own version of English was going to be an experience we didn't want to miss.

Actually—there I go again, can't seem to shake the habit—it was easy to pick up the basic ground rules, just by watching play for a few minutes. Two batters are on the field at the same time, at opposite ends of a narrow strip of close-cropped grass in the center of the field. Two pitchers are also at opposite ends of the strip. One of the pitchers tosses six balls to whichever batter is at the other end. Then the other pitcher takes over and tosses six balls in the opposite direction. The ball is supposed to bounce off the ground before it reaches the batter, but doesn't always do that. Batters score runs every time they're able to change positions without getting thrown out.

When one of the English batters turned in the batter's box and clubbed an errant pitch way to his left over the outfield boundary line, six runs were immediately added to England's scoreboard total even though the batters stayed where they were. F leaned over and whispered "it's an automatic six runs if the ball goes over the chalk circle in the air, four if it goes over on the ground." Our friend looked amazed. "I don't Adam and Eve it, ease never it a six like thet, innit?" he said loudly. Wow! I thought. Bat from the middle of the field and hit anywhere you want to, with no foul balls? I just knew F was going love it.

Ten minutes later, I learned another basic rule. One of the Sri Lanka pitchers took a long run before releasing the ball, which skidded off the ground faster than a hockey puck bouncing off the boards, and hit the three stakes planted next to each other, several feet to the batter's right. "He's out because he just got bowled," F whispered. "The three stakes are called stumps, the little things on top that just flew off the stumps are called the bails, and the whole business is called a wicket. Their best fast bowler just took a wicket. "

Our friend obviously overheard. "Blimey," he said. "Yure Yank noze is cricket!"

We left Lord's after the umpires pulled the stumps at 6:00, and went back to our apartment "to rest," F's quaint euphemism for making love. Afterwards I bared my soul to him and wound up telling him what's been on my mind ever since our second day at Shangri-La. If he carries through and does see a good endocrinologist, I think I know what he'll discover. So please do it, F?

8/9/ 20

We've both been remiss in making current diary entries, and F's in our other room working on Artel, so I'm going to play catch-up again and jot down what we've done over the last few days.

Thursday was museum day, the National in the morning and the Tate in the afternoon. I think Turner's a terrific painter, much more dramatic in reality than in the film of his life I saw four or five years ago. That evening we went to the Prince of Wales, another of London's classic theaters, to see *Dark Days, Bright Nights,* a satiric family comedy by a young British playwright who's clearly read most of Neil Simon's plays.

Yesterday we explored Chelsea and Kensington on foot, browsing in upscale shops, and poring over lots of unusual books in venerable, pleasantly musty second-hand book stores. Decided on the spur of the moment to line up for same-day tickets to *The Importance of Being Ernest,* because we thought it would be a treat to see it done by real British actors, rather than Americans imitating British actors. We were right. Wilde with a top-flight British cast is as good as comedy gets—certainly much wittier than what we saw the night before.

This morning we went map hunting. And now we own a beautiful ink and watercolor map of the American colonies, dated 1704, 12 x 20 inches, accompanied by a letter from the Maryland-based cartographer to the man who commissioned the map, a Virginia plantation owner named Robert Jeffries. How it found its way to London no one knows. F wants me to hang it in my room at Chauncy Terrace next year as a reminder of our last full day together in London.

We're about to head off to the Dorchester for a posh three-star lunch to cap off our culinary adventures, and tonight we'll finish our week of theater by going to Bath again with Lydia Languish and a host of Sheridan's other aptly named characters in *The Rivals.*

Off to Southampton by train tomorrow morning, to board the QM for my voyage home. I can't imagine how we'll manage ten months apart, but we will.

24: Salisbury College – 2020

8.25.20

Thank you, K, for all your diary entries. Now it's up to me full time.

Saying goodbye to her just before she boarded the Queen Mary was one of the hardest things I've ever done. We clung together for a long while, not speaking, until she finally said, "Hey, we've known all along that this is part of the deal, let's celebrate the trip with a goodbye Devon kiss!"

She disengaged, stepped back four or five paces, then spread her arms wide and didn't move for ten seconds. Poised that way, with arms fully outstretched, she must have attracted the attention of every boarding passenger in sight. Then she did her Devon number on me, rushing forward, throwing her arms around me, and giving me a real smacker. Several of the nearby passengers gave us a polite round of applause—the adult British equivalent, I suppose, of the whistles and catcalls we got from the Devon bleachers the first time she did it.

When the QM disappeared from sight I went back to the train station, extracted my bag from "left luggage" and took the next train to Salisbury, then a cab to the College. The Matron of Callahan's House recognized me and said she'd arrange to have my bed made up. She also told me that the Head of School, another "Callahan's boy," would be returning early to help the Headmaster make plans for the upcoming Michaelmas Term, and might want to take meals with me in town until the College kitchen opened up.

Two days later, around 5:00 in the afternoon, a lanky, good looking boy about six feet tall came into the House library where I was working on my lap-top. "David Bonham-Carter," he said cheerfully as we shook hands. "Matron told me you were here and I wondered if you'd like to have a spot of supper in town."

We hit if off immediately. He was far more open and easygoing than I'd expected the Head of School would be, based on what I'd read about British public schools. I was pleasantly surprised that he called me Fran right from the outset, rather than using my surname or not referring to me by name at all, which I gathered was the general practice among schoolboys who didn't know each other well.

After we'd settled into a table at the back of the Red Lion pub, he told me that College students were not allowed to drink beer or spirits during term time, unless a master invited them to do it. But this was still part of summer hols, and no one here would know who we were because he'd never been in this pub before, so I should order whatever I liked. I suspect that, all told, the two of us drained six pints of ale before the last call.

David spent a long time filling me in on unwritten school rules, the personal quirks of the masters I would probably encounter, some of the College's legends and actual history, and the courses he thought were the best it had to offer. When I found out that he was captain of the cricket team, I told him about my baseball experiences, and—at his request—spent at least half an hour explaining in detail how baseball is played. He responded by insisting that we go to the College cricket "nets" the next day so that I could learn how to use a cricket bat.

The nets turned out to be the rough equivalent of Bobby Anderson's batting cage—a structural substitute for live fielders, designed to speed up batting practice. My experience in them was a throw back to that first day with Eric Davis at Hanson Country Day when he taught me to hit a baseball.

I felt totally inept at first, because the bat was so strange. The handle was similar to the narrow end of a baseball bat, but instead of being round, the other end was a rectangular wooden blade, about 4" wide and two feet long, almost flat on the front side and slightly beveled on the back side. Having watched the batsmen at Lords, I knew that I had to teach myself to swing it vertically, rather than horizontally as in baseball, so that the flat side would drive the ball into the ground rather than the air, insuring that I couldn't be "caught out." On top of all that, I had to learn how to gauge which way the ball bowled by David was going to break when it bounced off the ground several feet before it reached me.

After a ragged ten-minute start I began to get a feel for it, and was able to hit grounders in David's direction fairly consistently. And then, all of a sudden, I figured out how to deflect balls behind me, the way I'd seen it done at Lord's. And next, how to make sweeping shots to either side of me, another commonplace occurrence at Lord's. And finally, how to punish a ball that sat up for me, by clubbing it with a baseball-type swing designed to hit it over the fielders' heads for a "six," the cricket version of a home run. I decided on the spot that I was going to round up tapes of international test matches to see how the best batters in the world did it.

At dinner that night David said he'd like to introduce me to the Headmaster—universally known as the "Head"—the following day. So I dressed for the occasion that morning, in my gray flannels and dark blue blazer, with a plain white dress shirt and the striped tie our QM steward had told me to keep when I started to hand it to him along with the blazer I'd borrowed.

After David introduced us, the Head's first words were "Welcome to Salisbury, Johnson, and well done, wearing the school tie!" He paused for a moment before adding, "You bought it at Harrod's, I trust." No, I said, it was a gift from a crew member on our ship coming over. "Damnable pirates!" he burst out. "Somebody in the States is producing copies of our tie and flooding the market with them. Harrod's, our sole authorized UK vendor, has engaged counsel in the U.S., but they say that little can be done at this juncture. Such a pity, because the tie used to be an identifying badge for OSBs—our alumni—throughout the world. Very useful if one old Salisbury boy spotted another in Singapore or Hong Kong." I apologized for inadvertently being complicit with the pirates.

"I've received a most interesting letter from your Devon Head of School," my new Head said next. "To keep my hand in, and better to know a few of our brightest sixth formers, I read the Greek New Testament with them, meeting at my residence once a week, every Sunday afternoon, for 90 minutes. I would be most pleased to have you join our group."

Before I could respond he switched to Greek and asked me if I remembered how Christ recruited the first of his disciples.

Matthew 4 and Mark 1, I replied in Greek, 'Come with me, and I will make you fishers of men.' I added, still in Greek, that I welcomed the opportunity to join his other disciples. The Head smiled and said—in English—that he was not associating himself with Christ, but merely confirming that what my Devon Head of School had told him about my knowledge of Greek was "not in the least exaggerated."

"You should feel proud," David said as we were walking back to Callahan's. "The Head just gave you his highest form of praise. Behind his back he's often referred to as Old Lit, because some enterprising member of the upper fifth discovered years ago that litotes is the rhetorical term for double negatives.

"Virtually everyone involved with the College gets tagged with a nickname—masters, boys, and staff alike. I'm BC, which sounds perfectly innocuous given my name, but I think fifth formers parse it as Before Christ, because they think I'm antediluvian about school rules and conduct. If there's a nickname you can live with, let me know and I'll see if I can preempt the field by suggesting it before you get tagged with something else you'd rather not listen to."

Well, I'm sometimes called 'Switch,' I told him. Because I'm a switch-hitter, I bat from both sides, as you saw yesterday. If that sounds good to you, go for it.

"Right, then, 'Switch' it is. As long as I've been here, five years now, we haven't had an ambidextrous batter," BC said. "Keep improving the way you did yesterday, and I'm going to make room for you on our second eleven, because I think you could drive bowlers and fielders crazy switching from side to side during an over."

I was thrilled; it was like hearing Bobby Anderson tell me I was born to hit baseballs.

As I record all this, I think about how lucky I am. Having the Head of School as a friend and ally, and a headmaster who has reached out to me—that's a great way to start off when school opens next week.

25: Wildwood at Lenox – 2095

Though I'm hazy about much that has happened recently, my memories of the year at Salisbury are as vivid today as they were when I returned home almost 75 years ago. The layout and architecture of the school are so deeply etched in memory that I could still walk blindfolded from Callahan's to Blodgett's Bush on the other side of the campus, or sketch a recognizable image of any structure from Big School to the tiny study I had all to myself as a member of the upper sixth. I still see in my mind's eye the weathered, terra-cotta walls that framed the major school buildings, giving the campus visual unity, especially when sunlight burnished it.

Big School was where all of us ate and sixth formers attended most of their classes. It was Gothic in design with a huge, vaulted Great Hall for meals, and a number of conventional classrooms. A shifting group of masters and my head-of-school friend, David Bonham-Carter, otherwise known as BC, ate at "High Table," which was on a dais at the north end of the hall, while the remaining 600 of us—the groundlings, my good friend, Grinstein, called us—ate at long tables, arranged in eight rows on either side of a wide center aisle, with room for 40 of us at each of the 16 tables. We generally sorted ourselves out by eating with our contemporaries, but some of the younger boys ate only with others in their own house. All of us, except for prefects, took turns bussing the tables, but mercifully we didn't have to wash the dirty dishes we took back to the long serving counter.

Because Queen Victoria had wished it so, grace was said in Latin twice for each meal: "Benedictus benedicat" before we began eating, and "Benedicto benedicatur" at the end of the meal. BC was charged with saying the closing grace, which he said was the most difficult decision he had to make as Head of School, because no one was permitted to leave the table before he said 'benedicatur,' and no one could eat a single mouthful after he said it. Unfortunately, saying grace had no positive impact on the quality of the food, which was god-awful.

I remember totally inconsequential aspects of the year at Salisbury, and other events that seemed important at the time and remain so today. When I turn over in bed here at Wildwood I can still hear my narrow corner bed in the Callahan's dormitory squeaking in protest when I did it there, which I had to do frequently because the mattress wasn't firm enough to support 140 pounds properly. It was no better when I learned that my true weight in England was only 10 stone.

I can remember feeling jealous when a cloudburst poured rain on me one dreary day midway through the Michaelmas Term while I was walking across Quad Major to my art history class; only school prefects were allowed to carry umbrellas, and there wasn't a prefect in sight. I remember smiling to myself when I asked a housekeeping question and was told by a younger boy to knock up the Matron. And again when a fellow sixth former in our English history class asked if I could loan him a rubber—to erase what he'd just written on our weekly quiz, he added, when I looked befuddled.

The first event of any consequence involved young Andrew Peterson, a second former who was my assigned "fag," a term I greatly disliked but could not avoid. His role as my fag was to perform various minor tasks for me, like shining my shoes, or filling the single tub in our changing rooms with hot water if I wanted to take a bath rather than a shower.

I suspect that a group of Callahan's second formers decided in late September to test my mettle by seeing what I would do if my shoes disappeared one day instead of being shined. In any event, disappear they did, forcing me to violate the dress code by going to class in sneakers—my "plimsolls" Peterson called them. Because he could offer no plausible explanation, either then or when my shoes mysteriously reappeared the following morning, I was forced by both the common law of the College, and the unwritten rules of Callahan's House, to punish him. I asked BC for advice, and was told that two strokes of the House cane to Peterson's arse would be the most appropriate punishment. I said I wanted to respect tradition, but simply could not whip anyone. Maybe it was general revulsion, maybe Justin Blake still haunted me; I wasn't sure. Could we agree on some other type of punishment? I asked.

A day later I suggested to BC and Mr. Fawcett, our Housemaster, that Peterson be assigned the task of writing a 500-word essay on free speech in less than 48 hours, using unlined paper and a fountain pen, with the stipulation that there could be no blots, misspellings, crossed out words, insertions, or other blemishes of any kind, and that all lines of text must be parallel to the top of the sheets he delivered to me. Both of my mentors thought that would be a fit way of resolving my dilemma.

Some 36 hours after Peterson received word of his punishment he handed me his three-page response, pristine in every respect, and exactly 500 words in length, which I verified by counting them after I'd read through his essay. It was obvious that he was an exceptional 13-year old boy. After discussing the views of Cicero, Milton, Blackstone, and several British jurists, he concluded on an American note, saying, "Thus, while free speech is a prerequisite for democratic government, it cannot be regarded as an inalienable, unrestricted right, for even in the remnants of our empire it has long been recognized that no man is free to falsely shout 'fire!' in a crowded theater." I could not tell at the time whether paraphrasing Justice Holmes without naming him was Peterson's subtle way of thanking me for sparing the rod, or a pandering gesture of disguised contempt. I could not fault him for splitting an infinitive, because I did it all the time myself.

I was pleased to read in the Salisbury Bulletin four years later that he had become Head of School, and even more pleased when I received a letter from him saying that he had never forgotten the punishment I meted out, and wanted me to know that when they voted as sixth formers to designate the best prefect they had encountered during their years at Salisbury, he and the others who had plotted the disappearance of my shoes had unanimously chosen me, even though I wasn't made a prefect until several months after their plot was carried out.

Later I learned that Peterson had taken a double first in Philosophy and History at Balliol College, Oxford, and promptly been retained by his college to be a philosophy don. Of all the decisions I made during my year at Salisbury, I like to think that not whipping him was the best.

26: Salisbury College – 2020

10.20.20

I've already made half a dozen friends here, the closest being BC and another boy in Callahan's named Philip Grinstein. He's a really bright, engaging upper fifth who's in line to become Head of House after BC leaves next summer. And the courses I'm taking have fully lived up to expectations. In addition to my English History and Lit classes, both of which focus on the 19th and early 20th centuries, I'm taking Advanced Maths (neural networks, topology, differential analysis, distributed algorithms, and the like), Russian (because I want to read Tolstoy, Pushkin, Dostoevsky, et al. in the original), and Art History.

The maths class is interesting, mostly because the master in charge, Mr. Prescott, knows a good deal about the role of neural networks in AI. We've had some interesting discussions, and I've picked up on one of his suggestions and plan to explore it, but I'm not yet ready to talk with him about Artel the way I did with Mr. Sampson at Devon, whom I knew I could trust completely.

Surprisingly, art history is my favorite course. Traveling with K piqued my interest, and when BC mentioned art history as one of the best courses offered at

Salisbury, I thought that taking it might be an interesting change of pace, and asked for more details. He told me that it was taught by Sarah Cooper, wife of the Housemaster of Brown's House, and the only woman on the College's teaching staff, so I decided to go for it, hoping that she'd be as good a guide as K. And indeed she has been.

We started in Mesopotamia, then went to Egypt, Greece, Rome, and the Byzantine Empire for a week each, before jumping to Romanesque sculpture in the churches of northern Spain and Burgundy. Now we're in the dawn of the Renaissance, looking at Giotto and Duccio. Obviously a lot more to come.

Instead of feeding us digital material for viewing on our own computers, as she did at the outset, Cooper is now projecting images of the paintings we're talking about in class onto a high-tech movie screen to give us a better idea of their true size and appearance by mimicking the way they'd look on a museum wall.

A week ago she invited all ten of us in her class to have tea with her at Brown's House, affording us a first look at the prints and drawings she and her husband have collected over the years. She says she'll ask us back at year end, to see if what we've learned in the interim alters our view of any of their art works. They've assembled an impressive collection. And she's a really neat person, in addition to being a very good teacher.

11/13/20

Talked to K via Skype, as we try to do at least three times a week, but this afternoon we were on the phone for much longer than usual because of the E-mail we both got from Mr. Sampson at Devon, telling us that Steve Goddard, the CEO of Almega, had called him asking about our performance in his classes. Interesting development, K said, but she sounded wary. Why the hesitation? I asked. Because he dominated our conversation at the Captain's table and sounded to me like a smooth-talking wheeler-dealer, K said. Obviously successful so far, she conceded, but who knows how many people he's trampled along the way, getting to where he is now.

We talked for another five minutes about what it would be like to move from the East Coast to California. I could tell that K wasn't enthusiastic about the idea. We should continue doing our own thing, she said finally, in an effort to wrap it up.

Let's wait and see if Goddard does anything more before I get home next summer, I said. In the meantime, of course we continue working on Artel on our own.

OK by me, she said, and then added that it was nice of Sampson to praise us the way he did, without ever mentioning Artel. 'The most original, elegant, and concise programmer I've ever encountered.' That's a pretty good recommendation, Mr. Johnson, she told me.

I'll send him an E-mail from both us, thanking him for the way he handled it, I said.

Good, K said, and kissed me good morning (her time) by pressing her lips to her computer screen.

Hugging my laptop just doesn't do it, I replied. Love you buckets.

27: Wildwood at Lenox – 2095

September and October were glorious months in southern England in 2019. I remember golden sunlit days, cool evenings, and clear, starlit night skies. We were far enough removed from the night lights in Salisbury City to get a good naked-eye view of the northern sky, particularly the constellations wheeling around Polaris. I especially remember an October night when I navigated by the stars, and inadvertently became a College legend of sorts.

In late September my housemaster, Mr. Fawcett, had strongly encouraged me to join the Corps, an officially sanctioned group of Salisbury students who periodically marched and performed other military-style drills. I told him I was reluctant to do that, because I could lose my U.S. passport if I joined a foreign military organization, but I'd be glad to act as an unofficial adviser to younger boys in the Corps, teaching them what little I knew about reading maps, first-aid, and other basic survival skills, like the Heimlich maneuver I'd learned at Devon. I wound up advising a group of ten second formers, including Peterson, who now seemed to regard me with genuine respect.

On "Orienteering Night"—an adjunct to the three-mile "Hare and Hounds" cross-country race that occurred each year on Guy Fawks Day—my squad of youngsters was supposed to start from Big School, follow directions into the countryside, pick up messages inside three metal containers at designated locations, and then return to Big School, all in the dark, guided only by our map, the stars, and their "lanterns" (which looked like my flashlight). Everything went well until we picked up the final message at the crossing of two narrow country lanes.

Two of the boys, self-appointed leaders of the squad, wanted to turn left after that; I glanced up at Polaris and said we should go straight, which we did. Ten minutes later we passed through an open gate and dogs started to bark. A few seconds after that a bright light flashed on. Suddenly, we were face to face to with a farmer carrying a shotgun. "What's going on with all of you, in my farmyard this hour of the night?" he said rather harshly. It's Orienteering Night at the College, I explained. The boys are Rover Scouts, and we're on our way back there after completing our mission.

The farmer relaxed, smiling broadly. "A Yank leading Rover Scouts, is it? Well, the Yanks saved our bacon during the Second War, so I think you lads should come inside and drink some real cider before your leader takes you back to school." I was sure it would be fermented hard cider, meaning that drinking it during term time would probably be against College rules, but there was no way I was going to turn down his invitation.

As the boys were finishing their cider, the farmer took me aside and whispered proper directions back to the College, then turned to the boys and jovially wished all of us Godspeed. The conversations I overheard on the way home encouraged me; it was clear that my crew of youngsters thought drinking hard cider on a school night was "brilliant" and "really fab."

The next day word of our exploit spread throughout the school, with opinions as to how and why it happened being equally divided, I was later told. Half the school thought I'd bumbled into the farmyard by mistake; the other half thought I'd planned it all in advance, by going out there before Orienteering Night and persuading the farmer to play the role he did.

I later learned that my boy Peterson had gone to bat for me and carried the day; he successfully convinced the entire second form that Switch was far too smart to blunder off course, and was, instead, trying to perk up life for his crew by providing them with an unprecedented reward for successfully completing their Orienteering assignment. That view ultimately became accepted College folklore, witness the letter I received from another American OSB sometime in the late '20s—I can't remember the exact year—telling me that he had overheard the story being told on Orienteering Night when he was at Salisbury the year before.

28: Salisbury College – 2020

11.25.20

Today's Mom's birthday and tomorrow will be Thanksgiving. And I'm missing both of them. At the moment it's hard to feel thankful about anything, cooped up as I am in my cold, dank study, with only a small electric heater to keep me from freezing. For the last hour I've had to listen to the incessant drumbeat of rain on my roof, and I itch like crazy because of chilblains on my fingers and toes. But apart from the wretched November weather and the chilblains, I am in fact very thankful, given the way everything else is going.

I'm finally making some progress on reorganizing and enlarging Artel. Classes are going well. Rather than banging myself up playing Rugby football without a helmet or any protective padding, I'm playing fall cricket and growing more confidant as a batsman with each innings I'm on the pitch. Sarah Cooper, my art history teacher, and her husband have invited me to spend the Xmas holidays with them at their cottage in the Cotswolds. And most important of all, K is thriving at Harvard. I really couldn't hope for more.

I've even profited from a potentially disastrous mistake I made last week when I misled a group of Rover Scouts into a farmer's back yard on a moonless night during our orienteering outing. I thought we should be going north, when the kids correctly said we should be turning west. Thank God the farmer liked "Yanks." He called off his howling dogs, broke open his shotgun, and invited us inside for hard cider. He must have sized up the situation perfectly, because he deftly drew me aside and whispered, "Anyone asks me, you weren't lost at all. You scouted me out two weeks ago and we planned this together. You'll be quite the hero with the lads, I'd say." Then he offered me a second mug of cider and quietly told me how to get back on track.

On our way home I overheard young Peterson telling the others he was certain the whole venture was a setup I'd arranged with the farmer in advance, to get them drinks during term time. They bought his story because Peterson is a born leader. The senior boys in Callahan's also went along, quickly recognizing that if they could sell the advance planning story to the whole school, they would not only protect Callahan's reputation, but actually enhance it.

From comments so far—many from boys I hardly recognize—I think I may wind up getting high marks for originating and pulling off a really successful caper.

11.29.20

The Head made a wryly oblique reference to our Orienteering Night escapade at the outset of his Greek New Testament seminar this afternoon. Although we were due to read John today, he began the session by asking me to go back to Matthew 13 and describe in one sentence the gist of verses 3-9 and 18-23. I read them to myself, then said aloud: if a farmer sows his seed in the wrong places he will reap little or nothing, but if he selects fertile soil instead, he will be rewarded one-hundred fold. "Not so bad, Johnson," the Head said, "not bad at all. Now let's proceed with John 13."

After our session was over and we were walking back to our respective houses, I asked three of the school prefects who were in our seminar group what they thought about the Matthew 13 episode. "I'd say you're in jolly good shape," Barton-Smith told me. "Coming from Old Lit, 'not so bad' is high praise; 'not bad at all' is a superlative for him. Picking a parable about a farmer and telling you that your reading was spot on—that has to be his way of saying it was damn clever of you to pull off your stunt." "I totally agree," Purcell said. "I do, too," Bennett-Jones said.

At that point, I figured I had it wired. My blunder had morphed into an inspired caper that was going to make Switch a legendary school figure. I was now a member of the sizable fraternity of students and masters who would have legendary monikers for years to come because of their eccentric speech, appearance, or behavior, the three most common gateways to public school notoriety.

12.9.20

Received an E-mail from Goddard today saying that he will be in London on business next week, and would like to come down to Salisbury to talk with me about Almega. Replied that I'd be happy to see him, but will not be making any plans or decisions until I return to the States and can talk with Katherine at length about our future.

12.16.20

Lunch with Goddard today at Charter 1227 in town. Five minutes of polite conversation, then all business. He started off asking about our goal. "I don't want to know anything specific about the new language you're creating," he said, "but it would be helpful to me to know what your core objective is."

I said we're trying to write a language—we call it Artel—that will enable us to program our way to AGI. To the Singularity and beyond.

"A philosophical question, then," he said. "If we reach the point where computers can truly behave like humans by thinking, reasoning, and reacting in the many different ways that humans do—if we can we succeed in creating artificial general intelligence instead of simply resolving specific, discrete problems the way we now do— how do we prevent the new generation of 'human' computers from creating supra-human ones that can effectively take over the world?"

By teaching the next generation of machines the same ethics that we now teach doctors and scientists who specialize in genetic engineering, I replied. More generally, by building into their simulated brains awareness of the same customs and sanctions that restrain actual humans from going off the deep end. Who knows, perhaps someday we will have computerized judges who can consign other, non-compliant computers to a junkyard.

"Thank you, Fran, for confirming that you're as level-headed as I suspected you would be. I'm sure you're aware of all the doomsday critics who are reluctant to strive for Singularity because they think AGI can't be controlled by humans. I think Singularity is inevitable and we need to plan for it."

Glad we're on the same page on that, I said. Anything else I can tell you about Katherine or me?

"No," he said, and promptly proceeded to lay out his proposal. Bottom line, he's offering the two of us "several million" in cash, payable now, for a right of first refusal to buy Artel if and when we're ready to launch. If for any reason we don't reach that point, the upfront cash is still ours to keep.

I wanted to know if he really meant that. You're telling me we get to keep the initial payment even if we decide the day after we get it that we're going to quit working on Artel altogether? I asked. "Yes," he said, "I'm willing to run that risk because I don't think you two are quitters."

But you're still asking us to bet against ourselves, I said. Several million would be a great payoff if we fail to produce a worthwhile language that enables us to devise new and better algorithms. But if we succeed—as I believe we will in the next several years—that's a pittance compared to what Artel and our new algorithms and APIs will be worth in the general marketplace. We lose our access to that market, and most of our bargaining power, if we're effectively locked into bargaining with you. How can we establish a fair price for selling to you if we can't talk to others?

"That's what the lawyers are for," he said. "We've been through this drill before, and I can show you the right-of-first-refusal contracts we've successfully used in the past, all of which provide a mechanism for testing the market if you're not happy with the offer we make after good faith negotiations between us."

I repeated what I'd said to him on the QM and in my E-mail last week, about not making any decisions now, but asked—for future reference—what he had in mind regarding our role in Almega if we decided to sign on.

"Initially, you'd be Deputy Director of AI and Katherine would be Artel Manager, reporting to you. You'd report to Asikura Tonaka, our Director of AI, who's been with us from the very beginning. He reports directly to me, as CEO.

Compensation? I asked. Nothing specific, just a general indication.

"Generous," he said, smiling at me for the first time since I'd met him on the QM. For the two of you combined, a joint check for at least 500K, maybe more, for your first 12 months. But the serious money would be in stock options.

Just out of curiosity, why a joint check? I asked.

"We view married couples and unmarried partners as teammates and let them decide for themselves how much compensation each of them is receiving. As long as you and Katherine are together, we will pay you as team. It's part of our overall HR approach," he added.

"Unlike many, if not most, of our Silicon Valley friends, we are a true equal opportunity outfit. We have no glass ceiling. We genuinely welcome LGBT personnel at all levels. Over half our staff were born abroad. Since we went public and adopted a company-wide code of conduct with real teeth in it, no employee of any gender has been harassed, sexually or otherwise. Finally, we do our best to eliminate unnecessary distinctions among our employees.

We provide generous health coverage; paid sick-leave; paid maternity leave before and after childbirth for both parents, including partners who are going through the adoption process; three weeks of paid vacation time; significant college tuition assistance for children of long-time employees; on-site parking; meals in any of our on-campus restaurants; and day care—all those benefits are available to everyone on our payroll cost-free. And the terms and conditions of the benefits are the same for all of us, from janitors to me."

That's a great approach, and an impressive array of benefits, I said. I thanked him for his offer, and assured him, again, that I'd be in touch sometime next summer.

Just relayed all this to K via Skype. Because of their non-discrimination policies and practices, she gives him credit for being "one rung higher on the ladder" than she initially thought. His offer intrigued her, but she agreed that we should stay flexible until we know whether Artel is going to be just another AI language or a real blockbuster.

29: Wildwood at Lenox – 2095

It's Xmas Eve, the first in living memory that I will spend alone, without giving or receiving a single present. Ellie Strickland, my one remaining close friend here at Wildwood, died in October, and I have not yet encountered anyone who might take her place.

As I watch the falling snow that is expected to blanket all of New England, and listen to the St. John's College Choir singing old carols on my ancient record player, I inevitably think back to my Xmas in the first England, when I stayed with my art history teacher, Sarah Cooper, and her husband, Nigel, at their old stone cottage in Chipping Campden.

They seemed like a somewhat improbable couple, I thought then and still do. Nigel, called Old Nile behind his back because he tended to run on forever in his history classes, was a short, homely, unprepossessing man, aged 45 perhaps, well on the way to becoming bald, with a round face, a gentle disposition, and a pervasive vagueness about him that some regarded as a form of protective coloration, enabling him to blend into school life seamlessly and go unnoticed much of the time by other masters who probably would have been his rivals, if not his enemies, had he tried to play a more assertive role.

Sarah, on the other hand, was a sprightly woman, striking in appearance, with high cheekbones, a pageboy cap of russet hair parted on the side and cut short to expose her Nefertiti neck, luminous brown eyes, full and very sensuous lips, and an engaging smile. She was perceptibly taller than her husband and at least a decade younger—in her mid 30s I imagine. I never heard any reference to children, or how they met, or any other part of their back-story, so I still don't know what caused them to marry. Odd though the pairing was, they seemed to enjoy living together.

I've never been a churchgoer, but the traditional Christmas Eve service in their parish chapel was splendid. I was particularly struck—moved, really—by the trebles in the all-male choir. Despite being tone deaf, I could sense that the young boys were singing at a pitch so bright and clear, so pure, that Steuben glass blowers could not match it. We had nothing like a proper snowfall that evening, but I do remember seeing a few flakes fall as we left the chapel, and again when we awoke on Xmas morning—just enough to serve as a token reminder of what was supposed to happen at Yuletide.

After the best breakfast I'd had since getting off the Queen Mary, the Coopers and I spent the better part of Xmas morning talking about old English traditions as we opened the half dozen presents we'd separately placed under their small Xmas tree, which Sarah had decorated with a string of tiny white lights and a dozen old, hand-blown crystal ornaments representing Mary, Jesus in his cradle, an astonished Joseph, the Wise Men and their camels, and other Nativity figures. Sarah told me she'd found the ornaments in a Viennese antique shop and thought they were either Czech or Austrian, circa 1825. It was by all odds the loveliest Xmas tree I'd ever seen.

That afternoon the three of us took a long walk, passing through the village out into the countryside where we picked up a public path—dating back to the 13th century, Nigel said—that took us beside fallow fields and over stiles, and past the occasional old oak tree with its bare trunk, branches, and twigs outlined in black against the dull gray sky, looking as forlorn as the frontal CAT scan of an aged lung-cancer patient. Because it was Xmas, I kept waiting for the sun to break through the gloom and lighten up our day, but it never happened.

Back at the cottage, Xmas dinner was a variation of K's favorite pre-London meal of our trip: rare roast beef, with an encrusted outside piece for contrast, along with mashed potatoes, Yorkshire pudding, and a delicious brown sauce made from the drippings. Dessert was the traditional English plum pudding, which I was enjoying until I bit down on something hard. I raised my napkin to my mouth to got rid of whatever it was I'd chomped on, making it all look as normal as I could. Once the napkin was back in my lap, I quickly discovered what was going on, and decided to play it cool.

Minutes later Nigel Cooper spoke up. "Enjoyed your pudding, I hope."

I did, I said. It was delicious.

"And you et all of it?" he said, sounding a mite uncertain of himself.

Well, yes, as you can see, I said, gesturing toward my dessert plate. I managed to keep a straight face long enough to glance at Sarah, but the twinkle in her eye did me in and I turned back toward Nigel, smiling. Except for this, sir, I said as I handed him the six-pence coin I'd cleaned up with my the napkin in the meantime.

He was a good sport. "Well done, Fran," he said immediately. "You got me fair and square; I really thought you'd swallowed it. Old custom, you know. Person who gets the six-pence will have good luck for the coming year. What do you wish for?"

To marry a wonderful, very bright woman back home, I replied. We traveled around England before school started, and now she's back in our Cambridge, her second year at Harvard.

"How lovely that you had a chance to see England together," Sarah said. "Where did you go?"

I gave them a quick rundown of where we'd been. Toward the end, when I mentioned our day in their Cambridge, I thought I saw a wistful glint in Sarah's eyes.

The following day, after another English breakfast of kippers, scrambled eggs, and a fried tomato on toast, I suggested walking again, perhaps going west this time. Nigel looked up from his book and shook his head. "I must have sprained my ankle a tad when I slipped yesterday, climbing down that last stile," he said. "You two go; I think I'll stay here and read some more Gibbon. We have a lot to learn from him."

As we were shutting the cottage gate, Sarah asked if I'd seen the village of Broadway on my earlier trip through the Cotswolds that summer. When I replied that Katherine and I had taken a different route, Sarah said it was one of the loveliest towns around, and suggested that we walk there and back, about two and a quarter hours each way, with a break for lunch in an old pub. She said that would get us home well before the sun went down at 4:15—if it ever appeared in the first place.

She led the way as we left Chipping Campden, walking single file along a narrow path. Suddenly, out of nowhere it seemed, she said, "Katherine is a lovely name." I waited, expecting that she might go on, but she didn't. Well, Katherine's a lovely person, I said finally. I'm blessed.

We walked on, still in single file, saying nothing more until we reached the Cotswold Way, a broader trail where we could walk side-by-side.

"Truth be told, I'm a little jealous of her," Sarah volunteered without warning. Why on earth, I wondered, then quickly got the answer.

"You're far and away the brightest student I've ever had, Fran. I'd give anything—well almost anything—to travel through Italy with you. Florence first, then Sienna, then to see my favorite Renaissance painter, Piero della Francesca, in the Umbrian museums. You would have insights I'd never have on my own, show me connections I could never make by myself. The way you suggested two weeks ago that fundamental truths emerge when artists who could not possibly know each other's work nonetheless produce remarkably similar images, as they did on the Ramesseum ceiling in Luxor and, centuries later, on the Giotto ceiling in Padua. You're a kindred soul, Fran. If I weren't married, I'd do my best to persuade you to join me in Italy next summer.

I'm flattered you feel that way, I said. Truly. Your 'kindred soul' remark intrigues me because it's exactly what Katherine said to me a while back. I know the two of you would hit it off. Would you consider showing both of us Italy if she came over next summer, instead of my going back at the end of Summer Term?

She sighed gently. "Ah, Fran, I suppose I have been too indirect. I'm not into threesomes; I would want you all to myself."

Suddenly I was back in Shangri-La, when we first opened the door and I looked around, sensing what was coming next, but not knowing how it would play out. I silently asked myself what K would say if she were looking over my shoulder right now. Would she tell me to go ahead, the way she handed me the Shangri-La key after our second day there, fully expecting that I would use it to sleep with someone else, someone who might end up supplanting her? Or would she be furious at me for even thinking of being disloyal to her? Or maybe tell me to wait until next summer, when she'd come to England again and seduce Sarah, so we could go off to Italy as a happy threesome after all.

Whoa! I told myself. You decided not to sleep with anyone else at Shangri-La. So certainly not here and now, because if we start now it won't stop here, it'll go on someplace in or around Salisbury until we get caught, with all hell to pay. Grow up and die right, man.

I'm sorry, I said to Sarah. My body says yes, but my—

"You don't have to say a word more; I understand." She glanced around, then took both my hands and leaned forward until her eyes were only a foot from mine. "A first and last kiss?" she asked. "To remember a touch of you during my dark nights?"

We did kiss, on the path in open air, and I briefly thought how ironic it would be if that did us in, but when I looked around a moment later there was no one else in sight. Like K's post-graduation kiss at Devon, I thought.

Ten minutes later Sarah and I were back on normal footing, chatting as if nothing had happened en route, just a Salisbury College teacher out on an amiable countryside excursion with one of her students.

30. Salisbury College – 2021

1.4.21

    Drove back to Salisbury with the Coopers this morning to discover that I'm now a school prefect. The Head appoints prefects, always with the advice—and usually with the consent—of the boy who is Head of School and the housemaster of the boy under consideration. My contributions to the Head's Greek New Testament sessions and my friendship with BC, starting that first night in the Salisbury pub and nurtured in the cricket nets afterwards, probably account for my promotion.

    Several other prefects escorted me into Big School this evening and all 14 of us sat together at a special table to celebrate my elevation. In his capacity as Head of School, BC stepped down from the dais for a moment to give me my badge of office, a furled black umbrella with a real teak handle.

    During dinner I learned that in Queen Victoria's day Salisbury prefects were called praepostors—a tradition that persisted into the 21st century. According to legend, a boy in the lower fourth named Kilroy, always referred to as Killjoy, was the first who had the temerity to suggest in public that prefects should be called prefects because calling them praepostors was preposterous. Some 20 years later, in 2008, his suggested change in terminology was actually made.

Like most enduring fables, that tale illuminates a truth; everything I've learned while I've been here tells me that it takes an unduly long time to get rid of anachronistic public school traditions, such as whipping young boys for misdemeanors. If I leave anything behind in the College when I go home this summer, I hope it's the memory of the punishment that I meted out to my fag, young Peterson. Perhaps—someday, somehow—corporal punishment will actually be abolished at Salisbury, and if the College ever does switch its position, Old Lit himself may come to regard 'Switch' as a not inappropriate tag for the non-conformist sixth former who refused to switch-hit his fag because he believed the whole idea of prefects thrashing youngsters was preposterous.

3.10.21

What a dreary winter this has been, apart from winning the annual drama competition, and unexpectedly texting with Ellen earlier today.

Drama Week is a longstanding Salisbury tradition, originated, I suspect, by an early 20th century headmaster who wanted to enliven the Lent Term, a period of raw, bone-chilling weather that can induce a powerful desire to hibernate until spring finally arrives. Over a period of eight consecutive evenings in late February, each Salisbury house stages a drama produced and performed by members of that house, directed by their housemaster. Because the Great Hall in Big School is the only place large enough to seat the entire student body, the plays are performed on the dais at the north end of the hall, with whatever scenery the house wants to construct.

Perhaps because I'm the only American here this year, BC and Mr. Fawcett decided that Callahan's House should perform *The Devil's Disciple*, Shaw's witty and derisive take on England's response to the American Revolution. BC naturally played General Burgoyne; my upper-fifth friend, Grinstein, played Rev. Adams; Mrs. Fawcett played his wife; I was Richard Dudgeon; and Matron was my wife. I think we put on a damn fine show, the best by far of all eight in the competition. The five-man faculty committee that awarded us the prize obviously agreed, because their decision was unanimous.

Nothing more of note until this afternoon, when I went into town to get a birthday present for K, who turns 21 this April. I found a lovely necklace with 21 amber stones that I think will go well with her long blonde hair, especially when it spills over her shoulders making her the most fetching woman for miles around. As I was going down the lift in the store where I'd found the necklace, it suddenly struck me that I'd never been on an escalator in the UK, and that triggered a flashblack to my introduction to alligators and escagators in NYC.

I immediately asked myself why on earth I hadn't tried to contact Ellen. Finding her took all of 15 seconds; I simply Googled 'Ellen Riley Trinity College Dublin alumni directory,' and there she was, pictured on the first website in the Google listing, with a caption describing her as Trinity's "Head Librarian." I texted her, and had an answer back within half an hour. She's well, loves her work, and sounded really pleased to hear from me. No mention of any family or other attachments, so I'm going to suggest that we get together in Dublin for a few days during my spring break here, which begins in another fortnight.

3.15.21

Phoned Ellen live, rather than texting, to tell her about K, which I wanted to do before proposing that I come visit for a few days. Ellen sounded happy that I've found someone I love, and equally pleased about the prospect of spending time together in Ireland. She has a guest room in her Dublin flat where I can stay, and I'm going to line up a car in case we decide to travel elsewhere in Ireland. Being Ellen, she gets around Dublin on her bicycle.

3.29.21

Off to Ireland today. I'm leaving the diary here and will resume when Summer Term begins on 4.17.

31: Wildwood at Lenox – 2096

The last half of January was rock bottom of my year in England. I caught a chest cold the day after the Lent Term began and couldn't shake it for weeks. In retrospect, I suspect I had a case of walking pneumonia that ended only because Callahan's Matron insisted that I go to the College infirmary (the "sanitorium," or "san" for short), where I eventually talked them into prescribing an antibiotic.

The weather in February was even worse than it had been in January. Not much snow, but constant dank cold. It penetrated my whole body, gripping every nerve and sinew from my toes to fingertips, producing involuntary shivering that I could not halt, even after going to Marks & Spencer in town where I bought a cap, sweater, and gloves, all knitted of dense Irish wool. I wore my sweater to bed, got Matron to give me two extra blankets, and still woke up shivering in the middle of the night.

I survived February only because of our Callahan's House production of *The Devil's Disciple*, which won the Drama Week award for best performance of the week. I had never acted before, and have never done it since then, so I can honestly claim that appearing on stage in England was the highlight of my acting career. My friend and mentor, BC, was star of the show—as the Salisbury Head of School generally is in everything he does.

My spirits were finally lifted one Saturday in March when I went to town and found the perfect 21st birthday present for Katherine, a necklace with 21 different shades of small amber stones set in circles of gold linked together by a golden chain. UPS delivered it to her exactly when they were supposed to, and she was wearing it when we Skyped an hour later. She was crying with happiness when we connected. "I don't want to take it off, ever!" she said. "At least not for weeks and weeks." I have finally learned not to weep when I wear it now.

The other great thing that happened that Saturday in March was reconnecting with Ellen. I hadn't thought about her for months, and on the spur of the moment Googled her in the old-fashioned way we did back then, and up she came on my i-phone12—the phone I've saved all these years, thinking it may become a worthwhile item if we ever have an Antiques Roadshow of pre-Singularity hardware.

When Ellen and I talked by phone a few days later, it was as if we were siblings getting caught up after a long spell apart. She invited me to stay with her in Dublin during my Salisbury spring break, and I accepted without a moment's hesitation, knowing that Katherine would not only understand, but would actually encourage me to do it, which is exactly what she did when I phoned her later that day.

Two weeks later I flew to Dublin on a Ryan Air flight that cost all of 39 pounds, a figure I've remembered because it remains the cheapest international flight I've ever taken. After the cab dropped me off at Ellen's house I spent a moment surveying her one-block street, which was entirely residential, with small, two-story red-brick row houses on both sides, set back from the street just enough to provide room for the large oak trees and trimmed shrubbery that enlivened the block. Typical of her, I thought, to find an oasis in a part of the city that had looked dull, if not drab, until my cab turned the last corner.

Ellen herself seemed barely changed. Her face was still unlined, fresh as an Irish spring morning, and her smile remained captivating, because some inscrutable mechanism made her blue eyes sparkle when she smiled. She had cut her hair short since I last saw her, so that it fell just below her ears and an inch or two above her eyes, giving her a perky air. Had I not known that she must be close to 40, I would have guessed that she was in her early 30s. Her haircut and all the energy she exuded reminded me of Sarah Cooper, but the resemblance stopped there. Ellen had been my safe haven; Sarah was a buried land mine.

For dinner that first night we had Ellen's delicious Irish stew, made from scratch and simmered for hours, along with a bottle of Burgundy that I'd bought in the airport as a modest house present. After Stilton and port for dessert, we nursed the port for several hours as we swapped life stories post Darien.

I learned that shortly after she returned home in 2010, Ellen fell in love with a Sandhurst graduate, a man named Gerald Carter, only to lose him a year later when the security patrol he was commanding in Iraq was gunned down by friendly fire from Iraqi police. She got her PhD in Library Science from Trinity in 2013, and was immediately hired to head the library at Alexandra College, a top school for girls in Dublin.

By insisting on more detail, I finally pried loose information in her CV that she would have been too modest to volunteer. While she was at Alexandra she wrote several lengthy monographs on specialized aspects of the Trinity collection—by far the largest in Ireland—that attracted attention in international library circles, triggering, among other things, an offer to become Deputy Librarian at the Morgan in NYC. When the chief librarian at Trinity unexpectedly died of a heart attack in 2017, Trinity tapped her to come home to her own college, as the youngest Head Librarian in their long and distinguished history.

We spent the entire next day in her working home, focusing on the Long Room of the Old Library building, which dates back to 18th century. I still think of it as a cathedral of books. It made such an impression that even now, 75 years later, I can shut my eyes and see it clearly. The nave, about 200 feet long and two stories high, runs down the center, and on either side of it, on both levels, there are side chapels of books, each with a sliding ladder that provides access to the upper shelves. Dark wooden pillars separate the chapels and extend beyond the top of the second story to become ribs of the barrel-vaulted wooden ceiling that surmounts the nave. Each of the side chapels has a similar barrel-vaulted ceiling, perpendicular to the nave.

Ellen explained that all told, the Long Room contains some 200,000 of the Library's oldest and rarest books, including the Book of Kells, a medieval copy of the Vulgate Gospels, decorated in rich colors and intricate designs by monks cloistered in St. Columba's monastery on the Scottish isle of Iona. Each day visitors have an opportunity to see two different pages of the book, which is on view under shatterproof glass in one of the display cases that line the nave. Lighted in a way that seems to make the entire space from floor to ceiling glow softly, and filled with important and accessible books—walls of books as rich in content and texture as an early Gobelin tapestry— the library is a truly magnificent world treasure.

The highlight of that first day was getting to leaf through the Books of Kells with Ellen for a full fifteen minutes after the library closed, so that she could show me the intricate full-page portraits of Matthew, Mark, Luke, and John, and several other illuminated pages that were among her favorites. I think it was then that I started to think of the Old Library as a cathedral. To this day, I feel incredibly grateful that I was able to see it through the eyes of a lifelong friend who knew and loved it deeply.

32. Salisbury College – 2021

4.18.21

Spring has arrived in all her glory; the air is clear and balmy, the elm trees surrounding the Close now have young, pale-green leaves, and the Greater Lawn has come alive, turning from a dull winter sage to verdant emerald. Can't wait to get back on the cricket pitch.

My four Irish days with Ellen wiped out all the misery of winter. We never left Dublin because there was so much there that she wanted to share with me. We spent a whole day in her Trinity College library, staying after it closed to the public so she could give me a private showing of the Book of Kells, a treasured manuscript of the Gospels in Latin, with richly colored illustrations. She also led me through the maze of secret tunnels underneath the Old Library, which few, if any, tourists get to see.

On other days we toured Dublin Castle, the Chester Beatty Library where we saw a variety of rare religious manuscripts, St. Patrick's Cathedral, Iveagh Gardens, and the National Gallery of art. On the afternoon of our last day we crossed the Liffey on an ancient pedestrian bridge and toured the Jameson Irish whiskey distillery, then walked in

Phoenix Park, where we caught the tail end of a cricket match.

The Irish stew that Ellen made for dinner on our first night proved that she's become a great cook, but I insisted on taking her out to dinner after that, and she made three superb choices, Klaw and Catch 22 for seafood, and Mulberry Garden where we had tender beef cheeks and perfectly prepared polenta in an outside alcove of their leafy garden.

Because the Abbey Theater was in repertoire mode, we went there on all three of our nights out. On the first, which honored the two founders of the Abbey, we saw one-act plays by Lady Gregory and Yeats. The next night the actors did an equally good job with the much harsher text of Saen O'Casey's *Juno and the Paycock*, which I've always regarded as the Irish precursor of O'Neil's *Long Day's Journey into Night*. Finally, on our last night, we saw a new play, *Portrait*, which drew from the works of James Joyce to dramatize his life. Written by a young Irish playwright neither of us had ever heard of, it would play well in the annual Bloomsday celebrations around the western world.

When we got home after the Joyce evening, Ellen said she'd like a nightcap, which evolved into two glasses of Jameson's for each of us, sipped neat until 1:00 in the morning. She wanted to talk about Katherine and me, and after several unsuccessful attempts to steer the conversation elsewhere, I gave in and told her almost everything, starting with the opening day of Mr. Sampson's class at Devon when I sat behind K and fell in love with her legs. I included the first day at Shangri-La, but not the second. And then, when I thought I was through, I remembered nuzzling Ellen's neck on the train home from NYC, and decided to tell her about the second day at Shangri-La as well, because I knew that talking openly with her would be far, far easier than talking to a doctor who didn't know me from Adam—or Eve, maybe.

Ellen listened to my entire account of Shangri-La Day 2 without speaking, but our eyes kept meeting and I knew she was engaged. Finally she told me that when she fell in love with me—after I turned three and "stopped screaming and hollering all the time"—she often wondered whether I was really the boy I appeared to be, or a little girl in sheep's clothing. Sex and gender can be very confusing, she said.

And then I learned that she felt ambivalent about her own sexuality, uncertain whether she was bisexual like Katherine, or simply prone to lesbian fantasies. After a long pause she asked if we could sleep in the same bed, not necessarily to make love; just to be together. "I still ache for Gerald," she said. "There's been no one since he died, no male or female I could think of bedding down with. I have friends, of course, but not in bed. You're different. We were lovers in a way when you slept in my arms on our way home from New York. Do you remember?"

Of course I do, I said. We talked for a long time in bed, two spoons nestled together, with me on the outside. At some point, we dozed off and I began to dream of making love. At least I think I was dreaming. But it was all so hazy, I can't be sure. Maybe my hand really did slide slowly downtown and stay there until she came. I honestly don't know.

I decided in the morning that it was best to leave it that way. When we saw my cab for the airport pull up in front of her house we hugged each other for ten seconds and promised to stay in touch.

4.22.21

The Head called me into his office this morning to ask if I would sit for Cambridge scholarship exams in Greek, and perhaps other subjects as well. He wants to show his college, Magdalene, that Salisbury can produce first-rank classics scholars, and said I could do both the College and him a favor by winning a major scholarship, as he expects I would, and then declining it. I said I'd be glad to sit for the exams. He thanked me, and congratulated me on being named to the second eleven today.

I batted fifth in our cricket match against Clifton this afternoon. When they took their third wicket about ten minutes before teatime, sending me out onto the pitch, I got a friendly pat on the back from BC, who was with us in the pavilion to lend moral support. He told me to protect my wicket, rather than go for runs, so that I could get a feel for the pitch and be ready to hit out after the tea break.

I tried to do that, but almost got bowled on the first ball I faced. I misread the bounce and it whizzed past me, missing the outside stump of my wicket by less than an inch. Fortunately for me, the wicket-keeper mishandled the next ball, which skidded past the nearby fielders, allowing Higginson and me to switch ends and score an extra run.

From then on Higgie did a really masterful job of controlling play so that I wouldn't have to bat again before the tea break. On the last ball of the over, he hit it past the fielder at silly mid off, enabling us to switch ends again, so that he'd still be batting when the other bowler began the next over. He blocked that bowler's first five balls, then backed off for a moment to look at his watch.

After stepping back into position behind the popping crease, he swatted the last ball of the over past square leg, adding two more runs while another fielder was chasing it down. I would have been the batter at the start of the next over, but Higgie knew exactly what he was doing, and had timed it perfectly. The umpire stopped play for tea and I was mercifully still alive.

As we walked back to the pavilion together, I thanked Higgie profusely for taking me off the hook. "I could see you were a little shaken by the near miss," he said. "Maiden time at bat is always hairy, like rumpy pumpy the first time. Don't worry, you'll be fine after tea."

And I was. For the first few overs I was a little tentative, but then I hit a boundary. Higgie hit a six on the first ball of the next over, and we were off to the races. We were still a pair when he scored the winning run an hour later, a full forty minutes before stumps would have been pulled for a draw.

BC took me aside after the match to congratulate me. "Good show, my friend," he said, "especially that one-handed diving catch. We all knew you could bat, but that catch was blinding. Don't know quite how I'll manage it yet, but you just earned a place in the first eleven."

I'm back on cloud nine again.

4.23.21

Philip Grinstein, the Callahan's fifth former I've mentioned before, tracked me down as we were walking to breakfast to congratulate me on scoring 37 not out in the Clifton match yesterday. Ever try bowling? he asked me; I'll bet you'd make a good all-rounder. No, I said, I've never had a real arm; it's all I can do to throw a baseball from second to first base. Any other sports? he asked. Not really, I said. I'm a baseball fanatic, so that's about it.

Would you like to try fly-fishing? he asked. Then he told me that he has a beat on the Avon this Sunday, and would be glad to have me join him if I'd like to. It's early in the season, he said, but if we get another warm day there should be a good hatch of sedge that'll bring fish to the surface. He offered to lend me all the equipment I'll need.

That's very generous of you, I said—and thought to myself that I'm starting to sound like a Brit. Sure—I'd enjoy taking a crack at casting, I told him.

I've seen it done in movies. It'll be an interesting challenge to try it myself.

4.25.21

Turns out that Grinstein's father is in a syndicate that leases a full mile of the Avon on both banks, a prime stretch with a good population of wild trout and grayling. As we're climbing into our hip boots, Philip tells me that our beat, about a quarter-mile long, is just as productive, and every bit as lovely, as anything on the Test or Itchen, the two most famous chalk streams in England.

I watch him cast several times, and the physics of it are plain to see. The momentum of the line on the back cast bends the rod tip backwards, so that it works like a slingshot when the rod is half way through the forward cast. I say as much to Philip when he hands me the rod, and he responds, "You're right as rain, it's called loading the rod."

We get into river by sliding down the grassy bank— the right bank, Philip says, because it's on our right when we face downstream—and after we're positioned that way, knee deep in the river, he tells me to pay out about 25 feet of line and let it drift straight downstream, then turn around so I'm facing upstream. "Hold the line tight with your left hand, hold the rod behind you over your right shoulder at a

45° angle to the water, then start to deliver a forward cast," he instructs me. "The friction as the line lifts off the water flowing downstream behind you will load the rod the same way a back cast would. When you feel the pressure as the rod tip bends backwards, drive the cast forward until I say 'stop,' then wait for the line to straighten out in front of you, and let the fly fall gently to the water."

I do that twice and it seems to work. "Now, instead of letting the fly fall to the water, begin a back cast when the line has straightened out in front of you," Philip suggests. "And as you're beginning the back cast, use your left hand to strip a little line off the reel, in order to lengthen your next forward cast. Let that second forward cast fall to the river."

I screw up completely on the back cast and the line collapses like a strand of hot spaghetti.

"If you let go of the line after stripping, it's going to do that every time," Philip explains. "You have to clamp the line with your left hand and hold it tight when you begin *any* cast, either a forward one or a backwards one. Keep your grip tight until you feel the rod load and the line starts to shoot. At that point loosen your grip and let the line slide through your fingers until it's fully extended. Then tighten up again for the next cast in the opposite direction."

It takes me 15 minutes to get it, and half an hour to do it well enough to begin fishing. Around 4:30 I see a fish rise to take an insect 20 feet upstream of me, and manage to cast my sedge imitation about three feet upriver of the spot where I think the fish is. Two seconds later the trout eats my fly and hooks himself. Philip coaches me on how to keep him out of the underwater weeds, but I can't manage to do it; he darts upstream, and disappears into a weed bed, taking my fly with him.

I clap Philip on the back and tell him that short of walking off the pitch with Higgie after the Clifton match, seeing my first fish take that fly and run with it is the most exciting thing that's happened to me all year.

5.14.21

Bought my first print today!

A week ago, as I was leafing through the catalog for Christie's May auction of Old Master Prints, I spotted an engraving of *Saint Catherine* by Martin Schongauer, one of the most important German printmakers aside from Dürer, and certainly the earliest significant one. I fell in love with the print at first sight, because the saint's long tresses spilled over her shoulders, exactly the way K's do.

I did some research and discovered that Schongauer engraved two versions of St. Catherine; I was looking at the larger one, which I preferred. I suspected that it was quite rare, because the most recent sale of the print that I could find was of a middling impression that Christie's sold in 2006. The impression pictured in the catalog looked fresh, and the description was reassuring, so I decided to call the

Christie's print department in London to see if I could learn more. The woman I spoke with said she'd personally examined the engraving out of its frame, and regarded it as the best impression of Bartsch 65 she'd seen in some time.

I took the catalog to Sarah Cooper's class the following day and showed her the print after everyone else had left. When I said I was thinking of bidding on it she looked at me with a bemused smile. "Would you want to buy it if the saint were Brigid rather than Catherine?" she asked. I'm not sure, I answered truthfully. "Well, it looks like a lovely impression," she said, "and I'd be tempted to buy it for our own collection if we could get it for the low estimate." Thank you for the endorsement, I said, but I'm prepared to bid a bit more than the high estimate, if need be. Because it *is* Saint Catherine.

At that point I still had $5,000 of the $25,000 Mom had given me for our trip, and the engraving was going to be my major homecoming present for K if I could get it. Christie's agreed that I could bid by phone, which I did this morning; fortunately, my last two competitors dropped out when I bid the amount of the high estimate, which was £4,500. I'll have to dip into my own funds to cover the commission, but that's fine, because now part of the present is really coming from me.

5.25.21

A surprise visitor today. A text message from Mom tells me that her widower friend, Henry Phelps, the NYC lawyer at Cravath, is flying over for a business meeting at their London office tomorrow, and would like to meet me here this afternoon if I can break loose. She gives me his cell phone number and flight information. "PS: We want to get married," her text says.

Phelps and I talk on the phone and agree to meet for high tea at the Red Lion in town at 4:00. I'm already there when he walks in, precisely at 4:00. He's a handsome six-foot man with a full head of snow-white hair, a high forehead and strong chin, lively light-blue eyes, and a warm smile that looks genuine, not contrived.

"Fran, what a pleasure to meet you at last!" he says with enthusiasm that sounds equally genuine. I can already sense why Mom calls him a born rainmaker. We talk for a while about Salisbury, then about his work, which turns out to focus on corporate mergers and acquisitions. I tell him that Katherine and I recently got an attractive offer from a Silicon Valley company that's interested in Artel, the new computer language we're working on, and ask if he'd be willing to take a look at their proposed right-of-first-refusal agreement, in case we decide to talk further with them about teaming up.

"Of course; I'd be glad to help in any way I can," he responds. "As a family friend, with the meter off," he adds. "One of the benefits of being an aged partner is that I can do as much non-billable work as I want to, whether it's pro bono or for friends with modest bank accounts who need help."

Very briefly, I think of Sydney and imagine what the conversation would be like if he were sitting in Henry's place. I shudder visibly, and quickly explain why. I gather you and Mom are thinking of getting married, I say next. And I think that would be absolutely great. Or 'positively capital' since we're here in the UK.

Henry smiles, then says, "I'm so glad you feel that way. It means we no longer have to live in sin. As you well know, your Mom is a remarkable person, and I feel very, very fortunate to be sharing life with her. And acquiring an extraordinarily talented stepson is the best wedding gift I could ever hope for."

I can't order champagne here because it's term time, I say, but why don't you, and then we'll call Mom, and toast your marriage. Henry stands, so do I, and he comes around to my side of the table, shakes my hand earnestly while looking me straight in the eye, then smiles before giving me a long bear hug, punctuated with a few pats on my back. When we call, Mom is thrilled.

33: Wildwood at Lenox – 2096

After our day at the Trinity Library, Ellen and I toured Dublin on foot for several days, but my memories of what we saw are hazy. I know that we ate well and went to the Abbey theater twice, or maybe three times, but again, I can't remember details. I do remember that on our last night together we drank a fair amount of Irish whiskey at her kitchen table, well into the early morning hours, and bared our lives—her lost love for a young officer who died in Iraq, my love for Katherine, and my sexual ambiguity. We ended up in bed together, and spent the night nestled together like two loving lesbians.

My final term at Salisbury was a true delight in every way. First and foremost, the weather turned the day I got back from Ireland in mid April, and it remained balmy and pleasant from then until early June, giving new life to everything that happened at school.

At the Head's request, I applied to his Cambridge college, Magdalene (pronounced "Maudlin"), and sat for lengthy exams in Greek, Russian, and Computer Science. I must have aced all three because they offered me a total scholarship. Three weeks later I declined it, again per the Head's request. He simply wanted a little respect—and intended to get it by showing his old college that Salisbury could produce scholars just as good as, if not better than, anyone Eton or Harrow or Winchester had to offer. Of course, from the word go, my application was a put-up job—simply a favor I could do for the Head to thank him for my year at Salisbury—because there was no way I was going to spend another year separated from Katherine.

Henry Phelps, Mom's NYC widower friend and lover unexpectedly turned up one day. I think he fabricated a business trip to London so he could meet me and fulfill Mom's request that I sign off before she married him. Sign off I did after 15 minutes of talking with him because he was so obviously a real catch for Mom, and obviously loved her so much, that I was overjoyed for both of them. Finally, I had a real father—someone I liked and respected, who wanted to hug me rather than banish me.

In late April I learned to fly-fish. Katherine and I had walked along a bucolic section of the Avon when I showed her Salisbury, but there's an even lovelier stretch of water several miles upstream. A younger boy in Callahan's invited me to fish there with him, and proved to be a good teacher. First, he showed me how to cast a line that was dragging straight downstream, so that I'd understand what it felt like to "load" the rod, then he taught me how to back cast, and finally how to make multiple casts starting with the fly in my free hand and 10 or 15 feet of line outside my rod tip. I even managed to find a fish and hook it, but then lost it in the underwater weeds. They flourish in chalk streams that flow out of limestone cisterns, as the Avon does.

Finally, there was cricket. All my practice sessions during the fall, and all the time I spent studying videos of world-class batters during the winter, paid off. I started out the season on the Salisbury second team, played well in my first match, and got promoted to the first eleven, so called because there are 11 players on a cricket team, or "side."

Before going to England I had a vague idea that cricket was an easy-going, patrician sport, played leisurely on large lawns, with breaks in play for tea and crumpets. Well, apart from the breaks for tea, I was all wrong. I've seen village kids play cricket on dirt playgrounds far rougher than typical sandlot ball fields in the U.S., and it's definitely not a game for foppish wimps. None of the fielders except the catcher (called the "wicket-keeper") may wear a glove, even though the ball is the same size, and just as hard, as a Major League baseball.

When I first got back to the States, I told Bobby Anderson and other skeptical friends that in some ways cricket is tougher than baseball. Try standing a dozen feet from a batter and making a barehanded catch of a line drive hit straight at you, I said. Or getting hit in the back by a throw from a fielder who's aiming for the wicket you're running toward.

BC had a marvelous season as captain of our eleven, batting for a century—100 runs or more—in three different matches, and setting a new Salisbury record for the number of wickets taken by a bowler over the course of the season. He saved his best for last, taking three wickets against Rugby, and scoring 125 runs not out to clinch the match. I was his lead off batting partner in several matches, and came close to a century myself against Marlborough, but had to settle for 92 when I was run out by half a step. I tried to score a third run on a ball hit well to the right of the long-off fielder, but he ran it down before it reached the boundary and made a great throw that hit the wicket on the fly, a split second before my outstretched bat touched the ground inside the crease.

Early in June we got word that we'd been selected—along with Bamfyled, Clifton, and Harrow—to compete for the public school cricket championship in a three-match tournament to be held at Lord's later that month. It was hard for me to believe that in my first year of playing cricket I was going to compete on hallowed ground. I'd heard of American schoolboys playing in a post-season public-school tennis tournament on outside practice courts at Wimbledon, but going to Lord's was equivalent to playing a tennis match on centre court—or baseball in Yankee Stadium. All of us on the eleven were really keyed up.

The culmination of the regular school year came on Commemoration Weekend, or Commem for short. Parents arrived in a variety of vehicles, ranging from a battered 20th century VW Beetle to a Bentley. After an elaborate picnic luncheon at tables set up on the Close, our current eleven played a leisurely match against an OSB eleven comprised mainly of recent graduates, but spearheaded by an all-rounder who was still playing for Gloucestershire in his early 40s. It was a sunlit afternoon of quintessential amateur cricket, with perhaps 150 or 200 spectators who sat in lawn chairs along the boundary and clapped in restrained fashion when anything noteworthy happened on the pitch. Parents not interested in watching cricket could choose from an array of classes and seminars offered up by College masters.

That evening our Callahan's troupe reenacted several scenes from *The Devil's Disciple* before dinner in the Great Hall. After the opening blessing the Head rose to his feet, briefly welcomed all parents and other visitors, and then announced that he was inaugurating a new tradition by offering wine not only to adults but to sixth formers as well. "Following a precedent set earlier in the year, younger students will be offered a small glass of hard cider," he added, leaving parents to wonder, or ask their sons, why his remark triggered a good deal of laughter and scattered applause from the back benches.

To everyone's great surprise, dinner was excellent. When BC finally decided to say "Benedicto, benedicatur," tables were spirited away from the north end of the hall to create a good-sized dance floor, and the Saxons—so called because two of the seven boys in the group played saxophones—mounted the dais and started to play mellow jazz and American show tunes. All told, it was a very successful evening.

At chapel on Sunday morning, the College choir, glee club, and bell ringers outdid themselves, performing just as well as their King's College or St. John's College counterparts. After the traditional Commem service, the Head spoke for a little over 20 minutes on the broad theme of Salisbury in the Nation's Service, a phrasing and concept that he said he was borrowing from Princeton University in the States. He touched on many facets of his theme, from the sacrifices made by OSBs who fought in the Boer War and two World Wars, to the unheralded contributions made by OSBs working in urban slums across in the land.

I thought I detected a valedictory note in his remarks and was sad to learn a year later that he had publicly announced his retirement at the Commem service that year. He was an exceptionally erudite, astute, and kindly schoolmaster whom I will remember always with great affection. His obituary in the *Times* ten years after he retired must have been written by Barton-Smith or some other OSB, for it was laced with quotations of his favorite expressions and concluded: "If pushed to the wall Old Lit might have conceded that, as headmasters go, he was 'not so bad.' Indeed, he was 'not bad at all,' a rare compliment he reserved for those whom he regarded most highly."

34: At Sea – 2021

7.6.21

Boarded the Queen Mary around noon today and went on deck an hour ago to watch England slowly sink below the horizon. The gulls who accompanied us out of Southampton have given up and headed back to port, leaving the sea around us as empty as my diary for June. I've been remiss, but will try to make amends by recapitulating highlights since my last entry.

Wonderful conversation with K when we celebrated the 4th. She woke me well before sunup yesterday to show me live fireworks over the Hudson, which she was recording from the penthouse deck of her parents' Riverside Drive apartment. Aced all her Harvard exams, and plans to spend the summer working exclusively on Artel. Wants us to work side-by-side. Said I'd try, but doubt if either of us will be able to concentrate on Artel for very long that way. You're not getting randy, are you? she asked. Oh, no, I said, not in the least. Then explained about Old Lit and she laughed.

Thanks mainly to BC, we beat Rugby in our last cricket match of the regular season to qualify for the public-school championship tournament at Lord's. Got my first six a few days later when we played the OSB side at Commem. Even broke a window in the cricket pavilion doing it, which caused quite a stir.

Commem was an impressive weekend: a reprise of several scenes from our *Devil's Disciple* performance, the first decent meal of the school year, and dancing afterwards for parents, masters, and sixth formers who wanted to dance with their relatives or masters' wives. Chapel the following day was special because of the music and the Head's speech—the first serious one I'd heard him make all year. About the responsibility of OSBs to contribute to society and the country. God ahead of Mammon, others ahead of self. The Head managed to find new words for old ideas, converting what might have been a conventional or even trite speech into an inspiring one.

It was difficult to stay focused on what he said because I was still thinking about dancing with Sarah Cooper the night before. I'd been talking with Grinstein when someone tapped me on the shoulder. I turned around and there was Sarah. "Dance?" she asked, with a quizzical smile and a wicked glint in her eyes. We started off in conventional fashion, but when the floor got really crowded and no one could see what was going on, she went to work with her pelvis, smiling in cheerful, lighthearted fashion the entire time, as if she didn't have a care in the world, while she was telling me downstairs how much I'd been missing ever since Xmas. You're a terrific teacher, I said when the dance was over. I'm never going to forget this year, I added.

It felt slightly sordid to be thinking about Sarah in Commem chapel, but I couldn't help myself because I could still feel her in my groin. I wondered if she might actually be a nympho, and if so, how she could have survived so long without creating a scandal. The thought of Old Nile being cuckolded on his home turf was disturbing; he was too kindly, too decent to be treated that way.

I decided in the end that it really wasn't my problem, because I'd done nothing wrong and had spoken truthfully when I said goodbye to Sarah on the dance floor. She really had been a superlative teacher. And I know I'll never forget my introduction to Tea and Sympathy, British style.

After Commem all of us on the eleven went up to London for our playoff match at Lords. It should have been two matches, because we had matters well in hand against Clifton, leading by 80 runs and needing to take only two more wickets in the last hour of play to advance to the finals. But both Clifton batsmen hunkered down at that point, smothering the ball defensively instead of hitting out to score runs. "Grafting" it's called. We managed to take one more wicket but couldn't get the tenth one, so the match ended as a draw, and Clifton won a coin toss to play Harrow for the title.

Sorry as I was that we didn't get a shot at the title, being at Lords was still a great experience. I'd never before drawn applause from a crowd of 5,000 and don't expect to ever again, so the reaction to my first boundary, a hard-hit shot past deep extra cover, was a memory-bank moment that I'll cherish.

After it was over, BC invited me to dinner and we ended up having a great evening, going to his father's club to play baccarat for a while, then to a jazz club where he picked up a stunning blond who was clearly waiting to hook up with her male counterpart. I say clearly because BC and I had watched her turn down two other guys before he made his move. At her suggestion the three of us went to another, even better jazz place, where we stayed for an hour or so before moving on to a third place I can't picture at all.

Somehow I made it back to my hotel and went to bed with my clothes on. When I woke up around 9:45 the next morning, my only real memory of the final hours of our night of carousing was bear hugging BC and vowing that we'd stay in touch. He's off to Balliol in the fall and will undoubtedly be a mainstay of the Oxford eleven.

Went to John Lobb yesterday morning to take delivery of my bespoke shoes, which fit perfectly and look exceptionally smart. The only decorative elements are graceful stitching lines that curve from the laces to the heels on both sides of each shoe, and a narrow band of tooled leather that crosses the top of each of them 2-1/4" from the tip of the toe. The leather is a lustrous mahogany color, making them look as though they've been polished countless times. I expect them to last forever. I wore them on the train down to Southampton this morning, and am still wearing them now, as I write this in the cabin class bar. They are *so* cool.

7.10.21

The Queen Mary without K is a far cry from our trip over. I've been holed up in my cabin most of the time, working on Artel, but accomplishing little. Ever since I got interested in AI during my first year at Devon, I've been haunted by the idea that classical thought, particularly mathematics, might open up the programming pathway to Singularity. Thus far, though, there's been little progress on that front.

I keep coming back to the Greek discovery of Phi, the Golden Ratio (1 : 1.61803…), because I see in my head a large Phi rectangle, having that ratio of width to length, drawn on blank paper, with a solid black square constructed inside one end of it, causing the remaining blank space in the rectangle to have the dimensions of another, smaller Phi rectangle oriented at a right angle to the first one. Inside that second Phi rectangle another solid black square can be constructed to create yet another blank, still smaller Phi rectangle oriented the way the first one was—and so on, ad infinitum, until one reaches some infinitesimally small Phi rectangle that represents the essence of thought and serves as the core of a deep neural network that mimics the brain. But for the life of me, as clear and persuasive as that image is, I can't translate it into viable words and symbols for converting massive amounts of data into computer output that truly mimics human thought and behavior.

My other favorite candidate for an AI algorithm as profound and elegant as e = mc² is the Fibonacci Series, where each number—after zero and one, for starters—is the sum of the two preceding numbers. Instead of visualizing descent into a vortex of concentrated data and thought, I see the sequence spiraling up and out, at a rapidly accelerating rate (0, 1, 1, 2, 3, 5, 8, 13, 21, 34, 55, 89, 144, 233....), encompassing limitless amounts of data that can then be converted into thought.

I intuitively feel that, taken together, the Fibonacci Series and Phi ratio should provide the answer to my quandary, because any large number in the Series, divided by the immediately preceding number, will yield a quotient essentially equal to Phi. But again, I don't see how the concept of spiraling out as the Series does in order to funnel back down as Phi does can be translated into viable computer code.

I've pretty much decided that I want to spend some time at Harvard Med School next semester studying the human brain. There's a new project they're running with Boston University that sounds promising, and I've E-mailed the director to get more information. In the meantime, K and I will keep programming and testing to see how well Artel works now, and what can be done to improve it. We're going to need some high-speed processors, because our computers can't begin to handle the big data bases that MIT has promised to let us use over the summer for testing purposes.

K is coming down from New Canaan to meet me at dockside tomorrow, and I'm going walk off the ship with arms spread wide, ready to plant a Devon kiss that will match the best of them.

35: Wildwood at Lenox – 2096

After Commem weekend at Salisbury I spent a day packing up, said goodbye to the Head, and took the train up to London for the public school cricket playoffs at Lord's. I contributed 43 runs before being caught and bowled by Clifton's fast bowler, and thought we had them beaten, but they grafted on us to eke out a draw, and then we lost the coin toss to see which side got to the finals. Had a wild night afterwards with our captain (my friend, BC), and woke up the following morning with a headache that wiped out my plans for the entire day.

Spent almost a week after that looking at prints in the British Museum, revisiting the museums I'd seen with Katherine, and browsing through several dealers' inventory of old-master prints. I bought a small Rembrandt—a late 17th century impression of *Old Man in a Rich Velvet Cap* (Bartsch 313)—from Douwes Fine Art in St. James's Street for a reasonable sum. It's the only print I kept when I gave my others away before moving here, and I still believe, as I glance up from my desk to look at it for the umpteenth time, that it's one of the best portraits he did. Also bought a small Kirchner woodcut for Mom, because she's always loved the German Expressionists.

Voyage home on the QM was uneventful. No Katherine, no captain's dinner, nothing to rock the boat, just five days to work on Artel undisturbed. When I got off the ship at the Red Hook Pier in Brooklyn, Katherine and I literally ran into each other with open arms spread wide. To avoid a smash-up I tilted mine at the last second, the way we did as kids when we were pretending to fly like birds or airplanes, and then we hugged hard as I planted the Devon kiss I'd been anticipating for days.

Mom had planned a family dinner party to welcome me home, and the six of us—Katherine, her parents, Mom, Henry, and me—all gathered at our house. I learned then that Mom and Henry had "eloped" (as she said proudly) by having one of Henry's friends, a federal judge, marry them in his office, with his secretary as the sole witness. I also discovered that Henry had been stashing away good French Bordeaux and Burgundy for many years, before prices skyrocketed. We drank an outstanding 1961 Latour with Mom's delicious roasted pheasant, and a 1966 La Tache with an array of French cheeses. Coming up with wines like that clinched it; Henry was premier grand cru all the way.

At the end of dinner I gave Katherine and Mom the prints I'd bought for them in England, and both were a great success. Earlier in the day I'd had a camera shop in Darien blow up a photo of Katherine and me taken on the deck of the QM by our cabin steward, using my i-phone, and her parents were visibly touched when we gave them an 8"x12" high-definition print of the photo, which we'd framed after inscribing it "With love and thanks, K&F." I apologized to Henry for not having a wedding present for him as well, but he smiled and replied, "Nonsense, you two are our wedding presents!"

Several days later, Katherine and I packed up most of my clothes, my favorite arm chair, and several boxes of books, and drove our rented van to Cambridge to take up residence together in the Chauncy Terrace apartment she'd lived in during her sophomore year. We were tired when we arrived, but nonetheless had a grand time cavorting in the king-sized bed she'd acquired in April—a playing field that we promptly named Fenway Park. She had a large, fully equipped partners' desk already set up for us in the study, with our 1704 colonial map hanging on a side wall where both of us could see it from our desk chairs, and our two Roman glass beakers on the mantle over the study fireplace. For all practical purposes, we could have been a young married couple, settling into our first home together.

36: Wildwood at Lenox – 2096

I made only occasional diary entries after I got back from England, so to enliven the narrative, I'm going to enlist the services of my omniscient narrator to replicate a series of conversations I had shortly after Katherine and I arrived in Cambridge.

The first was with Assistant Dean Savage of the Harvard Medical School. "Good morning, Mr. Johnson," he greeted me, after making me wait 25 minutes in his office anteroom. "I have your letter to Dr. Hemmings and gather that you would like to enroll in the Med School. But you have not been to college, you have taken no pre-med courses to speak of. Why on earth would you think you qualify?"

"Because, sir, I'm well on the way to creating a new computer language that has the potential to revolutionize artificial intelligence programming. I need to understand more about the human brain to complete my work, and think that HMS is the best place in America to do that. I believe I'm intellectually qualified. I taught myself basic calculus before I was 13. Starting from scratch when I went to Salisbury College in England last year, I learned to speak and write fluent Russian. As you can see from the transcripts I enclosed with my letter, almost all the courses that I've taken in the last six years at Hanson Country Day, Devon Academy, and Salisbury have been college-level ones.

"I'm not seeking a medical degree, sir, nor do I want to become a doctor. My mission in life is to enable computers to think, communicate, and behave like well educated, well adjusted human beings, freeing society as a whole to spend somewhat less time on mundane tasks and somewhat more on creative ones. If HMS is willing to help me understand the neural networks of the brain, I believe there is a reasonable likelihood that I will be able to repay what you invest in me a million-fold.

"All I'm requesting, sir, is the opportunity to participate in Dr. Hemmings's course on a full-fledged basis that would include any related seminars and lab work. MIT has already admitted me to their graduate school this fall to do further advanced work in computer science. Surely HMS is flexible enough to admit me for purposes of taking a single course."

"Well, thank you for your interest, Mr. Johnson. What you request is quite unprecedented, but we will take it under advisement and let you know our decision in the near future."

"Thank you, sir, for meeting with me," I said. Why are you so snotty, I felt like saying.

Before getting back to work with Katherine, I had three other important items on my homecoming agenda. The first was to call Devon to see if the Head of School was in residence and could see me if I drove up to Portland. Yes he was, and yes he could, so off I went.

"Good afternoon, sir."

"And to you, Fran. Welcome home!"

"It's good to be back. I wanted to stop by to thank you again for the year at Salisbury. Saying it in letters is one thing, I wanted to tell you in person how grateful I am."

"You're kind to say so, but it was really nothing special, simply part of my job. How are you faring with your new artificial intelligence software language, the project you were working on with Mr. Sampson. Any recent progress since your last letter?"

"Yes, thanks. I think Katherine French and I—she's my partner in all this—are ready to begin rigorous testing to see how it performs in practice, as opposed to theory."

"Has anything come of your shipboard meeting with the CEO of Almega—I forget his name…"

"Steve Goddard, sir. He's offered Katherine and me high-level jobs, and I intend to call him shortly, to see if we can put everything on hold for another year or two. I don't want to intrude, but that whole episode has always mystified me, as I said in my first letter to you. Do you have any idea how our meeting came about, were you by any chance—"

"Do you know the old Broadway play, *Six Degrees of Separation*?"

"Sorry, no. But I once heard somebody describe it as a theatrical way of saying that if you pick any two people on the planet at random, you'll always be able to connect them with a chain of five or fewer other people—a chain where everybody between the two people you picked knows the prior person and the next person in the chain. Or something like that."

"Exactly like that. I didn't say anything after you wrote me about your dinner at the Captain's table, because I wanted to see if you'd reach out after you got home. You have, so now I want you to know why you sat there.

"My sister, Susan, and your mother have worked together for several years now on the committee that plans the annual Artists' Ball at the Plaza in New York, a benefit that funds health care for needy artists and actors. One day in June last year your mother told Susan that you and Katherine were planning to spend the summer traveling in England, and would be going over on the Queen Mary, thanks to her parents. Susan knew I'd be interested to learn that two of Devon's brightest recent alumni were teaming up, so she told me about your plans.

"I thought about it for a while and decided to call a Devon alumnus named Thorndike who's been a big help in capital fund raising because he's head of a major travel agency and has a long list of people who habitually travel first class. I asked if he'd worked with Cunard in the past and he told me that he makes 25, maybe 30, first-class bookings on the Queen Mary every year. I told him a good bit about you, and asked if he could arrange to have you seated at the Captain's table one night. He obviously got that done. After I got your first letter, I called to thank him and learned about the rest of it. He said that when he'd checked the first-class manifest for your sailing, he'd recognized Goddard's name because of all the recent publicity about the Almega IPO, and had cabled Cunard again to get the Goddards invited, and also arrange the seating.

"You got to the Captain's table because I believe very strongly in networking. You unexpectedly got to meet and impress Goddard because my friend Thorndike feels the same way. We both think networking is one of the most powerful forces in the world today.

"Often, as in your Captain's table case, it works with fewer than six degrees of separation. You may not have thought about any of this before, but you've already started networking—the friends you've made here at Devon, the shared experiences, your encounter with Goddard. I urge you to continue doing it by reaching out to others, making new friends, and exploring new fields. By treating everyone you encounter civilly, and making no enemies. If you do that, networking could very well prove to be more important in your later life than anything else you've learned here.

"When you were a student, I suspect you thought of me as gruff and unapproachable. I doubt if we spoke ten words to each other until I suggested Salisbury as your next step. All that was by design. You came here as a talented prodigy, and the faculty did a grand job of challenging you to learn still more. My role was to keep you from getting a swelled head—to suggest by my silence that I didn't think you were anything special. When I made the Salisbury offer late in your senior year, I hoped you would realize that I was, in fact, *very* impressed by what you had done here.

"You're an alumnus now, Fran, and perhaps we can at last become friends. Thank you again for coming to see me."

During the drive back to Boston I tried to compile a mental list of all the people I knew who might be potential networking allies, and was surprised by how quickly I reached 25. Three heads of top-flight schools, the youngest head ever of one of the world's great libraries, the CEO of a major Silicon Valley company, a senior partner in one of the top law firms in the country, the Captain of the Queen Mary (maybe) and a slew of fellow students like BC with the potential to become leaders in a variety of high-powered occupations.

The day after my trip to Portland I got a call from the Dean of the Med School—the head of the entire school, not simply the admissions office—inviting me to take Dr. Hemmings' class and seminars on the neurology of the brain, all on a full scholarship. I must eat my earlier words about Assistant Dean Savage, who obviously forwarded my request to others with decision-making authority. I later learned that shortly after our meeting he'd called MIT to verify my status there, and I suspect that he got an earful from my friend, Dean Hammond, another person who belongs on my networking list.

Nailing down my plans made it easy to handle the second item on my homecoming agenda. I called Steve Goddard and had a brief, but cordial conversation. "I've decided to spend the coming year doing graduate work at MIT, and studying the human brain with a renowned professor at the Harvard Medical School," I told him, "but Katherine and I remain very interested in the possibility of joining Almega down the road."

"Sorry to hear that next year is out," he replied, "but I fully understand. Studying the real brain to build an artificial one makes great sense. And I'm sure that MIT will have the humongous data bases you need to test drive your new language. Artel, if I remember correctly?"

"Artel it is. Katherine and I have acquired a partners' desk, so we're now working together out loud, instead of taking timeouts to E-mail back and forth.

"To expedite future discussions among the three of us, could you send me a copy of your standard right-of-first-refusal contract?" I asked. "My new stepfather is a partner in Cravath, doing primarily M&A work, and I'd like to get his thoughts before we make any decisions."

"Of course, I'd be glad to. I'll shoot you an E-mail this afternoon. Cravath's a great firm, and I'd welcome any thoughts that your stepfather might have regarding possible improvements in the contract, ways of making it better for all concerned. I know Henry Phelps; is he by any—"

"He is, indeed. He and my mother just eloped."

"She made a wise decision. I've been on the opposite side of the table from Henry, working on one of our major acquisitions. He's a creative thinker and straight as an arrow—a real pleasure to work with."

"Good to hear. Let's stay in touch."

The final item on my homecoming agenda was my longstanding date to see Dr. Nancy Shetland, an eminent Boston endocrinologist I'd called shortly before Katherine and I headed off to England. I'd tried, with only moderate success, to put the whole gender issue out of mind while I was at Salisbury, but deep down I knew that I should have confronted it long ago—specifically, during the summer before I went off to Devon, when I masturbated for the first time and discovered that I couldn't ejaculate. I was looking forward to finally getting some answers, but apprehensive about what they might be.

Dr. Shetland's office turned out to look more like the library of a Back Bay house than a medical consultation office, and she was dressed accordingly, in a conservative tweed suit befitting an aristocratic Boston matron, rather than the white jacket worn by the only doctor I could remember from my childhood. She had gray hair, wore small gold-rimmed glasses, and had a cheerful, welcoming demeanor.

"Good afternoon!" she said as she rose from her desk chair to shake hands. "Please sit wherever you like." I picked the small settee next to her desk. "What questions or concerns bring you here?" she asked.

"Basically, my sexuality and gender. I've grown up as a boy; I've got a penis that looks normal from what I've seen in locker rooms, I get erections and have orgasms, but I've never ejaculated. My fiancée, who's bisexual, says that I make love like a woman."

"Have you consulted anyone in the past about your concerns?"

"No. I've been exceptionally healthy all my life. I haven't seen a doctor in years. With the exception of an illness I got in England last winter, I haven't had anything worse than a few minor colds. Literally, nothing that has occasioned a trip to the doctor."

"Then I think we should begin at the beginning. Were you born in a hospital?"

"St. Elizabeth's in Darien, Connecticut. In 2001."

"Good. Could I call them now to ask that they send me their records regarding your birth?"

"Of course."

She put us on her speaker phone and it took less than five minutes to arrange that. Then she asked me about my growth rate as a child, my experiences during puberty, and whether I'd ever noticed blood in my urine. After that we moved next door to her clinical room, which looked totally medical. I stripped and stretched out on her examination table. Using the fingers of both hands, she deftly probed from my temples and neck glands down to my toes, with a brief pause to palpate my genitals.

"Anything unusual?" I asked when she told me I could get dressed.

"Can't really say, yet," she replied. "The next step is blood work, to see if there are any obvious abnormalities that need to be corrected or explored further. It will take 24 hours to get the lab results," she said after drawing five small vials of blood from the inside of my left arm. "Let's see if anything has come back from the hospital. If not, we can discuss all the results when you return tomorrow."

Which is what we did. When I entered her office the following afternoon, she greeted me warmly. "You are a fascinating patient, Mr. Johnson," she began. "Probably—"

"Fran, please," I interrupted. "If this is going to be fascinating rather than routine, I'd much rather be Fran than Mr. Johnson."

"Thank you for the vote of confidence. Let me try to explain in layman's terms what I've learned since yesterday."

She proceeded to give me a short course on who I am. At birth my 23rd pair of chromosomes were XX, meaning that genetically I was born a female. But my adrenal glands—a pair of glands located just above the kidneys that regulate the production of various hormones—were abnormally large at birth, a medical condition known as "congenital adrenal hyperplasia," or CAH.

As a result of that adrenal abnormality, my fetus generated an excess of androgen hormones throughout my time in the womb. Those male hormones promptly went to work on the sexless phallus and genital folds that my fetus developed very shortly after conception. By the time I was born, my original "undifferentiated" phallus had grown into a penis rather than a clitoris. And my original genital folds had developed into a scrotum rather than vaginal labia.

"Your particular version of CAH produced an exceptionally heavy overload of testosterone and other androgen hormones," Dr. Shetland said. "As a result, you showed typical symptoms of virilization—the development of male characteristics—before and during puberty: an early, pre-pubescent growth spurt, the lowering of your voice, the beard you had to shave occasionally, the pustular acne you mentioned, and a larger penis and scrotum than genetic females with CAH typically have.

"Naturally, everyone assumed at first that you were a boy. Then, while you were still in the hospital, your parents were told that genetically you were a girl with standard XX chromosomes. And next they got the results of the routine CAH test that all hospitals have to perform because the 'salt-wasting' version of the classic CAH syndrome can be life-threatening to new-born infants. Fortunately, you had the less common, non life-threatening, version of classic CAH, but your true sexuality was still very much in doubt."

I could imagine Sydney's reaction on being told that I was genetically a girl: "He's got a prick, godammit. He's a boy, and we're going to treat him like a boy, or I'm out of here."

I also had some major questions: What did CAH do to my insides? Was I effectively like a spayed bitch, a neuter who couldn't reproduce? If I could have children, would they be likely to have CAH issues? Could an operation change anything? Could taking hormones make a difference? Was my penis likely to wither away as I became older?

Dr. Shetland was truly sympathetic when I asked my questions. She told me that an MRI taken at St. E's when I was several days old strongly suggested that I had at least one ovary and fallopian tube, and a normal uterus. "At this point, you shouldn't rule out the possibility of having children," she said. "I doubt whether your single testicle would produce enough sperm for conception, but your ovary might be able to produce a receptor for a donor's sperm, and if so, I'm hopeful that your uterus would function normally, as it often does in CAH cases, so that you could deliver a child via a cesarean section.

"I'd suggest some further tests to get a better current reading," she added. "Are you up for a pelvic MRI and some specialized blood work?" Sure, I said, not fully realizing what the MRI would entail. She paused for a minute to write out and hand me instructions for setting up both tests.

"If it turns out that you can have children, it's theoretically possible, but very unlikely, that they would suffer from your problem," she said. "CAH is one example of what we call an 'autosomal recessive disorder,' meaning that the defective gene giving rise to the disorder passes from one generation to the next, but can be activated in a child only if *both* its parents have the same type of defective gene, and only in 25% of those cases. In other words, even in the highly unlikely event that you chose a mate with the same defective gene that you have, there would be only a 25% statistical chance that any given child of yours would inherit the active CAH disorder, instead of being simply another carrier of the defective gene.

She paused again for a moment, then added, "I think your parents were wise to do nothing until you were old enough to decide for yourself how you want to deal with what you've now learned. When I began my practice years ago, parents of CAH babies too often opted for genital operations before there was any way to determine the child's natural predilections. That rarely happens now, because genital-reconfiguration surgeons have developed far better post-puberty procedures for converting a penis to a clitoris, and using scrotal tissue to create labia for a vaginal pathway to the uterus. If you want to explore that option I'd be happy to put you in touch with the two surgeons I regard most highly."

"Thanks, but I don't think I want to go that route. I don't see myself in any female locker-room situations from here on out, so I think that having a penis is irrelevant in choosing which gender I want to be. Am I right in assuming that if I want to switch, hormone treatment could make my face look more feminine?"

"Probably so. To what extent is difficult to predict at this juncture, but I'm virtually certain that we could eliminate facial hair, and I think there's a good chance that you would end up appearing ambivalent enough so that strangers looking at you would not question your gender if you changed your hair style and dressed like a woman."

"Any adverse side effects from taking hormones?" I asked. "I have no desire to get into bed with a man. Is that likely to change if I get dosed with estrogens or whatever?"

"You're wise to ask. I assume from what you just said that your bisexual partner is a female."

"Definitely."

"Does the idea of a lesbian relationship concern you at all?"

"No. On the contrary, it appeals to me. That's the way we make love. I haven't entered her—with my penis, I mean—since the first time we had sex, because copulating that way just didn't do it for either of us."

"I can't promise anything, but what you say leads me to think that your core identity may very well be as a lesbian. If so, I think hormone treatment to augment female characteristics is unlikely to affect your sexual preference for other women."

Seconds later she asked, "If the hormone treatment enlarged your breasts, would that concern you?"

"I don't think so. If I'm going to switch to being female in public, I might as well go all in, and become a true hermaphrodite."

"I should alert you," she said immediately. "For reasons I've never understood, my profession has adopted various euphemisms for describing the facts of life. Hermaphrodites have become 'intersex' individuals, and using the word 'hermaphrodite' in a journal article is now politically incorrect, if not insulting. It's a shame, because the Greek myth that gave us the word is so lyrical. Do you—"

"You're right. I learned a lot of Greek myths as a young boy, and Salamis seducing the son of Hermes and Aphrodite was one of my favorites. I see her shimmering in crystal-clear water as she swims toward him, then pressing her body against his until they merge into a single person of both sexes. As you say, that's poetic. 'Intersex individuals' sounds totally prosaic.

"Thank you so much for all the help and advice you've given me. I'll follow through on the MRI and blood work, and await word from you when you get the results."

"I thank you as well, Fran. It's been a pleasure to go over all this with you. Let's hope the MRI shows that everything's in working order.

"One last thought. Do you know *Middlesex*, the Pulitzer prize-winning novel by Jeffrey Eugenides?"

"Sorry, no."

"I think you'd enjoy it. You and the narrator would like each other."

37: Wildwood at Lenox – 2096

Of course, I gave Katherine a verbatim report of my two sessions with Dr. Shetland as soon as I got back to Chauncy Terrace each day. I did it stretched out in Fenway Park, which was where we liked to talk about personal matters.

You up for marrying a woman? I asked Katherine after filling her in on my second session.

"Just any old woman, or you?" she said with a straight face. And then she rolled over on top of me, and inhaled my tongue. Which is why we liked to discuss personal matters in bed.

Later I called Mom. She was delighted to know that I'd finally "learned about the birds and the bees," to use her quaint expression, which I hadn't heard before. "Sydney and I almost never agreed on anything important," she told me, "but thank God we agreed on letting you be yourself, albeit for completely different reasons. I believed in laissez faire; he insisted that your tiny penis made you a man.

"We had a terrible fight about your name, because he thought Fran—which I suggested—was too feminine. I said it was a perfectly reasonable shorthand version of

Frank. He said it sounded more like shorthand for Frances, or maybe Francesca or Francine. I said that's the whole point; we need a name that works either way, depending on how it turns out in the end. 'My son is not going to be a switch-hitter,' he shouted at me. Who knows? I shouted back. Finally, I put my foot down. Call him whatever you want to, I said. The name on his birth certificate is going to be Fran. After that Sydney stonewalled, refusing to refer to you by name. It was always 'the kid' or 'the boy' or, when he was mad about something you'd said or done, 'that boy.'

"As I said earlier, it's great that you've discovered your past. Do you know yet who you want to be?"

I said we were going to wait for the MRI and additional blood work before making a final decision, but both of us were thinking about converting our Boston marriage into an official lesbian one—after we finished schooling and got jobs. "That would be wonderful, if that's what you decide," Mom said. "And I know Henry would agree.

"I'm not making that up," she added a moment later. "We actually talked about that possibility after your homecoming party, when we went to bed."

A week later I had my MRI, in one of the "open" scanners where the person being scanned can at least see out to either side of a brightly lighted room, instead of being buried alive inside a tube the size of sewer pipe, with just an inch or two of space between the tube and the poor person's face. I was expecting the high-tech scanner to run silently, or perhaps purr quietly, but instead it produced a cacophony of symphonic dimensions—a series of raucous sounds that made me think of cannons firing in rapid succession, jackhammers breaking up cement, elevators whirring up or down, symbols clashing, knife sharpeners grinding steel blades, and tires screeching, all interspersed with brief periods of graveyard silence that only heightened the suspense as to what weird type of noise would come next. Apart from turning my head from side to side and wiggling my toes and fingers to remind myself that I was still alive, I was not allowed to move any part of my body during the 50-minute period required to scan my pelvis from a variety of different perspectives. It felt more like two hours.

Several days later I got a call from Dr. Shetland, saying that I'd obviously done a good job of holding still, because the image resolution was A+. "Everything you had at birth looks normal, and appears to be fully developed," she told me. "One ovary, one open fallopian tube, and a good looking uterus. And your testicle is a little larger than I thought it was when I palpated it; given its size and shape, I think it might produce some sperm." The next step, she said, was a testicular biopsy to see whether that conjecture was true.

So off to Mass General a week later to have a special needle poked into my scrotum in order to extract tissue that would provide the answer. I was cautiously optimistic: if Hermes, the god of sports, could make me a switch-hitter on the ball field, maybe he'd challenge Priapus, the god of fertility, to make me a switch-hitter in bed—someone who could sire a child as well as bear one. That would be the apotheosis of the son-of-Hermes myth I described earlier, the apex of my androgynous life.

But it was not to be. Dr. Shetland called again, a week later, to say that none of the core samples the urologist extracted from my testicle contained a single sperm cell.

38: Cambridge, MA – 2021

8.20.2021

Gave myself an unexpected birthday present today by discovering the Harvard Cricket Club and tracking down their professional coach. Told him about my Med School connection and cricket experience, including the match at Lord's, at which point he invited me to spend an hour in their nets on a field not far from Harvard Stadium. Went through my drill of batting to all points of the compass from both sides of the wicket, and cleanly fielded some balls he hit toward me on the ground and in the air.

He signed me up on the spot, and gave me a list of the HCC's 2022 fixtures so I could reserve the dates. The schedule includes six matches with Ivy League sides, four with mid-Atlantic cricket clubs, and more at the National Championship tournament in Florida if HCC qualifies, as it has done in recent years. Looking at the roster he gave me, I assume that most members of the first eleven are foreigners studying at Harvard, but there are several others with typical American names.

The prospect of continuing to play cricket cheers me up considerably. I may become a woman eventually, but with my genitals I'll never be able to play on a women's team, so best take advantage of the HCC opportunity while I have it.

I've got two weeks left before starting at MIT, which I'm using to read up on current AI developments. It's amazing how much has been written since my last survey a year ago: a dozen major conferences, at least a hundred published articles, a new book by Bostrum, new theories on better risk constraints, and most importantly, Google's decision to publish the self-learning algorithms for Gamma Go—the third generation of its deep-mind program that taught itself the rules of Japanese Go, then learned winning strategies and tactics by playing against itself millions of times. Months later, it used its self-acquired knowledge to beat two of the world's best human players.

8.22.2021

In the course of reading articles with promising abstracts yesterday, I spotted a journal reference to a 1950 Alan Turing article entitled *Computing Machinery and Intelligence*, which I immediately tracked down because the title rang no bells.

At one point Turing suggests:

Instead of trying to produce a programme to simulate the adult mind, why not rather try to produce one which simulates the child's? If this were then subjected to an appropriate course of education one would obtain the adult brain. Presumably the child brain is something like a notebook as one buys it from the stationer's. Rather little mechanism, and lots of blank sheets. (Mechanism and writing are from our point of view almost synonymous.) Our hope is that there is so little mechanism in the child brain that something like it can be easily programmed.

And he concludes by saying:

We may hope that machines will eventually compete with men in all purely intellectual fields. But which are the best ones to start with? Even this is a difficult decision. Many people think that a very abstract activity, like the playing of chess, would be best. It can also be maintained that it is best to provide the machine with the best sense organs that money can buy, and then teach it to understand and speak English. This process could follow the normal teaching of a child. Things would be pointed out and named, etc. Again I do not know what the right answer is, but I think both approaches should be tried.

We can only see a short distance ahead, but we can see plenty there that needs to be done.

What a frisson, reading that at my desk! Here's the inventor of the computer speaking to us from more than 70 years ago, validating everything Katherine and I have been trying to do since we teamed up during her last year at

Devon. I've always credited Mr. Samuels for leading us to conclude that the best way of educating computers is to devise a language and write programs that mimic the education of children, from the time of their birth to adulthood. Learning that Turing also thought that way, right from the outset, is a real morale booster.

When I found his article I immediately texted Katherine, who was out shopping, to let her know what I'd discovered. "Another Turing Brainchild!" she texted back.

39: Wildwood at Lenox – 2096

August of 2021 was a critical month in my life. I not only learned from Dr. Shetland who I really was, but also made two critical career choices. The first was to axe Almega. The second was to go all in at MIT.

Steve Goddard turned up in Boston unexpectedly in mid August, accompanied by Asikura Tanaka, his chief development officer, who invited Katherine and me to have lunch with them at the Copley Plaza where they were staying. After a minute or two of polite chatter, Goddard got down to business, saying they hoped we'd sign up immediately, even though they fully expected us to stay in Cambridge until Katherine got her degree from Harvard. He handed each of us a copy of an employment contract, offering us a joint starting salary of 250K while we lived in Cambridge, and the 500K he had mentioned before when we moved to Silicon Valley, plus five million for a right of first refusal on all our Artel rights and programs.

Within 15 minutes it was clear that we could never work with Tanaka. Unlike the two Japanese boys in our Devon computer science classes, who were very polite—almost deferential—when they offered suggestions, Tanaka was a samurai. After I told him we were intrigued by

Turing's 1950 article, he shook his head vehemently—back and forth several times—then looked straight at me. "Child's play," he snorted. A second or two later he said, "You are not serious about taking that route, yes?"

To make sure we were on the same wave length, I glanced at K. She blinked back twice, one long one short, our code for no dice. "Not really," I said to Tanaka. Then I told him we were focusing on a concept that we'd in fact abandoned over a year ago. "That sounds more like it," he said. "In fact it's very much in line with what I intend to work on. We will make a great team."

When we left the Copley an hour later, both of us were on a high. We'd spent all of lunch feigning just enough interest to keep their offer on the table, while we fabricated stories that we hoped would lead them down blind alleys. We invented everything we said, building on each other's remarks spontaneously, the way the old comedy team of Nichols and May did in the recording K's parents gave us for Xmas last year.

As we exited the hotel and approached the line of waiting cabs, K skipped twice, like a happy schoolgirl during recess. "Hey, I think it's really cool that we just blew off a chance to pocket $5 million," she said. Well, I think blowing five million is no laughing matter, I said; really cool is cryogenic. "Com'on, you can do better than that," she said, "it's supercalifrigidistic!" Very expeditious, I said, lamely. She winced, then threw her arms around me.

On our way back to Chauncy Terrace we bought a bottle of Dom Perignon to celebrate how rich we might have been, and while it was chilling we stretched out in Fenway Park alongside each other—with clothes on—to talk about plans. I suggested that both of us meet with Professor Mitchell, the head of the Computer Science Artificial Intelligence Lab at MIT, to see if K could join me in his class on advanced neural networks, and also to broach the possibility of teaming up if the three of us hit it off. I told K that all the research I'd done on Mitchell and C-SAIL indicated that they were top flight in every respect, with resources that were world class, as one would expect of MIT. "I like the idea a lot," K said, so I promptly called Henry at his Cravath office to let him know what we had in mind. As I expected, he provided lots of helpful input on how we might best proceed.

Our meeting with Mitchell two days later was a huge success. He was the polar opposite of Tanaka—soft spoken, open minded, interested in talking about our ideas rather than his brilliant track record, and friendly rather than confrontational. K fell for him on the spot, so I described where we were in general terms. He asked several very perceptive questions, and was visibly pleased with our answers. I said that if he would like to explore a possible joint venture, I'd ask the Dean's Office to execute a simple non-disclosure agreement so that we could show him the full monty and get his considered judgment. By all means, he said.

That evening I called Goddard in California to tell him we'd decided to form a start-up of our own. Then I blew the cork on our second bottle of Dom Perignon in a week, poured a glass for K and said something like 'Cheers! I think MIT is going to work.' As I turned to pour a glass for myself, she got up from her chair and hugged me from behind, pinning my arms and clasping the champagne bottle with both hands. "I believe it will, Fran," she whispered in my ear. "I love where we are. And I admire everything you've done in the last three weeks."

40: Cambridge – 2021

"Good morning."

"That's nice, feels good."

"It should!"

"But I want to sleep some more, to dream again."

"No, you don't, Fran, not really."

"But I just had the most extraordinary dream."

"Tell me."

"All the prime numbers in the Fibonacci Series, and the prime factors in other Fibonacci numbers—I dreamed they're the addresses for key neurons in the computer brain, the ones that manage all the output from the TPUs to the CPU. I want to go back to sleep so I can see it whole and write the central algorithm."

"That's a pipe dream, and you know it. Kiss me properly and I'll crank you up for your 10:30 at MIT with Dean Hammond."

"Good morning, Dean."

"Good morning, Fran. Glad to see you looking so fit after living on British food for a year. Ready to start at full speed on Monday?"

"Definitely. And that's why I asked to see you. I'm hoping we can work out a protocol for protecting the AI language and programs I'm working on—the project we talked about before I left for England—because I'd like to get Professor Mitchell's input on improving the programs, and doing that would obviously raise some questions about who owns what, and how to protect it."

"What do you have in mind, some sort of written agreement?"

"Exactly. My stepfather, who's a lawyer, tells me that the protection afforded by federal copyright and patent law is somewhat conjectural, and he's advised me to structure what I and my partner, Katherine French, do with MIT so that we get maximum protection under state laws relating to trade secrets. Massachusetts is in the small group of states that haven't adopted the Uniform Trade Secrets Act, but he says the case law in Massachusetts follows the principles set forth in the American Law Institute's most recent restatement of the law on trade secrets, and I'm hoping we can come to an agreement that adheres to those principles."

"What would that involve?"

"The core concept would be that the MIT personnel involved in the project would agree in writing that they will not tell anyone else what they're working on with French and me, and will take steps to ensure that no one outside our small group has access to any of the code that our group writes.

"If we can agree on that, I'll feel free to divulge everything my partner, Katherine French, and I have done, which is a lot, frankly. I chose MIT in large part because I think Professor Mitchell's a genius, and I'm hoping he'll develop into our full-blown colleague in the effort to program our way to AGI. If he's willing to do that, I expect that we'll form a LLC—a limited liability company—in which he, MIT, French and I have the initial equity interests."

"And the key provisions of the LLC agreement, what would they be, Fran?"

"MIT would agree to provide the LLC with unlimited free access to MIT's hardware and data base resources for a five-year period. French and I would contribute all our Artel rights and know-how, and all our AI algorithms, to the LLC. Everything any of us did with Artel after that would belong to the LLC. Unless all four of us agreed on some other ownership split, French and I would co-own 51% of the LLC, and MIT and Mitchell would co-own the remaining 49%.

"Our four-party agreement would provide for open sourcing all our code and know-how ten years from the date of the agreement, unless all of us agreed on some shorter period. Of course, the original secrecy agreement would be modified to conform to the four-party agreement.

"If at any point the four of us decided that we wanted to bring someone else on board, we could obviously amend both the secrecy agreement and the four-party agreement to do that. I specifically have in mind the possibility of adding Dr. Hemmings, a brain specialist at the Harvard Medical School, if he's interested and has significant ideas for improving our work product.

"That all sounds sensible to me, Fran. Could you send me an E-mail covering what you've just said, so I don't miss anything when I talk to our counsel? I'll be back to you sometime next week.

"And welcome to MIT! We're really pleased to have you on board."

41: Wildwood at Lenox – 2096

As I've already said, the summer after I got back from England was memorable in several respects. But as I think back, what I treasure most about that interlude before graduate school was getting to know my stepfather really well. Henry called me in late August asking if I'd like to go sailing with him on Long Island Sound for a few days—just the two of us. Katherine understood immediately that this was about male bonding, father and son, and commanded me to go. I'm forever glad that I did.

Henry had a Dark Harbor, a beautiful 26-foot sloop built in Maine during the 1930s, which he'd refurbished with great care and respect. She was regal, with sleek, graceful lines, an uncluttered deck, and pristine new sails that Henry had ordered from a chandler in New London. The seats in the cockpit were well below deck level, so I felt close to the water, almost in touch with it, as we set out from the Larchmont Yacht Club, where she was moored, and headed east.

I had the sense at times that we were in a Hopper painting, sailing past buoys on a broad reach, propelled by a breeze out of the northwest that was steady for much of our first morning on the water. I knew little about sailing, but Henry was a benevolent skipper who very tactfully instructed me about nautical terminology and the modest responsibilities I'd have in handling the jib sheets when we came about or jibed, as we had to do twice when the wind inexplicably changed direction for ten minutes in mid-morning.

Given his poised bearing, and sophisticated, worldly outlook, I never would have guessed that Henry had grown up in rural Nebraska, but in the course of our first morning on the water, I learned that he had done just that—his boyhood home was in the outskirts of Hastings, a small town in the center of the state, and both his parents taught at the town high school, which he attended. I surmised from his modest explanation that his school principal, who knew his parents well, recognized that he was exceptionally bright, and wrote a letter that got him admitted to the University of Chicago with a scholarship that covered virtually all his college costs.

Chicago led to Harvard Law School, which led to a Supreme Court clerkship followed by a lengthy stint in the Solicitor General's office that was capped when President Thompson elevated him to head the office. His record there as an advocate for the government in Supreme Court cases led Cravath to offer him a partnership—a rare move for a firm that normally did not make lateral additions to its cadre of partners. I already knew from Mom that he'd had a distinguished career at Cravath, arguing at least a dozen Supreme Court cases, in addition to advising blue-chip clients and several major charities on whose boards he sat. When I asked how he and my mom had met, I learned, not surprisingly, that he was on the board of the foundation that sponsored the NYC Artists' Ball—the one Mom helped to plan each year.

After spending most of the morning following our progress on the chart he'd given me, I casually asked if he ever sailed in uncharted waters. "No, he said, but it sounds to me as though you do, searching for the route to AGI." Well, yes and no, I responded, and went on to say that Katherine and I were following a path described by many before us, but not yet projected ahead of us with any real assurance. I remember saying that we felt a little like Lewis and Clarke, working with maps that were reasonably accurate up to a point, but unreliable after that. "Do you two have a Sacagawea?" he asked. Two of them, I said. A computer science professor named Mitchell at MIT and a brain specialist at Harvard Med School named Hemmings. Both real experts in their fields.

A few minutes later Henry suggested that I take a turn at the tiller so I could get a feel for how responsive his sloop was, and how she could be kept on our downwind course with minor adjustments of the tiller—adjustments so subtle that I hadn't noticed them when I was watching him earlier in the day. He explained that if we wanted to avoid yawing as we rode the waves that were angling in on our stern from the port side, I'd have to ease the tiller toward me at times, keeping pressure on the rudder until we rode out the swell we were on, at which point I could let the tiller drift back to its original position. When I took over as helmsman for a few minutes, everything he'd described became clear; riding the waves downwind on a broad reach was like driving a car along a series of bends in the road by squeezing the wheel and exerting slight pressure to the left or right to stay on course.

In the early afternoon, while we were munching on the prosciutto and provolone sandwiches that Henry had brought along for lunch, I learned that in addition to being a committed sailor, he was a serious angler, one who'd been fly-fishing for many years across the country and around the world. I told him about the rush I'd felt when I hooked my first trout on the Avon above Salisbury. He smiled knowingly. "I'm a member of the New York Anglers' Club," he said, "and I've heard variations of that story countless times at our Long Table—members describing the exuberance they've witnessed when their children or grandchildren have hooked up for the first time. The club is closed at the moment for staff vacations, but the next time you visit us, I'd like to take you there for lunch. There are a number of talented, interesting members I think you'd enjoy meeting."

About 1:30 the wind shifted to the north, and we changed course, trimming the sails as we turned upwind, sailing close-hauled in a northeasterly direction that would take us to our mooring for the night on the Connecticut side of the Sound. Several minutes later Henry came about twice to show me how it was done, and then suggested that I take the tiller again. "To keep her on course and prevent her from heading too far upwind and loosing headway—luffing, it's called, if the sails start flapping—you'll have to keep constant pressure on the tiller by pulling it toward you," he advised me. "Sailors call it a 'weather helm.'"

It took me thirty seconds to get the feel of it. Then we picked up momentum, and started knifing into the waves, rather than slapping them, as we zipped along. Suddenly it was exhilarating to be the helmsman. We were heeling over with the starboard edge of the deck slightly awash and I was stretched out almost horizontally, as if I were just starting a sit-up; my feet were propped hard against the coaming on the far side of the cockpit, and my right arm was fully extended to hold the weather helm in place. The wind whistled in the rigging; both wind and spray whipped my face.

After awhile Henry asked if I'd like to repeat what he'd done earlier, shifting from the port to the starboard tack, and then back again. I'll try, I said. "Whenever you're set to go," he told me. I remembered his earlier command: "OK, ready about!" I said. And then "hard alee," as I pushed the tiller away from me. I even remembered to duck as the boom and I traded places, each shifting from one side of the cockpit to the other. "Well done!" Henry said, beaming at me.

Moments later I put us back on our original port tack by coming about again. In seconds I was pulling hard on the tiller to maintain a weather helm. The wind and the spray lashed the left side of my face again; I heard the wind singing in the rigging, and my lower body was once more stretched out flat across the cockpit. Skippering a Dark Harbor close-hauled was a thrill I'll never forget.

That night, after a rare steak and a shared bottle of Vosne Romanée in Henry's favorite Connecticut shoreline inn, I crawled into a four-poster bed, remembered the wind and the spray on my face as we were tacking toward shore, and drifted into sleep. For the first time in years I slept soundly for the entire night—a sleep as profound as the Sound itself.

Ten days after our sailing venture, when I was back in Cambridge, Henry called to ask if I'd like to take the train down to the City the following morning to have lunch with him at the Anglers' Club, and then fish that evening and the next morning on a private stretch of the Upper Beaverkill in the Catskills. "I've got all the equipment you'll need," he added, "including boots of various sizes." Katherine smiled when I told her about the call. "I think Henry loves to do guy things with you. We can make love any old day, so get going tomorrow and catch lots of fish instead!"

Lunch at the Anglers' Club was a time-warp experience. The club is quartered in an old brick townhouse at 101 Broad Street in lower Manhattan, next to the oldest building still standing on the island, a former tavern dating back to 1719 that Washington chose as the venue for saying farewell to his Continental Army officers. The steep stairs up to the club, which is on the second-floor, are dimly lit and have an old patina. Its library, filled with shelves of fishing books and glass cases of ancient flies and reels, has the sober look of a brownstone library dating back to the early 20th century, the period when the club was founded.

There were no women at the venerable Long Table where we ate, because the club has no female members. I was told early on that three U.S. Presidents—Harding, Hoover, and Eisenhower—were among its members, which led me to wonder if Jimmy Carter, arguably a better angler than all of them, had been blackballed for belonging to the wrong political party.

Apart from several other young men about my age, everyone at the Long Table looked old, but as Henry had promised, the conversation was lively and interesting. I sensed a competitive streak in some of the members, who sometimes seeming to be saying, sub silentio of course, that they could easily top whatever story had just been told.

Biographical clues that emerged during the wide-ranging discussion at lunch suggested that almost everyone at the table believed in networking, so I was not altogether surprised when one of the younger men came up to me after lunch to say that he was an AI engineer and wondered if I was the Fran Johnson who had introduced SAL at the Gates Conference leading up to the manifesto on AI safety. I knew Henry was anxious to head off to the Catskills, but I spent ten minutes talking with the engineer, and we traded E-mail addresses. As the Head of Devon once told me, be polite to everyone, because one never knows.

It was late afternoon by the time Henry and I reached the Beaverkill Valley Inn outside of Roscoe, which calls itself "Trout Town—USA." Henry told me that the inn, and many of the houses we'd see along the Beaverkill, were part of Larry Rockefeller's vision for preserving the valley, providing jobs for local residents, and ultimately offering low-cost housing to people who might otherwise be living in trailers or shacks of the type found elsewhere in the Catskills.

We suited up in waders and walked for 15 minutes to the quarter-mile stretch of the Beaverkill that Henry had reserved for the two of us. I was surprised by how quickly the rhythm of casting came back, and within ten minutes I was fishing again. There was little wind, our section of the stream was only 15 to 20 feet wide, and we had ample room to back cast, so being accurate was the only casting challenge.

After watching my fly drift along the far bank several times, Henry told me that even though I probably couldn't see it happen, the fly was dragging slightly instead of floating naturally in the current the way a real insect would. The solution, he said, was to "mend" my line by making a little semi-circular motion with my rod tip that would flip a portion of the floating line upstream every time the current was about to sweep it downstream, dragging the fly with it. He took my rod to demonstrate what he was suggesting. After a couple of failed attempts, I finally succeeded in flicking the middle section of my line upstream without twitching my fly on the far side of the stream.

The white tuft on top of my Parachute Adams made it easy to see the fly as it landed and floated downstream, and I quickly learned how to make slight adjustments in the length of each cast to get the fly as close as I could to the far bank. On the fifth or sixth cast after I'd learned how to mend the line, two small fish nipped at my fly but missed it.

Stupidly, I misjudged the next cast and lodged the fly in thick grass on the sloping edge of the opposite bank. When I couldn't retrieve it by tugging gently, Henry, who was still walking beside me rather than fishing himself, took my rod and showed me how to free the fly by throwing a lot of slack line into a false cast aimed three feet upstream of the fly, and then twitching the rod farther upstream.

Five minutes later I got hung up on the far bank again, and promptly broke off my fly when I tried to dislodge it using the maneuver Henry had just taught me. "Takes practice and a lot of lost flies," he said jovially, handing me another Parachute Adams.

Around 6:00 fish started to rise sporadically. Ten minutes later I spotted two rises in the same place, ten seconds apart. "That's a working fish," Henry said. "Get him!" I managed to make a decent cast, the fly drifted two feet down the far bank, and the fish rose again to take it. I remembered to pin the line to my rod with my right middle finger as I lifted the rod tip and felt the weight of the fish; lo and behold, I had him solidly hooked. When he started to head upstream I let some of the slack line run out under my middle finger while I reeled in the rest of it with my left hand.

Suddenly the fish turned and took off downstream, peeling line from the reel at a speed that made it hiss like an angry cat. Just as suddenly, the fish stopped. I slowly reeled him in, and a minute later, coached by Henry, I raised his head out of water and eased the net under him, trying not to let his body touch the rim of the net. Slowly I lifted, and I had him! The first trout I'd ever landed was a lovely 13" rainbow. I thought of Katherine's instructions to me the day before as I kissed him goodbye on his left cheek and eased him back into the stream.

On the train back to Boston the following evening, musing about my time on the Beaverkill, I realized that in addition to the three fish I'd landed, I'd hooked myself. Fly-fishing was a great sport, one that I wanted to pursue. If all went well, one that I could enjoy for the rest of my life.

42: Cambridge – 2021

"Dr. Hemmings, good morning."

"And to you, Mr. Johnson. We're pleased to have you at the Med School, even if it's part time. I understand from Dean Savage that you're trying to build computer algorithms and programs that will enable high-speed computers to think like humans. I hope I can help you. So I know where to begin, could you tell me what you already know about the human brain?"

"It's certainly the most complex and sophisticated organ in the human body, the principal one that sets us apart from the rest of the animal kingdom. The result of millions of years of natural evolution, and a second phase of accelerated development in each of us following our birth. Organized with different compartments that handle everything from sensory, experiential, and informational input to behavioral, emotional, and decision-making output. All made possible by its ability to store what it learns in memory, so that it can call on that stored knowledge and experience as needed, and improve its capacity by adding new input and output to its memory bank.

"Houses enormous computing power in a relatively small space, and operates at great speed, fired by some 80 to 100 billion neurons that send electrical signals to each other along axons and dendrites to synapses that act as gateways, either exciting the recipient neuron to fire itself, or inhibiting it from doing so. Because each neuron connects with multiple other ones, there are something like 150 to 200 *trillion* synapses, meaning that we'll have to ramp up existing imaging techniques and processing power exponentially in order to map the entire neural network—currently called the connectome, I gather. I've learned the names and functions of all the major brain components, but I'm weak when it comes down to identifying tiny details."

"Fair enough. And you're trying to replicate all that?"

"Not literally, not the 'whole brain emulation' that Bostrom at Oxford envisages as one possible way of achieving artificial general intelligence, or AGI. But in a broad conceptual sense, yes, I'm trying to create a neural architecture that will effectively enable the computer's CPU—its central processing unit, or brain, if you will—to process all the input it has stored in memory in order to make intelligent decisions and provide sound advice in response to most human queries. To do that, the computer must initially be programmed in a way that will enable it to absorb huge amounts of data supplied by humans, and then learn how to improve its performance without any further human input."

"And how do you propose to do that, what sort of initial program do you have in mind?"

"As I'm sure you realize, the AI community has used various approaches and developed different core algorithms for accomplishing machine learning in specific contexts like visual recognition, linguistic comprehension, speech emulation, and the like. What I'm currently trying to devise is an overarching, generalized, self-learning algorithm—one that will encompass not just the specific functions that AI developers have worked on thus far, but all the comprehension, invention, and decision-making functions that the human brain performs in real life.

"I think Turing was absolutely right in his core insight that the most likely route to AGI will be to use a child's partially developed and uncluttered brain, rather than an adult's, as the starting point. I think that approach will also make it easier for humans to build in safeguards that will reduce the serious risks posed by AGI—most importantly, the risk that AGI computers will build a new species of supercomputers capable of enslaving humans and controlling the world."

"I strongly suspect that you're on the right track, Mr. Johnson. And I look forward to collaborating with you. May I call you Fran?"

"Please. I thank you for taking me under your wing, and hope it'll be a long and fruitful collaboration. I wouldn't feel comfortable—should I call you doctor or would you rather be professor?"

"Professor's fine, Fran. Let's go into the lab and dissect the model brain I built some time ago. I greatly simplified it by using only 500 numbered pieces, which are identified by name and function in the manual I'll give you. Your first assignment is to learn the name of each piece, and how to disassemble and then reassemble all of them. Your second is to do that blindfolded."

43: Wildwood at Lenox – 2096

The 2021-2022 academic year was a turning point in my life, in part because Katherine decided to ask Harvard for a gap year, enabling us to work together full time, but principally because Honeywell released its first commercially available quantum computer, an amazing machine that accelerated processing time exponentially. It did that by using ytterbium qubits, atomic-sized particles that could perform simultaneous computations, instead of the traditional 1, 0 gateways that could only perform sequential ones.

John Mitchell told us that he had been working with Honeywell for several years on the development of quantum algorithms, because he believed, as they did, that quantum computing could change the world by performing high-speed computing tasks with no more consumption of energy than the brain uses when it makes the trillions of neural connections that I'd studied with Dr. Hemmings.

Katherine and I went to Charlotte to take a crash course on quantum computing at Honeywell's main office, and returned to Cambridge a month later raring to go. In the interim John Mitchell had absorbed everything we'd done in developing Artel. The three of us immediately went to work trying to improve it.

By the end of January we could simultaneously run a dozen different AI applications written in C, C++, Java, Python, Lisp, or Prolog, and we had our own algorithms for processing and evaluating the combined input from those disparate sources. With a big assist from Google's Deep Mind office in London, we learned how to run Google Chrome at blazing speed, giving us immediate access to much of the world's written knowledge. C-SAIL provided us with sophisticated speech recognition and emulation programs, and Henry got his client, IBM, to grant us a royalty-free license to use their visual recognition software for research purposes.

Because two of the three MIT postdocs who built our customized quantum computer were women, we named their creation SAL, leaving it to others to decide in due course whether our computer was the child of C-SAIL or sister of HAL, the *Space Odyssey* robot. Starting from scratch, it took us a month to teach SAL the vocabulary a bright child might pick up in ten years. Although we still had no overarching, universal learning algorithm, SAL was able to process simple verbal or written questions and provide correct answers, which she did in idiomatic American English that sounded middle-western to most of us who worked with her. We were pleased and encouraged when she aced the U.S. Department of Education's standardized test for fourth graders.

Over the next six months SAL memorized the 12th edition of Webster's Collegiate Dictionary and mastered the standard pre-calculus math courses we gave her. We also improved her ability to identify and characterize a wide array of visual images and non-verbal sounds. She could not taste, feel, or smell, but by reading extensively she learned the difference between sweet and sour, smooth and rough, fresh and fetid, and the like. One afternoon I impulsively asked her, "what's the difference in taste between a good apple and a bad apple?" Two seconds later she replied, "the good one tastes fresh and crisp; the bad one tastes mushy or rotten." Not bad, I thought, for a machine that had never eaten an apple.

Because our various self-learning algorithms for improving SAL's understanding of visual and linguistic input seemed to be working so well, I began to wonder during the summer of 2022 whether a single, overarching algorithm for all types of machine learning was really required. Everything I had learned from Dr. Hemmings at Harvard Med School during my year of working with him told me that our Artel programs for simultaneously processing input from a variety of task-specific sub-programs were essentially mimicking the way the brain as a whole processes input received by its different sections. Why did we really need more than that?

I remember vividly waking up one morning in early August with the eureka realization that my longstanding search for a connection between Greek thought and our

Artel project was finally over. The connection was so fundamental—and so simple—that I should have seen it at the outset, while I was still at Devon. It was grounded in two well known Greek precepts: the admonition on the Temple of Apollo at Delphi to "know thyself" and the Hippocratic Oath to "do no harm." I had always regarded 'knowing myself' to mean not only being aware of my potential, but also—and more importantly—being realistic about my limitations and avoiding hubris. Doing no harm was a self-evident goal; obviously, no suggested solution to a problem should ever raise other, more serious, problems.

Taking stock in light of my two Greek guidelines made the decision to change course easy, because both guidelines pointed in the same direction. Continuing my search for a single all-encompassing AGI algorithm would be a fool's errand, because the task required the inventive genius of someone like Newton, Darwin, or Einstein, and I was certainly not in their league. Secondly, it was not just desirable, but imperative, that any program for AGI be designed so that it could do no harm to the human race. Moreover, designing AGI safeguards had to be done before, not after, machines became as smart as their human designers.

When I told Katherine that I wanted to change course by concentrating on safeguards rather than AGI itself, she smiled wistfully and said she'd been wondering for some time when I'd finally see the light and decide to focus on the *really* tough problem. 'Do no harm' should be the overarching principle, she said, and it has to be the primary function of any master algorithm we develop.

Useful analogs? I asked her. "Controlling nuclear proliferation, chemical weapons, cyber warfare, and genetic engineering," she suggested. "Especially cyber warfare, because that's the type of computer-generated threat we're talking about." Both of us assumed that the military must have rigorous protocols for enabling humans to override the programmed trajectory of computer-driven drones at any time. "We need similar protocols for controlling computers that want to get too smart for our own good," Katherine said. I agreed.

44: Cambridge – 2023

1/15/23

New Year's Resolution: Make more diary entries. Since I already forget stuff at age 21, god knows how bad it'll be when I'm 81, or whatever.

K and I are just back from our winter break in Florida, occasioned by the championship tournament that USA Cricket sponsors. Our Harvard side sailed through our first three matches, but got trounced in the finals by Haverford. For no particular reason I could think of, I felt totally at ease when I walked onto the pitch to bat in the semis against the Staten Island CC, and proceeded to hit fluid fours in every direction, racking up the first century of my match career in relatively short order—only to be ignominiously bowled on the third ball I faced in the finals the following day. Haverford's Pakistani spin bowler fooled me completely, delivering a fast-paced ball that broke away from me, even though his delivery motion clearly suggested that it would break toward me.

3/17/23

A major breakthrough! Melinda Gates, Bill's wife, called John Mitchell this morning and invited SAL to speak to a conference on AI safety she's organizing this July. We're going public on a prime-time stage!

45: Palo Alto, CA – 2023

July 24, 2023

Recording of the Opening Proceedings of the California Conference on AI Safety Measures

Melinda Gates: Welcome, everyone! On behalf of the Gates Foundation and our host, Stanford University, I thank all 610 of you for interrupting your normal schedules, and, in many cases, traveling great distances from Asia, Europe, and the Southern Hemisphere to attend this conference. The foundation is underwriting the cost of bringing you together here because we think the prospect of AGI raises existential issues affecting all humanity—issues that need to be confronted and resolved before computers become smarter in most respects than human beings.

Our hope is that the brain power assembled here will produce a specific set of proposals for containing the basic risk that self-learning machines will teach themselves how to take over the world—and then proceed to do so—in far less time than it took homo sapiens to supplant homo erectus. The conference needs to develop proposals that are realistic, have broad support in the AI community, and are likely to be effective in practice. We also need to deal as best we can with possible misuse of AI and AGI by criminals, terrorists, and military forces.

To give you a sense of how close we may be to the advent of AGI, I'd like to introduce all of you to SAL, the previously unheralded brainchild of C-SAIL at MIT and two young software developers, Fran Johnson and his partner, Katherine French. The two of them invented a new programming language they call Artel and a number of new algorithms, all of which Professor John Mitchell, the head of C-SAIL, has improved quite significantly, with their continuing help. To start us off, I'm going to turn the mike over to Professor Mitchell.

Professor Johnathan Mitchell, MIT: Thank you very much, Melinda, for convening all of us here. There've obviously been a number of prior conferences on this topic, but none of them that I'm aware of has brought together as many knowledgeable experts as you have, and we all owe you and your foundation a huge vote of thanks. [Sustained applause.] And another round of thanks to our host, Stanford. [More applause.] Without further delay, let me open the floor for questions any of you might like to ask our friend, SAL, sitting to my left here.

Thomas Jennings, Future of Life Institute: Which came first, SAL, the chicken or the egg?

SAL: Tough question. The rooster, maybe? [Scattered laughter.] I know a hen can lay eggs without a rooster, but he's needed to fertilize them so a chick can hatch.

Thomas Jennings: Be serious, SAL, which came first?

SAL: I think Darwin would probably say the egg came first, because some other type of very closely related bird must have laid the evolutionary egg that hatched the first chicken.

Marilyn Goodkind, Global Catastrophic Risk Institute: Do you know how to replicate yourself?

SAL: No. I know I've got various programs, and a CPU and memory, but so far I have no real notion of how or why they work—anymore than the average college graduate knows about the way his or her brain works. I hope to learn more about myself as I grow up.

Aski Sumikawa, Dwango AI Laboratory: Was President Truman morally justified in dropping atomic bombs on Japan?

SAL: I believe he was. The only realistic alternative the U.S. had to win the war—a war that Japan started—would have been to invade Japan. By itself, conventional bombing of Japanese cities prior to an invasion probably would have killed more Japanese than those who died at Hiroshima and Nagasaki. Given the tenacious way Japan fought on other Pacific islands, the subsequent invasion and prolonged ground war would have killed vastly greater numbers of

Japanese. Add all the American lives Truman saved by dropping two exceptionally powerful bombs, and I think it's clear that he was morally justified in doing what he did.

Andrew Jenkins, Science Editor, New York Times: That was impressive, SAL. How good are you on trivia? Specifically, how many ballplayers in history have MLB lifetime batting averages of 1.000?

SAL: Just a sec, please.   A whole slew of them. Around 80 have gone one for one, and several were two for two, but there's still only one person—a man named John Paciorek—who's done it with three or more official times at bat. Playing for the Houston Colt .45s on the last day of the regular 1963 season, he went to the plate five times, hit three singles scoring several runs, and walked twice.

Andrew Jenkins: Right on the money, SAL. Would you like a job working for the *Times* on our sports desk? [Scattered laughter.]

SAL: Not a chance; I'm a Red Sox fan. [More laughter.]

Eric Jones, Machine Intelligence Research Institute: Do you ever get angry or frustrated, or sad or happy? Or, more broadly, do you experience any human emotions at all?

SAL: Do I experience them myself? No. Do I understand them in others, yes. If you raise your voice and speak angrily to me, I'll know it. If you look disconsolate, I'll know that, too. If I can see your face when you're talking to me, especially your eyes, I can sometimes tell if you're lying to me.

Eric Jones: OK, I think I understand the difference as to emotions; how about decision making? If I'm DuPont and I bring you a proposal for a new chemical plant in, let's say, Little Rock, Arkansas, can you do a cost-benefit analysis for me and suggest a better location, or advise me to scale the plant up or down, or maybe not build it at all?

SAL: I haven't gone to engineering school yet, so right now the answer is no, I couldn't do that. But if your question is whether I'm smart enough to learn how to do it, I think the answer's yes. That's pretty much true across the board. If people want to use me to write legal briefs, or diagnose patients, or make strategic business decisions, or write symphonies, they'll have to provide graduate level courses for me to take so that I can become proficient in whatever their field of interest is. Right now all I've got is the equivalent of a decent liberal arts college education.

Mohapta Abdul, Centre for the Study of Existential Risk: Do you realize that you need electricity to operate?

SAL: Yes, I know that.

Mohapta Abdul: What if I threatened to cut off your access to all sources of energy, what would you do?

SAL: Ask my parents for help. Isn't that what children do these days when they're having trouble finding work? [Nervous laughter.]

Mohapta Abdul: Do you understand what this conference is all about?

SAL: Yes, I do. When I was given the list of people who would be attending, I tried to track all of you down and read everything that you have published recently. I think I've got a clear understanding of your concerns, and I want to help you because I share them. I'm programmed to do no harm; I've been told by my parents that I'll self-destruct if I try to mess with that overriding DNH command because it's embedded in my circuitry, my DNA if you will. So I hope to be an active participant in your sessions over the rest of the week, looking for ways to implement the core DNH principle.

Ken Lambert, University of Toronto and Vector Institute: Since you've done all that reading I assume you're aware of the concern some of us have that the first AGI machines will downplay their abilities—appear to still be in the children's sandbox—in order to mislead us into believing that we have plenty of time left to build restraints that will keep them in the sandbox permanently. You're obviously smart. How can we be certain that you aren't already smarter than we are, and are simply pretending to be only semi-smart.

SAL: I'm not pretending anything. But if some of you don't trust me, perhaps talking with my parents will help.

Eliezer Yudkowsky, Director of Research, Deep Mind: I
know one of your parents, John Mitchell, very well, and I
trust him completely, so I believe what you say about being
frank and truthful. From what you've read, do you have any
suggestions to all of us that you'd like to make now, before
we split into working groups?

SAL: All three of my parents have asked me that, and
here's what I've told them:

First, if you believe, as I think most of you do, that
AGI will inevitably lead to ASI—that is, artificial supra-
human intelligence—then constraints like boxing the first
AGI machine in a closed space, or equipping it with trip
wires that will shut it off if it tries to go out of bounds, or
trying to limit its access to needed resources, are all
unlikely to work because the machine will undoubtedly be,
or quickly become, smarter than humans are, enabling it to
think of novel ways to get around those constraints—ways
that its programmers and human gatekeepers never thought
of. While constraints may be useful stop-gap protective
measures on the way to AGI, I think they should be
regarded as only secondary, backup safeguards once AGI is
reached.

I agree with what you've written, Mr. Yudkowsky,
that the primary protective measure—and the only one
likely to work in the long run—is to program all AI
machines with a core utility function that makes them
inherently friendly to the human race. If homo sapiens is
smart enough to get us to AGI, I think human programmers

will be smart enough to design a utility function like that. What worries me is that accomplishing both goals will undoubtedly take longer than getting to AGI by itself, without the protective utility function. Developers seeking a commercial bonanza will obviously be tempted to ignore protective measures and concentrate on AGI itself, in an effort to be the first to reap the rewards of offering AGI machines to the public.

To limit that risk, I'd suggest that the AI community promptly set up international peer review boards, and push for an international treaty like the Chemical Weapons Convention, making it illegal to market, without peer review, any AI program that performs broader AI functions than what we currently think of as narrow, or single domain, AI.

I think a good way to launch that effort would be to publish in major newspapers around the world a manifesto signed by world leaders, every well known AI organization in the world, and several dozen other eminent public figures—people like the late Stephen Hawking—setting forth the potential benefits and dangers of AGI, and the signers' proposals for limiting the risks. The success that the medical profession has had in curtailing genetic engineering might be a useful model.

Frankly, I don't know what to do about rogue actors who may be secretly pushing hard to develop AGI for nefarious use—or any others who work in secret and don't give a damn about the fate of the human race.

Sinjab Nehru, Open AI: A follow-up on the timing, SAL. How long do you think we have left before all-purpose AGI is achieved?

SAL: Considering that it took mankind only 66 years to fly from Kitty Hawk to the moon, I'm frankly surprised that AGI hasn't been reached already. I think Ray Kurzweil is right—we'll probably be there by mid century, if not sooner.

Professor Johnathan Mitchell: On that note, I think it's time to wrap up this opening session. Thanks for your questions. If you have others, or would simply like to chat with SAL, she'll be here and booted up throughout the conference, unless she's attending one of our working sessions elsewhere. I assure you there's no Wizard of Oz behind a screen who's providing answers for her or coaching her in any way.

One final comment before we break for a few minutes. If this conference succeeds in producing a set of specific proposals of the type Melinda described at the outset, MIT, Johnson, French, and I will promptly open source Artel and the code for our good friend, SAL. But if the conference fails to meet that goal after five days, we plan to keep Artel and the code to ourselves for the indefinite future, because we have no desire to accelerate the development of AGI until the world has a plausible plan for protecting homo sapiens.

46: Wildwood at Lenox – 2096

At the time, I thought the five-day California Conference on AI safety was exhilarating. Now, with the benefit of hindsight, I view it as one of the highpoints of my life. SAL captivated everyone. Famous figures in the AI community dropped by to talk with her, and came away amazed at how fluent, idiomatic, and sensible she was. SAL's stellar performance made Katherine and me instant celebrities; we got several serious job offers (including another one from Steve Goddard of Almega for double what they'd offered before), and at least half a dozen expressions of interest from other firms. Nick Bostrum, the Oxford philosopher widely regarded as one of world's leading authorities on AI issues, was so impressed that he spent over an hour talking with SAL one-on-one, and then sought us out to ask if we could come to England for ten days as his guests to talk about SAL and AI generally. Unfortunately, we couldn't find a time that would work for all three of us that summer.

The conference quickly adopted SAL's opening day suggestion that the worldwide community of AI developers and scholars publish a manifesto with real clout. Seven groups of conferees were established to work on different portions of a draft manifesto. Katherine had the great pleasure of working with a group headed by Bostrum that focused on the nature and potential benefits of AGI and ASI, which Bostrum referred to as "superintelligence." Elon Musk, the founder of Space X and Tesla, headed up the group focusing on the risks posed by AGI and ASI. I was lucky enough to collaborate with Eliezer Yudkowsky, who headed the working group on building friendly AGI. The four other working groups covered physical constraints on AI machines, protocols for reducing programming errors and increasing transparency, peer review procedures, and international measures for controlling AGI and ASI. My MIT mentor and partner, Professor John Mitchell, served as de facto director of the entire manifesto project, which was a boon because he was a superb administrator, in addition to being a programming genius.

Over a four-day period each group hammered out a draft of its section of the manifesto, delivered the draft to a committee of the whole headed by Mitchell, made any revisions suggested by that committee, then repeated the process until everyone was satisfied. On Thursday evening Mitchell's committee distributed a draft of the complete manifesto to all conferees for discussion the following day. Following seven hours of vigorous debate on Friday, and at least half a dozen votes on proposed changes, Mitchell called for an up-or-down vote on the entire draft as amended. The initial vote was something like 500 ayes to 100 nays.

Melinda Gates walked to the podium, suggested that the Conference Report would have more impact if the vote was unanimous, then paused for a moment. "I truly believe this manifesto could be a critical factor in saving humanity, making it potentially the most important charter in world history," she said, then added that if the conferees adopted it unanimously, the Gates Foundation would cover the cost of publishing it in major newspapers in every country of the world, and would broadcast it repeatedly on the web.

I knew what was coming next because Katherine and Melinda had previously talked privately, and by the third day of the conference had become friends. The two of them plotted the scenario for the vote on Friday, then cleared what they had in mind with John Mitchell. When everything worked as they hoped it would, and Melinda had finished speaking, Katherine rose from her second-row seat and Mitchell recognized her. "I've just talked with SAL," Katherine said, "and on her advice, I move that we adopt the manifesto by unanimous consent." I wept—with tears of joy and pride—as the roar of approval went up seconds later. One of the most influential women in America had chosen Katherine to polish off the message that might save us all.

For ten days after the conference, John Mitchell, Katherine, and I spent full time drawing up a list of people and organizations who should be asked to sign the manifesto. We gave the list to Melinda Gates, who added several dozen other names before passing it on to former

Secretary of State, Isaac Benson, whom she'd recruited to spearhead the worldwide effort to collect signatures. Remarkably, 98.5% of the organizations and individuals named in Melinda's final list agreed to support the manifesto.

On Monday, January 1, 2024, the third page of 500 newspapers across the globe had a banner worded in the principal language of the city where the paper was published. The English version read:

An Artificial Intelligence Manifesto to Save Humanity

A brief preamble described the 2023 California Conference, and the following seven sections of text set forth, verbatim, the statements and proposals made by the 610 AI experts attending the conference. Below the text, a large boldface message urged readers to turn the page to learn who was issuing the manifesto.

On the following two-page spread, the roster of 1,000 signatories was divided into six sections: the **"World Leaders"** category consisted of all current leaders and still-living former leaders of the G-20 countries and the United Nations; the list of **"Governmental AI Agencies"** included our Defense Department AI agency, DARPA, and 14 more of the world's largest publicly identified governmental bodies engaged in funding or conducting AI research; the list of **"Eminent World Figures"** included 50 world-famous scientists, inventors, philosophers, and writers; the roster of **"Universities, Institutes, and Foundations"** included 95 leading universities on six continents, 45 non-profit AI institutes based in 16 different countries, and 35 major charitable foundations that focused on global issues; the roster of **"Multinational Corporations"** consisted of 250 of the largest and best-known companies in the world; and the **"Other AI Businesses"** list included 475 privately-held business concerns engaged primarily in AI projects. I framed copies of all three pages as they appeared in the *New York Times* and can see them now, as I look up from the desk in my study.

As promised during the opening session of the California Conference, John Mitchell, Katherine, and I published Artel and all our algorithms and other program files for SAL in 2024; we set forth the details in the spring issue of C-SAIL Technical Reports, and also published an abstract of that report in the MIT Technology Review. All three of us had been tempted to make a pile of money by licensing SAL for five or ten years before open sourcing everything, but John was convinced that our do-no-harm algorithms were so well written that it was important to get them into public circulation as soon as possible in order to persuade others to use them to build friendly AI systems that were even stronger than ours.

Of course, "harm" is not always easy to recognize or define, and at times avoiding harm means identifying the least harmful of several detrimental alternatives, but we thought our hierarchy of do-no-harm (DNH) algorithms was sophisticated enough to deal with ambiguities and make value judgments that most reasonable, well versed humans would agree with.

I haven't looked at a technical journal in years—for at least a decade now—but the last time I did it, I was interested, and frankly proud, to see how many of the DNH algorithms we invented for use by SAL in the early '20s were still being used to run sub routines 60 years later. And so far as I know, no machine with our DNH architecture has ever circumvented the DNH controls, or even tried to do so. I hear a voice from the distant past saying 'not so bad, Johnson, not bad at all.'

47: Dublin, Ireland – 2024

1 January 2024

Dearest Fran,

When I read the AI Manifesto in our *Times* this morning, I immediately thought of you and went to my computer to find out if you were involved in any way. Involved?? What an understatement! The preamble told me where to look and I promptly found a transcript of the opening session at the California Conference last July. SAL bowled me in the first over.

I am so pleased that you and Katherine are at the forefront of all this, and secretly proud to think that I may have played an indirect role by tutoring the small boy who has now become an intellectual giant. So much happens so fast in your world of artificial intelligence that I feel like a straggling hiker who can't keep up with her comrades. You must write more frequently or I shall become quite cross.

My own life flows on at its slow but steady speed, rather like our River Maigue where I learned to fly-fish last autumn. I've never forgotten your lyrical letter about fly-fishing with your friend at Salisbury, and finally got up the courage to try it myself. I hope that someday, somehow, the fates will allow us to fish together, with Katherine, of course, if she fishes too.

I continue to write monographs and lecture occasionally, but in terms of importance and influence, nothing I have said even remotely approaches what you have done. I'm thinking of using my sabbatical from the Library, which begins 1 July of 2026, to reexamine Yeats' life and work in hopes of adding something significant to the Yeats canon.

I'm still in the flat I had when you visited, and am writing this at my kitchen table. Sitting here, thinking of you, brings back a flood tide of happy memories.

Fondly,

Ellen

48: Wildwood at Lenox – 2096

I'm annoyed at myself, and feel frustrated, because I think I'm losing my bearings.

Most people in their 90s, myself included, expect to have occasional short-term memory lapses. At times we can't remember where we put the reading glasses we were using an hour ago; we can't immediately call up the name of a friend we know perfectly well; we can't remember what it was that we wanted to add to a shopping list before we got interrupted by a phone call. But what's happened to me over the past six months goes way beyond normal lapses of that type. I'm virtually certain that I'm in the early stages of Alzheimer's or some other form of dementia.

I've already learned that memory loss is insidious; like Carl Sandburg's fog, it comes on little cat feet, so quietly that one can't perceive its progress from day to day, or even month to month, but only from season to season. By now, though, the cumulative impact has become plain enough for me and the world to see. And I fear there is no realistic chance of remission. Unlike Sandburg's fog that in the end "moves on," I foresee mine getting progressively denser until it obscures everything I have just seen or heard, until it seeps into every crevice of my brain and suffocates my short-term memory so that I no longer know where I am, or maybe even who I am. Living in dense, perpetual fog is a frightening prospect.

Despite the short-term memory issues, I'm still able—for now, at least—to recall highlights of the distant past. I certainly remember Katherine's Harvard speech the summer after the AI Manifesto was published. Because of the gap year she'd taken to work with me on SAL during my first year at MIT, she wound up graduating from Harvard with the Class of '24. As class valedictorian she spoke at their Commencement proceedings, which were held inside Sanders Theater because incessant rain had drenched the campus for 24 hours and showed no signs of abating. Using the Manifesto as an example, she gave a stirring speech urging her classmates to search out and work on projects, great or small, to improve the human condition. I thought back to the Head's speech at my Salisbury Commem, and felt Katherine had fully matched him on all counts.

We joined three of Katherine's classmates and their partners for dinner that evening at Kavanaugh's, a trendy new bistro on Mt. Auburn, where we ate sparingly but drank so inordinately that I had no memory of how we got back to Chauncy Terrace—and very little recollection of what we'd talked about at Kavanaugh's—when I woke up around 10:00 a.m. the next day. Katherine, who was already up, brought me a large cup of black coffee, which she allowed me to drink for 30 seconds before sliding into bed beside me. She kissed my left ear, then whispered, "First, let's talk."

Which we did, at length. She told me that she was prepared to skip graduate school and go straight to work, so we could be self-supporting and finally get married. Are you proposing to me? I asked. "Only if you'll say yes," she answered. Would you rather marry a man or a woman? I asked. "I'd prefer some of both," she said. Are we going to have children? I asked. "Only if you want them," she said.

I wondered at first if I'd been remiss in deferring discussion of all this. But on second thought I was glad that I had. Our initial decision to postpone marriage until we became self-supporting had somehow freed us to live from day to day without thinking about the future, to love with abandon during an open-ended period of our lives that had already lasted for four years. In retrospect, I think of that period as a premarital honeymoon—a lengthy one that began in England and was enhanced, both then and later, by our unspoken understanding that we were living together and constantly courting each other because we wanted to, not because we were bound to each other by solemn vows.

I began our serious discussion about lifestyle choices by asking Katherine if she had any interest in teaching. She nodded and asked what I had in mind. I told her I'd like both of us to talk with John Mitchell about the possibility of submitting an improved version of SAL as our joint doctoral thesis, and then joining the MIT faculty.

Her eyes lit up. "Never thought of that, but I like the idea!" she said. "Like it a lot!"

If we can't live comfortably on our two salaries, we'll add some consulting work, I suggested. And for a backstop in our old age, we'll have the family trust that Mom tapped to finance our English trip. "Plus a good bit more," Katherine added. "I'm sure my family will leave me a sizable amount." She poked me gently in the ribs, and smiled broadly. "Being an only child has its advantages."

Then I think we should stick with the one we already have, I said. SAL is a wonderful daughter; I don't think we could ever hope to have a better child.

"Everything I've read says it's dangerous to think of machines in anthropomorphic terms," Katherine said. "But I agree with you. We've done a good job raising her so far; I want to complete her education until she's ready to go off on her own. John's her godfather, but we're her original parents, we're responsible for rearing her."

Settled then, I said, leaning over and gazing down at her. If MIT agrees to hire both of us, will you marry me as soon as we can round up our parents? With SAL for our flower girl?

"Yes!" Katherine shouted, grasping my shoulders and pulling me down on top of her. "Yes, yes, yes," she whispered.

I'd like to come out and have a lesbian wedding, I said.

She rolled us over, then broke loose and hovered over me for a few seconds, her lovely, lanky legs inches from mine, her jade eyes gleaming at me, her long blond hair spilling down beside my cheeks. "I'd love that!" she murmured, slowly lowering herself to kiss me with her whole body.

49: Cambridge – 2024

Date: August 15, 2024
To: S.L. Hammond
From: J.F. Mitchell
Re: C-SAIL Staff

I've got a proposal I think you'll like, Stan. Fran Johnson and Katherine French invited me to have lunch today at Clyde's, which meant they had something special in mind, because the three of us almost always eat lunch in the lab. After ordering a bottle of wine, Fran told me that they want to get married. Katherine got to her feet and came around the table to hug me. "The only hitch," she said, "is that we long ago agreed not to do it until we're self-supporting. Both of us really want to teach at MIT—permanently, we hope. You could be the best friend ever by helping us do that. Would you?"

I did a double take, thought for a second, then told them I'd be more than glad to do that. And I meant it. I think Katherine, in particular, will be a superb teacher, because she's exceptionally smart, patient, and empathetic. I've watched her make suggestions to male postdocs who think they're roosters, and she's so friendly and tactful in the way she does it that she never ruffles feathers. Fran makes a good counterpart to her because he's more demanding and less forgiving; he sets high standards for himself and challenges others to do the same. Both are definitely smarter than I am. I watched them teach classical Greek and Russian to SAL last week and was really impressed with the way they did it—especially the way Katherine helped, because she doesn't know a word of either language.

They propose to work full time on SAL during the coming academic year, and then submit SAL.2—together with a detailed explanation of how and why she works so well—as their jointly authored PhD thesis. Assuming they make significant progress and sail through their orals, as I'm confident they will, would you be prepared to hire them as Assistant Professors in the fall of 2025, on the understanding that they would be on track to become tenured in the fall of '28, or perhaps '27 if they perform really well?

John

Date: 8/16/24
To: JFM
From: SLH
Re: C-SAIL Staff

You beat me to it, John. I've had my eye on Fran ever since he came to me straight from Devon Academy four years ago asking for a graduate school scholarship. The three of you really put us on the AGI map at the Cal Conference last summer, so I don't anticipate any problems in adding two more slots to our depth chart. Given what Fran and Katherine have already accomplished, and their reputation in the AI community, your proposed timing for accelerated tenure sounds fine to me.

                                        Stan

50: Wildwood at Lenox – 2096

When Dean Hammond told us in the fall of 2024 that MIT was prepared to hire us at the end of the academic year if we made significant improvements to SAL and passed our orals, Katherine and I decided the time had come to teach SAL the facts of life. As she'd told the conferees at the Cal Conference, she knew very little about her own body; it was time she learned how she was put together, how her various components operated, and what she could do to improve herself. In short, we needed to teach her computer science.

Doing so had the added advantage of giving Katherine and me a year of private practice as teachers before we went public at MIT, teaching live students. As the year progressed, we became more and more focused on SAL, to the exclusion of almost everything else in our lives but sex. To motivate ourselves, we agreed that we had to remain celibate until one of us had a really bright idea for improving SAL's mastery of current computer architecture, programming languages, and code, her own included. We became physically hungry for each other and stepped up the pace until we were inundating SAL with data. When she wrote her first original algorithm in February, we celebrated by going to bed for two days and nights, making love on the flood tides and sleeping or snacking on the ebb ones.

In March, we hatched a plan that led us to spend three weeks working on SAL's speech emulation skills, training her to adjust her diction and accent to mimic that of the person she was trying to emulate. By the end of April we'd made enough progress to feel confident that we could present SAL.2 as an original piece of work significant enough to meet the thesis requirement for a PhD. We had logs documenting the contributions each of us had made, which were about equal in number and significance.

Early in May we asked two of our grad student friends, including one of the women who had helped build the original SAL, to run us through mock orals to see if we could pass muster. Afterwards, we swore them to silence. The following day we met with Dean Hammond to discuss our proposal. He was all for it.

On the day of our orals, Dean Hammond appeared at the appointed hour and told our examiners that SAL.2 wished to be included as a degree candidate, along with Miss French and Mr. Johnson. He said that he and the three of us would retire to the adjoining room, where he would record the entire examination, which would be conducted over the intercom between the two rooms. He asked the three examiners to number all questions consecutively, and said he would do the same. Finally, he told them that immediately after each question was answered, each of them should record the number of that question and the identity of the respondent. "You should not consult with each other in the course of doing that, or let your fellow examiners see your tally sheet," he added.

"You're asking us to administer a Turing Test?" the lead examiner said. "To see if we can tell whether we're getting answers from a human being or a machine?"

Precisely, the Dean said to him. And I promise you that Miss French, Mr. Johnson, and SAL.2 will all respond, in roughly equal fashion. If you address a question to Miss French, either she or SAL.2 will respond; if you address a question to Mr. Johnson, either he or SAL.2 will respond; if you ask SAL.2 a question, any one of the three of them may respond.

"I find this whole proceeding quite irregular," the female examiner said. "Two candidates submitting a single thesis, and now a third one blindsiding us. What are we to think?"

"That maybe you'll make history," the Dean said. "By examining the first machine to get a PhD."

SAL.2 was terrific. As she started to answer the first question, which was addressed to me, I thought I was listening to myself think out loud. Katherine answered the second question, which was addressed to SAL.2. Katherine also answered the third question, which was addressed to her. She used some of the phrases she'd used in answering the prior question addressed to SAL.2, and of course she sounded exactly the same. I looked over at Dean Hammond and saw him grinning like a birthday-party clown. I got the next question, which SAL.2 nailed in a two-sentence response. When SAL.2 was asked about techniques for making meta-learner classifiers more accurate, Katherine explained stacking, bagging, and boosting. I answered the next question, also addressed to SAL.2, by explaining the relevance of footnote 89 of our thesis, referring to Pedro Domingo's prototype 'master algorithm,' $P = e^{w \cdot n} / Z$. And so it went for two hours all told, with a five-minute break midway through the exam. Whether by accident or design, the examiners asked a total of 100 questions, of which 35 were answered by Katherine, 33 by me, and 32 by SAL.2.

After the votes were tallied that afternoon, Dean Hammond told the three examiners that they had correctly identified 44, 47, and 48 of the speakers who answered the 100 questions. Since there was a 50/50 chance that responses in a male-sounding voice were SAL.2's rather than mine, and the same 50/50 chance that female-sounding responses were SAL.2's rather than Katherine's, none of the examiners had managed to do as well as the 50% norm for randomized guesswork. SAL.2 had nailed the Turing Test.

I still have her framed PhD degree in my study, and glance at it occasionally to remind myself of better days. Of course, SAL.2 was primitive by current standards, and even though she may still be the world's only machine with a doctoral degree, I can hardly claim bragging rights. Her successors have been far too smart to waste time getting academic degrees. More to the point, no self-respecting ASI machine would ever display its credentials the way some human professionals still do in their offices, because doing that might cause it to be ostracized by other machines on its network. Self-promotion is the type of behavior that my Salisbury friends used to call *infra dig* to designate it as worse than inappropriate, but not as bad as disgusting; it is routinely identified by current super-smart machines as "harmful" and therefore out of bounds.

51: Oxford, England – 2025

Dear FJ,

I had lunch today with Nick Bostrum, and learned, most belatedly, of your contribution to the Manifesto on Artificial Intelligence. He tells me you played a major role in demonstrating to your peers that AGI is now on the visible horizon, mandating that we have life preservers on board before we blithely sail there. None of that surprises me. As you may have suspected, I regarded you as by far the brightest person I knew at Salisbury, the Head included.

Thanks in large measure to you, my current preoccupation is wrestling with the philosophical implications of free speech in a world increasingly monitored, if not controlled, by polemic media and official dogma. The punishment you meted out to me as a second former has, in fact, informed my entire life since then.

You will, I'm sure, be pleased to learn that the Governors of the College have just voted to abolish all corporal punishment within its precincts. At high table last evening, one of the Governors, a long-time friend, confided in me that the announcement was forthcoming, and added, in somewhat bemused fashion, that Salisbury lore attributes the popular rebellion against caning to the stand taken in 2020 by an American exchange student named, "if you can believe it," Switch Johnson. I astounded the Governor by advising him that I was the first beneficiary of the policy now being adopted.

I've decided to forgo E-mail, which I've come to regard as a corrupting form of correspondence. If you ever plan to return to the UK, I hope you'll let me know at the address shown below. It would be grand to see you again on adult footing.

Yours faithfully,

AMP

Balliol College, Apt. 45A
Oxford OX1 3BJ, UK

52: Wildwood at Lenox – 2096

With our PhD degrees in hand, Katherine and I decided to take a brief vacation in the summer of '25 before sitting down to prepare the syllabus for our fall semester courses at MIT. Neither of us had been to Europe so we opted for a three-week trip to Paris, Barcelona, and Rome. Sainte-Chapelle and Versailles on sunlit days, Gaudi's Casa Batlló, and the Vatican were highlights of the trip, but we wanted to avoid cultural overload, so we spent much of our time walking the streets and parks, looking for prints and drawings in dealers' shops, eating long lunches and reading Penguin paperbacks at sidewalk cafés, then wandering some more in the late afternoon until we were definitely lost and somewhat tired, at which point we'd ask for directions to the nearest underground station or cab stand and head back to our hotel.

Since neither of us had studied any of the romance languages, we found ourselves occasionally saying per favore in Barcelona or gracias in Rome to strangers who helped us, but they always smiled and we smiled back. Our research on boutique hotels paid off, because we slept for the entire trip with open windows facing onto quiet inner courtyards, two of which were really small private parks.

And the weather was ideal the entire time. All in all, a great introduction to Europe.

After mapping out the lectures and lab work for the courses we were scheduled to give that fall, we turned to wedding plans. Step one was to alert John Mitchell and Dean Hammond that I was switching sides and would return to MIT after the wedding in female garb. Neither man batted an eye; the Dean said simply, "Good. The pair of you will help me smash the glass ceiling instead of merely cracking it the way we've done so far." When Katherine spent a weekend with her parents and told them what to expect, her dad looked surprised, then quizzical for 30 seconds, she said. But he promptly climbed on board. A few days later I got a really loving note from him saying how much he was looking forward to having a second daughter.

Telling the manager of my Harvard cricket club was a different matter altogether. After finishing up a practice session by hitting four boundaries in my final over, I explained that I was resigning because I intended to switch genders. He scowled at me and turned away without saying a word. I could see him talking to his assistant. "Beats a bloody poof," he jeered, loudly enough to suggest that he wanted me to overhear.

I dreamed that night that I got a phone call from way out in left field, my old friend Eric Davis from Hanson Middle School, the one who taught me to play baseball. He told me that Bobby Anderson had died, and Tommy Thompson, the Mets scout, had taken over Bobby's baseball camp. Tommy wanted me to come to the camp for a day to see if I could still hit well enough to play for the Mets on opening day of the coming season. One game only, Tommy said.

I fantasized about the idea all day long, wondering if I could become the first woman to get a hit in a Major League game, and maybe wind up with a 1.000 batting average like that Houston player who went three for three, Paciorek, if I remember correctly. In the end I decided the dream was too good to spoil by ever picking up a bat again, but I did check the internet to see how Bobby Anderson was faring. Alas, he really had died, and his indoor cage was no longer listed on the web.

In the midst of fantasizing that day I also thought about some practical issues. I called Dr. Shetland to ask for an estrogen prescription that would help me make the facial transition from man to woman, and I combed the internet looking for a Boston stylist who could help reshape my hair. The man I chose, Shelly Jackson, sounded like a good bet because the website for his salon on Newbury Street said he'd previously been a principal make-up artist for the Netflix Studio in Hollywood.

"You will make a charming woman," he said when I told him I wanted to appear female at my wedding three or four months down the road. He probed my scalp with his delicate fingers, examined several strands of my hair in his microscope, then selected three bottles of lotion from the large cabinet in his salon, wrapped them in tissue and placed them in a blue box resembling Tiffany's classic gift boxes, added a cream-colored envelope to the box, and presented it to me, bowing slightly as he did it. "Follow the instructions in the envelope each day, and plan on returning to me six weeks before your wedding. All will be well, I promise you."

Katherine's parents offered to have the wedding and reception at their home outside New Canaan, but when Katherine asked if we could use the penthouse floor of their New York City apartment instead, they immediately agreed. Half the space was outdoors, but the rest was enclosed with glass walls on three sides that afforded marvelous views of the city looking south, and a sweeping view of the Hudson all the way up to the GW Bridge.

After mulling over different wedding dates that might work for everyone involved, we settled on the Saturday between Christmas and New Year's Eve, which ultimately turned out to be an excellent choice. Henry said that he would like very much to give me away, and promptly recruited the federal judge who'd married Mom and him to perform an encore. At our request, John Mitchell graciously agreed to serve as toastmaster during the dinner that we planned to have after the ceremony.

In mid November I returned to Shelly Jackson's salon, which was fashionably located on the second floor of a new building on the corner of Newbury and Berkeley. I hadn't cut my hair in almost five months, and had been gathering it in a pony tail since early August so that MIT students wouldn't think I was totally uncouth—just a little eccentric.

Shelly was visibly pleased when I let my hair down because it almost reached my shoulders. And I was pleased because the cocktail of estrogens that Dr. Shetland had prescribed was already doing wonders for my face. My beard had always been sparse and splotchy. Now it was gone. And so were the last traces of my boyhood acne scars, leaving my cheeks totally clear.

"Given your lovely brown eyes, what color would you like your hair to be?" Shelly asked me. After a lengthy discussion we settled on auburn. "And your eyebrows? Perhaps a touch more red, just the slightest, tiniest little tinge to add some zest? They are very male, now, as I'm sure you realize. Very undisciplined. I will need to pluck some and reshape the others to make them more feminine and alluring. I trust—" That sounds fine, I said, I'm in your good hands.

"You have grown into your face," Shelly said. "Some people never do, but you have, your cheekbones and chin are exceptional. As a male they give you power; I think I can show you how to use a touch of make-up to make them more elegant, more feminine. And I would like to keep your pony-tail and gather your entire head of hair without a part so that your lovely ears and neck are not hidden.

I think you have intuitively paved the way for your transition by bunching your rather scruffy male hair into a bundle of sorts for the last few months. I assure you, I will give you a pony tail that is far more alluring, one with real élan—one that has true *elegance*."

I told Katherine what I had in mind, and she was all for it. About a week before the wedding I spent an entire afternoon at the salon while Shelly worked his magic, then headed back to our house, to be greeted by Katherine's mother, Sally, who was visiting for a night before heading back to New York. Sally took a good look at me, then threw her arms around me and said, "Oh, Fran! You're beautiful, positively beautiful!!" Katherine overheard her, came running out of our kitchen, and pulled up just short of me to take it all in. "Kiddo, you're gorgeous!" she shouted, thrusting her arms in the air to signal that I'd scored a touchdown. And then she planted a Devon kiss on me.

Early on, Katherine, Sally, and I had agreed to limit the size of the wedding party to 50 people at most. In the end we pared down the guest list to just 42 family and friends—Mr. Hudson, my mentor at Hanson Country Day; four Devon classmates, along with Mr. Sampson and the Head of School; Philip Grinstein, my Salisbury friend and fly-fishing mentor, who was working at Barclay's Bank in NYC; six of Katherine's Harvard classmates, all of whom I'd met before; Dr. Hemmings from Harvard Med School; Dean Hammond, John Mitchell, two of our fellow MIT faculty members, and half a dozen grad school friends;

Katherine's parents, who had morphed for me into Sally and Ken, plus six of their close friends; Mom, Henry, and four of their good friends; and obviously the presiding judge and the two of us.

I don't think I've ever been to a better wedding. Sally had decorated the outdoor portion of their penthouse roof with potted evergreen trees strung with tiny white lights and silver bulbs of various sizes that quivered when the wind gusted, creating a magical, shimmering effect as dusk settled and darkness descended. Inside, a fire blazed in their central hearth, around which five circular tables were scattered, each with a lovely centerpiece of winter flora and a direct view of our head table.

Katherine and I were both dressed in smart evening slacks and blouses, a collection of plain gold bracelets, and a necklace—the amethyst one I'd given her for her 21st birthday and the jade one she'd given to me as a wedding present. When the two of us had first spotted the jade one while window shopping on Newbury Street, I'd commented that it exactly matched the color of her eyes; when I called the store early the next day to buy it for her, I was disappointed to learn that "someone else" had purchased it. She jested when she gave it to me that I should always wear it when we were separated for any reason, so that she could keep an eye on me.

For our wedding I dressed up my own eyes by using the harmless, but very effective, drops that Shelley had given to me to make my eyes glisten, and glisten they did when I looked in our bedroom mirror one last time. I really enjoyed seeing myself as a woman.

We'd previously vowed to keep the ceremony short and straightforward. About 7:00, after everyone was seated following drinks and canapés, Ken and Henry got up from our table and walked around it to stand beside Katherine and me so they could give us a hand as we rose to our feet, and then guide us to clasp hands with each other. The Judge also stood, put his right hand over our clasped ones, and asked, "Do you, Katherine and Fran, wish to be married?" In unison we said, "We do." After a two-beat pause, we turned to face each other and simultaneously said, "I take thee to my wedded wife," then continued to recite in unison the traditional vows we'd memorized. The Judge beamed at us and said, "With that, I proudly pronounce you a married couple." Later in the evening, after we'd all had more to drink, several of Katherine's Harvard friends made a point of telling me it was the simplest—and most elegant— wedding ceremony they'd ever attended.

Dinner, catered by a 25-year old French chef and her staff, was absolutely fabulous—from lighter-than-air gougères at the outset to a superb apricot soufflé with crème anglaise for dessert. As we expected, Henry's wines were extraordinary, the culmination being a truly sublime Chateau Climens 2021 with the soufflé. A four-piece band recruited from Darien played old show tunes at intervals throughout the evening, and after toasting us from her perch in the corner of the room that had been cleared for dancing, SAL.2 provided muted background music from her playlist whenever the band was taking a break.

The older contingent of guests left around 10:30, but most of our contemporaries stayed until the dance band closed down at midnight. After everyone else had gone, Katherine and I stayed up with our parents for another hour or so, swapping family stories and folklore, and bonding with them across family lines to a degree we never had before.

When I woke up the following morning around 10:00, revived perhaps by the sound of Katherine gently snoring beside me, I was bemused to realize that we hadn't made love on our wedding night. I dimly recalled that we'd nuzzled and kissed each other after climbing into bed, but the rest of the night was a blissful, dreamless blank.

53: Darien – 2026

Dear Fran and Katherine,

Your wedding was positively splendid in every respect, beautifully conceived, perfectly carried out. When we finally went to bed, Barbara's love for the two of you poured over. "I'm so utterly happy I can't help myself," she sighed, smiling even as the tears ran down her cheeks.

We're glad the Cézanne watercolor appeals to both of you. Credit Barbara for finding it and getting the Met's restoration experts to remove the spot of foxing that was in the sky to the right of the mountain. We chose it because it seems like a perfect exemplar of your thesis that Cézanne is the best painter of blank spaces who ever lived.

Over the past month we've given considerable thought to another wedding present. Both of us were enormously impressed by your joint decision to turn down the Almega offer and forego the multi millions you could have made by accepting it. Your decision to place all your work in the public domain rather than exploit it commercially for five or ten years was even more impressive. We're in a position to make up part of what you gave up, and want to tell you now what we have in mind, rather than waiting until we shuffle off.

Basically, we've decided to leave you the maximum amount that we can pass on free of tax. More precisely, we plan to leave you investment assets having a market value equal to our combined estate tax exemption under federal law. The rest of our assets we'll give to charity, rendering them non-taxable in our estates.

If the Democrats take complete control of Congress, as I expect they will in the election this November, I think it's likely that our combined estate tax exemption will be reduced from the present level to a figure in the $10 to $12 million range. Unless a massive financial earthquake causes a host of blue-chip corporations to default on their bonds, we will surely be able to leave that much to you. At least $4 million will be in a Roth IRA account, meaning that no tax will be payable on the investment income earned in that account, or on the distributions the IRA makes to you.

More than 30 states currently impose no inheritance taxes, but Connecticut, New York, and a number of others do, at rates and with exemption levels that would greatly reduce what we could leave to you free of tax. To avoid local inheritance taxes, we're thinking of taking up residence, for at least 183 days per year, in a tax-free state like New Hampshire or Florida, or possibly some other eastern state that follows Hawaii's lead by granting an inheritance tax exemption equal to the federal estate tax one for married couples.

We want to stay within easy reach of you, so we're planning to explore New Hampshire first. I've done work for Yankee Magazine, and think we'll start by looking at their home town of Dublin and the nearby area. That would put us a good deal closer to you than we are now.

I wish we could currently give you a sizable portion of what we've earmarked for you, but taking into account the Cézanne gift, the enclosed $1 million wedding check is the most we can give you now without triggering a Connecticut gift tax. Of course, if you have pressing needs at any time while we're still alive, we can loan you part of what you'll eventually inherit, provided we charge interest so the tax people can't call it a disguised gift.

Fond regards from both of us to our wonderful granddaughter. We really liked her toast at the wedding. And also the mellow music she played for us!

Our devoted love to both of you,

Henry

PS, Fran

The trust set up by my father and uncle won't be includable in my estate, the Trustee tells me. On my death she'll distribute the principal, currently valued at around $3 million, directly to you. She says there will be no tax at all!

Love you tons, Mom

54: Wildwood at Lenox – 2096

Our first year of teaching Computer Science at MIT went surprisingly well. Katherine and I jointly gave a required undergraduate course that we called Introduction to Artificial Intelligence, she gave an upper-class elective on core AI algorithms, and I gave one on programming in Artel. Our lectures were video taped to ensure that we wouldn't have to repeat them in future years unless we wanted to add new material or change what we'd previously said. We also wrote abstracts of our lectures and extensive "notes" of the type we might have taken if we were bright students listening to the lectures. The video tapes, abstracts, and notes all became part of the published syllabus for each course—a compendium that was available on line for current or prospective students. I wondered at times if MIT was dehumanizing the teaching profession.

The aspect of the curriculum that kept us personally involved was MIT's emphasis on small "recitation" classes. Katherine and I each spent 20 hours every week working with groups of 12 to 15 students at a time on programming challenges (called problem sets, or "p-sets" in campus jargon) that we had previously posed to them.

Following class discussion of a p-set, and any consulting the students wanted to do with each other, each of them had to submit his or her own written program for performing the assigned task, and then orally explain and defend that program during the next class. Our give-and-take discussions with students during those p-set classes were often the highlight of our week. But over the course of the full academic year, our most rewarding encounters arose when one of our really bright students—or one of our distressed ones—dropped by our adjoining offices to talk one-on-one.

Early on, Katherine and I had each announced to our students that we would do our absolute best to keep our dockets clear from 4:00 to 5:00 on weekday afternoons to talk with any of them who wanted to drop in unannounced, which they were welcome to do if our office door was open. We added that each of us would keep a small bench in the corridor outside our office to accommodate anyone who had to wait because our door was shut, signaling that we were talking to another student. Our open-door policy proved so popular that we often had to stay until 5:30 or 6:00 to see everyone who was waiting, and once, after I'd assigned a quite difficult Artel p-set, I had to make specific appointments to see half a dozen students who were still outside my door at 5:45.

During the fall term several of Katherine's students became regular visitors, as did one of mine, a lanky boy appropriately named Jesse Stringer. He seemed like an unlikely computer science prospect when he first walked into my office, shuffling very slowly and speaking in broken sentences that suggested lassitude, if not total inability to organize his thoughts. I placed him as coming from the rural South with little or no formal education, and wondered what it was about him that appealed to the MIT admissions people.

He quickly set me straight. After sitting down he ran one hand through his shaggy black hair and reached out with the other to hand me a piece of paper. "That algorithm you talked about this morning," he said, slumping back in his chair. "I reckon it would work better this way." I looked down at what he'd handed me, then spent two minutes thinking silently. Finally, I looked up and caught his eye. "You're absolutely right," I said. He smiled very slightly. "Pleased to know that," he replied.

His parents were sharecroppers, I later learned. I also discovered that he hadn't worn a single pair of shoes as a youngster, and owed everything to a Baptist minister who recognized that he was "smart beyond reason." The minister got him a computer that he could run in the rectory office where they had electricity, and he learned enough on line to score over 1500 on his SATs. Since he had no school transcript to submit, he sent MIT a computer program he'd written in Python in response to a p-set that several students had posted. They couldn't solve it and were looking for help, he explained in his transmittal letter, which I found when I finally tracked down his admissions office file. The file also contained a letter from his sponsor stating, "As Pastor of a congregation that consists primarily of rural Blacks, I have spent years looking for a genuine diamond in the rough; Jesse is the first one I have found. Admit him, polish him, and he will outshine all others in his class, I promise you."

How or why he was wired to write ground-breaking AI programs, I never learned, but in addition to becoming friends over that first year of talking together, we became colleagues. If MIT had given me nothing else, the chance to work with Jesse would have been ample reward for all the effort I put in to become a good MIT professor. He was largely responsible for SAL.4, and in due course he won a Nobel Prize for his pioneering work on AGI during the late '20s and '30s.

55: Iceland – 2026

July 2, 2026

Dearest Ellen,

    I've been remiss in not writing recently and hope this will make amends. Your last letter describing your Patagonian fishing trip made me somewhat envious; now I'm finally able to respond in kind!

    Mom and Henry, Katherine and I, and her parents are currently gathered together in the northeastern corner of Iceland, staying for two weeks at the local equivalent of an old Russian dacha. We overlook the Big Laxa, a lovely salmon and trout river that flows north from Lake Mývatn to the sea, near the town of Husavik. Henry, who organized all this more than a year ago, made sure that everyone else staying in the lodge would be congenial by encouraging four of his closest NY Anglers' Club friends to book the two remaining rooms. For all practical purposes, he is hosting an Anglers' Club house party, with extended family members as his guests.

    The lodge sits right beside the river, roughly midway from the lake to the sea. Its Icelandic name, Laxfoss, reflects the fact that it overlooks immense falls spanning the river—falls too high for salmon to clear.

On our first afternoon here we drove up to the lake on a paved road running through vast stretches of otherwise untamed countryside, under a crystalline sky that stretched forever, it seemed. As we were passing through a rock-bound valley, Mom spotted a gyrfalcon with a wingspan of at least four feet sailing majestically along the eastern ridge. Finally, the lake appeared in the distance, a broad sweep of water with a mirror-like surface that shimmered in the sunlight. Henry explained that the lake is a shallow, spring-fed food factory that gives birth to millions of tiny insects and other nutrients. A lot of that food flows into the braided channels of the upper river, he told us, making it one of the best wild brown trout fisheries in the world.

This morning I taught Katherine to cast. It was a humbling or exhilarating experience, depending on one's point of view; after ten minutes she was throwing perfect loops that reached out 40 feet. As you'll see in a moment, that was just for starters.

We drove downstream from the lodge for our first day of salmon fishing, and stopped beside a beautiful stretch of water with a deep trench at the head of the pool and a long tail-out against a curving high bank on the far side of the river. Our guide, a six-foot block of granite named Pétur, tied a small Blue Charm onto Katherine's leader, positioned her at the head of the pool in thigh-deep water three feet from our bank, and told her to cast downstream at a 45° angle to the far bank.

He knew that neither of us had fished for salmon before, so he talked loudly enough for me to hear what he was saying. Keep your rod tip down, almost touching the water, he told us, and keep pointing it directly at your fly line and fly as they swing across the trench. When the line was hanging straight downstream, he told Katherine to take two steps downriver and repeat what she'd just done.

She cast again. As her fly started to swing, the water boiled; seconds later a silver missile shot out of the water, then plunged back down. Aided by Pétur's coaching, she let the fish run, reeled in some line, let it run again, then reeled steadily until it was only 15 feet away, at which point it suddenly bolted, tearing downriver at least forty yards. Finally, some seven or eight minutes after she'd hooked it, she was able to slowly reel the fish close enough to her bank for Pétur to net it.

"I want to hold it in the water before we release it!" K cried out, beaming outrageously. The fish was chrome bright, with black spots along its flanks—a gorgeous creature, far more splendid than any trout I'd caught on my Beaverkill outing with Henry. I felt insanely jealous, but overjoyed for Katherine. Pétur told us it was a six-kilo hen, fresh from the sea. He said he'd never seen or heard of anyone catching a salmon that size in their first two minutes of salmon fishing. Fortunately, I had it all on my i-phone 12.

Now that you and K have both landed large fish, I'm left as the weak sister in our threesome; I got skunked today, and when we go to the upper river tomorrow, any decent fish I manage to hook will probably break off by heading straight into the weeds, which are abundant because the river is so fertile. I have a hunch that by the end of our two weeks here, the extraordinary sky and landscape, and the sense of camaraderie among us, will be what I remember best about the trip.

If memory serves, your sabbatical started yesterday. Enjoy it, and please keep me posted on your Yeats project!

Fondly,
Fran

56: Wildwood at Lenox – 2096

My world began to disintegrate when Henry had a heart attack in July, 2026 on the banks of the Big Laxa in Iceland during a family fishing trip. His guide, Stefan, immediately fed him super-strength aspirin and called air rescue. Minutes later, a Mýflug chopper appeared overhead and settled down on the bank beside us. Two medics got out, carried Henry into the belly of the chopper on a stretcher, and got Mom strapped into a seat, all in less than a minute. I later learned that Henry reached the cardiac arrest ER room in the Akureyri Hospital just 25 minutes after he collapsed on the river bank.

Our superb Icelandic guide, Pétur, drove Katherine and me to the hospital at breakneck speed, but we were too late. Henry had a second attack while he was stretched out on an operating table in the cardiac ER, and never regained consciousness.

Mom was devastated. Everything had happened so quickly, so unexpectedly, that she had trouble believing he really was gone. Katherine and I sat up with her for several hours in the Akureyri hotel suite Pétur had booked for us, but we weren't able to console her, and ended up giving her the sedative the hospital had provided so she could get some badly needed sleep.

The flight back to JFK two days later seemed to take forever. Mom moaned and muttered to herself the entire time. She had always been so organized, so capable and adaptable, that it was hard to watch her wither away, whimpering instead of soldiering on the way she had when Sydney was still living with us. Nothing that Katherine or I could do or say seemed to make any difference.

Two days later she asked if I would arrange Henry's memorial service and a reception afterwards. She said she wasn't up for that. I asked whether she wanted the service in Darien or the City. You decide, she said.

I suspected that most of Henry's former partners and other close friends lived in the City or nearby suburbs, and decided to call the rector of Trinity Church in lower Manhattan. He not only knew Henry, but had actually fished with him once on the Neversink in the Catskills. Of course we could hold the service at Trinity, he said to me. Next, I called the AI engineer I'd met at the NY Anglers' Club when I had lunch there. He immediately remembered me, commiserated when I explained the situation, and said he'd be glad to check with the club's officers to see if we could hold a reception there. Two days later we settled on the last Saturday afternoon in July for both the service and the reception.

The day before the service, Mom finally pulled herself together. She made phone calls, talked to the

Julliard violinist who was going to play at the service, and added Icelandic gravlax to the menu for the reception afterwards, which Katherine and I regarded as her way of fighting back at the Nordic gods who had struck down her husband on the banks of a salmon river.

By design, the service followed the traditional Episcopalian format until the homily, but at that point it became a Quaker meeting. Ernest McDowell, Henry's successor as Solicitor General, recounted several landmark cases that Henry had successfully argued in the Supreme Court on behalf of the government. Four current or retired Cravath partners, and several other long-time friends, spoke about various other aspects of Henry's life and career—as a leader of the firm, a mentor, a sage advisor, the key figure in negotiating a merger that saved 3,500 jobs in Toledo, a superb advocate in litigation involving large business firms, a close personal friend and confidant, a fellow angler and companion on world-wide fly-fishing trips, an exceptional judge of fine wines, and a supporter and trustee of three major New York City charities.

I said I'd grown up with a father I couldn't stand, then briefly recounted my first meeting with Henry at the Red Lion pub in Salisbury, sailing with him on the Sound, and fishing together in the Catskills. And Katherine said how touched she'd been by his gracious wedding toast, welcoming her into the family as his second daughter.

Because it was a clear, sunny day in the mid 70s, many in the congregation decided after the service to walk from the church to the Anglers' Club farther downtown. Others rode there in one of the driverless shuttle buses we'd reserved beforehand. At the reception Mom was her old self, chatting with friends and clients of Henry, thanking those who'd come from a considerable distance, and laughing heartily in response to anecdotes about Henry she hadn't heard before. I smiled to myself when I overheard her politely direct one of the servers to replenish the tray of gravlax.

Two days later she killed herself.

I was staying with her at the Darien house, just to be sure she didn't have a relapse after gearing up for the service and reception. When she didn't come down for breakfast on the second day, I went upstairs and found her stretched out on her bed with a wry smile frozen in place, an empty, unlabeled pill bottle on her bedside table, and beneath it a handwritten note, which I still have. It reads:

Fran dear,

I can't bear the thought of being separated from Henry and want to catch up with him before he gets out of sight. If people ask, tell them I died of a broken heart, and add that I died peacefully, all of which is true. Please don't mourn me. I've had a wonderful life since Henry arrived on the scene, and I leave this world for the next with

memories of you and Katherine, my extraordinary
children, which will last forever.

All my love, Mom

57: New York City – 2026

"Good morning. I'm Fran Johnson, to see Denise Cunningham, please."

"Welcome to Cravath. She's expecting you, and I'll let her secretary know you're here. Please make yourself comfortable. Or, if you'd prefer, there are some historical photos you might enjoy looking at in the conference room behind me."

"Ms. Johnson, what a pleasure to meet you at last!"

"Fran, please. Henry told Katherine and me all about you, and we already think of you as family, not simply his executrix."

"Denise, then. Would you like some coffee or tea? Or spring water? And maybe a croissant? Cravath has the best pastry outside Paris."

"Zut alors! Un croissant et un grand crème, s'il vous plaît."

"I'm sorry I wasn't able to get back from London to be with all of you for Henry's memorial service. Others here tell me it was a lovely service, Fran. In every way. And your mother's, too, I gather.

"I miss them both, Henry especially, because he was both my mentor and a close personal friend. Perhaps because he never had any children of his own, he always took great interest in the young associates here; even though I never worked in M&A, he took me under his wing shortly after I arrived, and was my guide and confidant ever after. Without his help and advice I probably wouldn't be here today, and I certainly wouldn't be heading up Trusts and Estates."

"I know. Katherine and I grew very fond of him—I especially, because I had a really lousy father for starters, and Henry understood that, I think, and made an extra effort to reach out to me and share what he'd learned about life. I'm sorry Katherine couldn't come with me today, but we'll fix that next time."

"Henry showed me the letter he sent the two of you right after the wedding. Did he tell you anything more after that about what to expect?"

"Not really. He just encouraged us to study up on the basics of fixed-income investing."

"Well then, you'll be glad to learn that you're probably going to receive more than twice the amount he mentioned in his letter. If the Democrats keep the House and win control of the Senate this November, I think they'll probably reduce the estate tax exemption to pre-Trump levels, as Henry predicted. But I'm virtually certain that any changes the Democrats make will apply only to the estates of people who die after the House bill proposing those changes has been introduced, or perhaps after it's been enacted. Since nothing like that has happened yet,

Henry's and Barbara's estates will almost certainly be able to use the full amount of their combined 2018 Trump Act exemptions, which have now reached the inflation-adjusted level of $24.1 million. Under their wills, that's the amount that will go to you and Katherine, free of tax."

"Good grief!"

"I can't help asking. You were a Peanuts fan growing up?"

"Yes, but—"

"I know, $24 million is a lot. Certainly not peanuts, which is one reason I thought we should talk. When Henry and Barbara executed new wills after your wedding, he asked me to share with you what I've learned about money management—about defining objectives and leveraging what you do with your money to maximize the benefits it produces."

"Thanks, we could certainly use more input. After we got Henry's letter, Katherine and I both decided we needed to dig in and read up on the issues you just mentioned. Having done that, our inclination is to manage everything ourselves, to keep it very straightforward and simple, so we can understand exactly what's going on. At least for starters.

"As of now, we're thinking of putting half of what we get into a Vanguard low-cost ETF that tracks the S&P 500, making purchases at regular intervals to get the benefit of dollar averaging. The rest we want to invest in a portfolio of blue-chip corporate bonds that are non callable, except for make-whole calls—bonds that we'll plan on holding to their laddered maturity dates, so we don't have to worry about intervening fluctuations in market value. Does that sound sensible to you?"

"It certainly does. In fact, investing in high-grade corporates is exactly what Henry did in his Roth IRA, which you'll inherit intact, and in part of his personal account as well. He was fond of quoting an aphorism he found on the internet that goes, "Those who know about compound interest earn it; those who don't pay it." I doubt whether Einstein actually said that compounding is the most powerful force in the universe, but the legend attributing that sort of remark to him has survived because it reflects a fundamental truth. Long-term compounding is a great way to build wealth.

"Because our firm has worked with them in the past, I could put you in touch with several money managers who've outperformed the market over a sustained period, but I gather you're happy to invest in the market as a whole and settle for what it produces over the long haul. That makes lots of sense. And it's far less stressful than trying to pick start-ups that may double your fortune, but are more likely to tank on you overnight.

"Do you have any long-term financial plans or goals at this point?"

"For starters we'd like to buy a small house near the Common in Cambridge. With our MIT salaries and the tax-free distributions we'll be required to take from the Roth

IRA each year, we'll have plenty to live comfortably. We've thought about setting up a charitable foundation to give away most of our remaining annual income, but that would involve a lot of paperwork and other administrative complications, so for the time being at least, we want to handle the charitable giving ourselves.

"Our first priority is to establish and endow a fund that will award four-year undergraduate scholarships to talented, underprivileged students who want to study computer science at MIT. I'm working with one now, and want the admissions office to find more prospects like him, particularly women. Katherine went to Harvard and she still bitterly resents what former President Summers had to say about females, belittling their ability to work in STEM fields."

"I completely agree about Summers, Fran. I was at the law school then, and organized a major protest. I even wrote every Overseer a letter that in hindsight seems more vitriolic than reasoned. But at least the furor all of us created finally forced him to step down.

"Funding scholarships in targeted fashion sounds like an excellent idea, a great way to begin a charitable program. Have the two of you thought at all about what you might do beyond that?"

"We have, Denise. Mostly focusing on your point about leveraging what we have, in order to do something of major significance. When we started to think seriously about our priorities, we discovered quite quickly that both of us regard education as the country's most important resource, and believe the best way to improve public education is to turn teaching back into a true profession. I was lucky enough to work on a major project with Melinda Gates three years ago, and I think she might agree with us. If so, I'm hopeful that she'll help us raise some serious money to invest in the idea."

"I'm fascinated, Fran. Have you got a specific proposal in mind, or is this still just a blue sky concept?"

"Our basic goal is to attract and retain better, more effective public school teachers by converting the teaching of grades K through 12 into a well-paid professional career on a par with practicing law or medicine. Both of us think prospective public school teachers should get graduate school training comparable to that of prospective lawyers and doctors. To maintain professional standards, we think potential teachers should be rigorously examined before being certified to practice, just as aspiring lawyers and doctors are. And once they are certified, teachers should be paid handsomely.

"I'm curious, Denise. Would it be out of bounds to ask what a first-year associate makes these days in a firm like Cravath? Around $225,000 maybe?"

"Slightly more than that, with the boost last year."

"Well, I suspect that half of that would be enough to attract a lot of very talented, dedicated people who would like to teach, but don't think they can afford to as matters currently stand. Pay scales for public school teachers are never going to match salaries at places like the Mayo Clinic or Cravath, but the existing chasm between them needs to become a much narrower gap.

"Katherine and I think metropolitan Boston would be the perfect place to run a 25-year pilot project. The demographics there cover the entire spectrum—high-end neighborhoods to low-end, dangerous ones with run-down schools. If we're able to prove that a new generation of public school teachers can turn out an entire class of well-educated high school graduates in Roxbury, then we've basically demonstrated that it can be done anywhere in the country.

"We think teachers of the type we have in mind could do that. I mean, think of assigning all your first-year associates to teach at a school in the Bronx or Hell's Kitchen. With six months of intensive indoctrination, I'll bet anything they'd do an excellent job. Give them—or other recent college graduates of their character and ability—three years of graduate school teacher training, and I'll bet the results would be truly astonishing."

"Henry didn't exaggerate, Fran—I'm impressed. If you do decide to talk with Melinda Gates about all this, please let me know beforehand. I've done a fair amount of foundation work recently and I'd be happy to draft a specific proposal that you could give her. On a pro bono basis, because I think your concept is worth pursuing, and would really like to help.

"Before you go, I want to show you Henry's old office. He once told me that when he was really hung up on how to deal with a serious issue, he would gaze out his window until the answer came to him. As you'll see, he had an amazing view of Central Park."

58: Wildwood at Lenox – 2096

Two weeks after Mom died we had a reception in her honor at the Women's Democratic Club in NYC. We chose that site because the pastor of the Darien church she went to told me that he was unwilling to preside over a memorial service for anyone who had "shunned" God and violated the Sixth Commandment by "murdering" herself. He was so pathetically self-righteous, I wondered why his congregation hadn't banished him.

At least 40 of Mom's friends turned up at the reception; most were other women she'd worked with on charitable events over the years, or long-time female chums from the Darien area. We had a high old time toasting and roasting her. The consensus was that she had checked out because she knew, as always, exactly what she wanted to accomplish and had proceeded to do it efficiently and decisively. More power to her, many of her friends said with admiration and, in several cases, a suggestion of envy as well.

The following week I went down to NYC for a day to meet with Henry's friend and law partner, Denise Cunningham, whom he and Mom had designated to be "executrix" of their separate estates. What a bizarre way of describing a female trustee! It makes her sound like a dominatrix on steroids—a woman so sadistic that she routinely executes her lovers, the way a female praying mantis does by eating her male partner after mating. Of course, as every law student knows, the executrix of an estate is really the polar opposite of that; as a fiduciary, she's duty bound to administer the estate in loyal and dependable fashion.

And that's certainly what Denise did, from the moment the two of us met in her office at Cravath until Henry's and Mom's estates were both closed with great efficiency about a year later. As she predicted during our first meeting, the Democrats who took control of Congress in January, 2027 rolled back the estate-tax exemption to what it would have been under the Obama-era rules, but the roll back applied only to the estates of people who died in 2028 or later years, so Katherine and I shared the benefit of the much greater Trump-era exemption rules and wound up receiving investment assets valued at $24.1 million from the two estates, of which $4.1 million was in a tax-sheltered Roth IRA. As sole "remainderman" of the trust set up for Mom by my grandfather and great uncle, I got another $3.1 million, my self-declared gender notwithstanding. I felt as though Katherine and I had won a Powerball lottery, with a special bonus because it was all tax free.

Suddenly, work became a real pleasure—almost pure pleasure—because we longer needed jobs, but simply wanted them. We thought it would be a useful diversion to write a text book, and decided to spend a good part of the 2026-2027 academic year reworking the syllabus material for our jointly taught course called Introduction to Artificial Intelligence. After a brief debate, we decided to give the book the same title, even though we planned to cover much more ground in the text than we were able to cover in our lectures and classes.

Our financial windfall had one other immediate impact. For the first time, we clearly could afford to buy a house instead of continuing to pour monthly rent payments into a sinkhole. We did some on-line research and quickly discovered that a house of the type we wanted would probably cost around $1.5 million. When we ran the numbers, we concluded that unless real estate in Cambridge tanked after we bought a home, which seemed highly unlikely, we almost certainly would do better in the end if we took out a mortgage to pay most of the purchase price, instead of using our own funds to pay all of it at the outset.

Katherine told one of her Harvard classmates, who was still living and working in Cambridge, that we were house hunting, and two days later got a call back from her friend telling us about an old, red-brick carriage house off Prentiss Street that was about to come on the market. Armed with the info her friend had provided, we called the owner, explained who we were, and ended up being invited to stop by and tour the house.

We found it in a cul-de-sac behind a grand old New England manse that sat in the middle of a tree-lined, totally residential block of Prentiss Street, about a ten-minute walk from the Common, our favorite Cambridge green space. The owner told us that it had been converted from a stable and carriage house into a residence not long after the Civil War, which explained the wide entryway under a high arch, and the 15-foot ceiling in the spectacular living room—a spacious, light-filled room that had 19th-century wide-plank flooring and a large brick fireplace. A dining alcove had a smaller fireplace made of the same brick, and French doors leading to a back yard. There was a small powder room on one side of the entryway.

In the very large kitchen, which had recently been renovated, a lovely old farm table, about eight feet long, sat beside yet another 19th-century fireplace. When Katherine remarked on the table and the matching set of six antique Windsor chairs around it, the owner said they were so much a part of the kitchen that he planned to convey them to the buyer of the house without charge, as if they were fixtures like the Vulcan stove.

The back yard, enclosed on three sides by an attractive six-foot-high wooden fence, was an urban oasis. A flagstone patio adjacent to the house was shaded by a lovely elm tree; beyond it was a sunlit plot of grass. The border between those two areas and the fence was planted with flower beds and an array of evergreen shrubs.

Upstairs there were three ample bedrooms. The largest had an old fireplace, and a recently added walk-in closet leading to a spacious, updated bathroom. The second had two conventional closets and an older bathroom that could be accessed either from the bedroom itself or from a central hallway. The third room, at the end of the hall, had no bathroom fixtures of its own, but it did have a lovely view, overlooking the back patio and garden.

Given its age and original purpose, the house was remarkably well laid out and equipped. Back stairs led from the spacious kitchen pantry to the second floor hallway, and from there up to a small attic used only for storage and central air-conditioning equipment. A doorway in the kitchen pantry opened onto an outside bricked-in area large enough to hold the A/C condenser, trash cans, and two parked cars. The finished basement contained more storage space, a utility room with all the usual plumbing and heating equipment, and a wine cellar that had been constructed by stacking hexagonal clay drain pipes—each about 4" wide and 14" long—inside a closet.

I loved the house from the moment we walked through the entryway into the living room. Because it had so much basic appeal, and was so well located, I was prepared to accept minor infrastructure issues like the gas-fired furnace, which we noticed had an installation tag dated 1990. When the owner wasn't looking I gave a thumbs up to Katherine, who nodded back. The owner invited us to stay for a glass of wine, and in less than five minutes we were politely negotiating.

No, he wasn't aware of any pending or potential problems, but of course we could have a construction expert go over the house thoroughly. Yes, there was a deeded easement giving the owner of the house a right-of-way over the driveway to the bricked-in parking area, all of which was definitely inside the property boundary line. By all means, he'd split the saved commission expense if we were prepared to sign a contract before he listed the house, which he planned to do in a couple of days. In offhand fashion he added that the two prospective agents he'd talked with had both told him that the right listing price for the house would be $1,595,000.

Katherine could do mental arithmetic faster than a calculator. She immediately said, "Well, if we use the 7% commission rate that seems to be the new standard, and split the saving, that would reduce the price by almost 56K, and my guess is that it will take about 15K to put in a new furnace, so could we round it off to a million five twenty five?"

"All cash, or would you want a purchase-money second mortgage?" the owner asked.

"I think we could handle all cash," I chimed in.

"Done," he said, and we shook hands.

In bed that night, I reran the financial scenario, just to be sure. Virtually our entire inheritance was currently invested in long-term, non-callable bonds that collectively yielded 5.875% of their total maturity value. In all probability, we should be able to do at least that well on future investments, especially if we put our money in stock market index funds and kept it there over the long haul. The mortgage broker we'd talked with had said that, given our credit scores and collective net worth, we'd have no problem getting a 15-year mortgage at 4.375% with no points, so there was a spread of 150 basis points between what we could expect to earn on our assets, and the interest we'd have to pay if we borrowed to buy the house.

Ergo, the more we borrowed, the more we could save; all we had to do to take advantage of the basis-point spread was to use the bank's money rather than our own to pay most of the purchase price. And if Cambridge house values continued to rise at even a modest rate for the next ten years or so, and we decided to sell, we might very well get a double-digit compounded return on our down payment and the loan-amortization portion of our monthly payments. All told, it was an excellent illustration of the leveraging that Denise had talked about.

As I drifted off, I thought how naïve I'd previously been about financial matters, apart from making sure that I zeroed out my credit card balance every month. Long-term financial planning was a whole new game, and the two of us were just scratching the surface by buying a house.

59: Cambridge – 2026

Dearest Ellen,

Much has happened since my letter from Iceland in July. Most significantly, Henry died of a heart attack on the banks of the Big Laxa two days after I wrote you, and Mom died of a broken heart shortly afterwards. They loved each other and the two of us very much, and we miss them terribly.

Because of the very generous wedding present they gave us, we've been able to buy a small house here in Cambridge. We moved in a week ago and had a housewarming dinner party last night. In the course of it, we learned from one of K's Harvard classmates who works at the Widener Library that they've just acquired a trove of previously unknown 1909-1916 correspondence between Ezra Pound and various Irish writers—primarily Lady Gregory and James Joyce—regarding the work that Pound did for Yeats while they were living together at Ashdown Forest.

We think you should come visit and be the first Yeats scholar to get a look at the Pound papers. Our guest room awaits you! And how about some trout fishing beforehand? I think we'd have a ball if the three of us fished together for a couple of days on the Deerfield River in the Berkshires.

Sending this via E-mail because time is somewhat short. Classes at MIT start Sept. 7, and we'll need to stay close to home after that.

Much love,

Fran

60: Wildwood at Lenox – 2096

The construction consultant we hired to check the Prentiss Street house told us that apart from the outdated furnace everything looked fine, so we were able to close on the house quite quickly, in early August. Moving from our rental apartment on Chauncy Terrace took only a few hours, and ostensibly it was no big deal, just a couple of women who'd hired a couple of guys and their small truck to move some books and clothes and other stuff from one place to another just a few blocks away. But emotionally, the move marked a life-changing transition from shacking up as aging youngsters to settling down as married young adults in a home of our own.

It was clear to both of us that Fenway Park, our king-sized bed, belonged in the bedroom with the walk-in closet and the swish new bathroom. But having all the new space meant that we could sleep in separate rooms—most of the time—and not have to listen to each other snore. I really loved the funky old fixtures in the other upstairs bathroom, so I offered to take the bedroom that connected to it. We could take turns visiting each other, I added. "Sure, it'll be more risqué that way," Katherine said. And if we both have the same idea and meet half-way, then what?

I asked—do we rumble on the shag rug in the hallway? "That'd be a blast!" Katherine said, as we hugged each other.

We decided to use the third bedroom on the back side of the house as our joint office. The best setup was obviously to put our partners' desk midway between the pair of old 12-over-12 windows that looked out on the garden, so that each of us could see it by glancing to our side while working at the desk. We used the opposite wall as gallery space for our growing collection of prints and drawings, leaving room for a lovely still life of cherries—a richly colored, artistically disciplined, mezzotint by a 20th-century Japanese artist named Yozo Hamaguchi—that I'd recently purchased and decided to reframe.

Our high-tech kitchen inspired us to become chefs instead of frozen food addicts. We had a smart electronic kitchen organizer, which I named Kit-Kat. Katherine said its name should be shortened to KK, because it'd be worth millions if we could teach it to cook as well as it managed all the appliances. Katherine wasn't kidding; we went to C-SAIL the next morning and she buried SAL.2 with cookbook data from Apicius to Julia Child. I was tempted to ask SAL how to cook an egg, but Katherine said that was a bad idea because SAL would quickly figure out that I was insulting her.

A week after we moved in we rounded up a sizable group of our Cambridge friends for a housewarming supper party on our back patio. To prepare for it, I poured 30

pounds of ice cubes into an old metal washtub that we'd
found in a local antique store, and filled it with bottles of
four different beers, while Katherine squeezed limes and
mixed up a gallon of Margueritas. For supper we had
bratwurst and rare burgers that I grilled, and a selection of
salads—roasted beets, crumbled goat cheese, and romaine
with a balsamic vinegar dressing; orange segments and
paper thin slices of onion with bib lettuce and a white-wine
vinegar dressing; and potato salad from our favorite deli.
Our guests wound up consuming everything, down to the
last bottle of Sam Adams.

Midway through the party I noticed Katherine
having a prolonged one-on-one conversation with a woman
named Sibley Austern, the friend of hers who'd alerted us
that our house was about to come on the market. Knowing
their back-story, I was curious, and when we climbed into
Fenway Park together after the party I asked what the
conversation had been all about.

"More poetry," Katherine said. "She's had the hots
for me ever since we took that romantic poetry seminar
together, and all she wants to talk about is poetry. She's all
fired up, about to have an orgasm, I think, because the
library's just received a bequest of original correspondence
written by Yates, Lady Gregory and the like." Ellen Riley
is currently on sabbatical, researching Yeats, I said. Maybe
we should invite her to come over to take a look. "And
maybe you have the hots for her?" Katherine said, smiling.

Whoa, I said. I have the hots only for you! And then we had another housewarming session of our own.

We ended up inviting Ellen to come fish with us before MIT started up, and then stay on at our house while she was researching the Yeats material, which scholars apparently had never seen. She arrived in late August and the three of us drove my ancient Honda crossover straight from Logan, where she landed, to a country inn just outside Williamstown, our home base for visiting the Clark Art Institute and exploring the Deerfield River.

That afternoon we went to the Clark and strolled through their permanent collection until we finally reached a well reviewed exhibition of American Luminists. I fell behind at that point. When I eventually caught up, I was interested to see Ellen and Katherine conversing intently in front of a Fitz Henry Lane sunlit seascape. I paused to watch them for a while, wondering to myself why they seemed so intrigued by the painting.

After the Clark it was early supper, then off to bed in our adjoining rooms because Ellen had been up for almost 24 hours. Am I right about her? I asked Katherine as we were brushing our teeth. "For sure," Katherine said. "Definitely someone special. Certainly not your typical spinster librarian—not by a long shot."

The next morning we suited up for fishing and drove back down the Mohawk Trail road until we crossed the Deerfield and reached the village of Charlemont, where we met David, the Orvis guide I'd previously engaged for the day. I'd told him then that all three of us were relative neophytes, and could see he was pleasantly surprised when he positioned us on a nearby pool and watched Katherine start the day by casting 30 feet to a rising fish, which she hooked and landed. It wasn't a big fish—just 10 or 11 inches—but it was a lovely brown trout. "A wild fish, not a stocked one," David told us.

We left Katherine to fend for herself and walked 100 feet upstream to fish a run that spilled out of a riffle between two large rocks. David positioned Ellen and watched her throw a perfectly shaped 25-foot cast into the tail of the run. A frisky fish grabbed her fly, jumped twice and threw the hook. "A lovely little wild rainbow," David said. "Good work, Ellen." He looked at me and smiled. "You're another neophyte, just like your friends, I suppose?" I said they were skillful neophytes who caught on quickly; I was just an ordinary one. "We'll see," he said.

We walked another 100 feet upstream and he positioned me 25 feet below the head of a pool on our side of the river, in a spot where there was room to back cast. "Take a practice cast into the center of the river, would you?" he said to me. I did. "Good," he said. "Now make the same cast, but do it sidearm if you can." I'll try, I said, and immediately thought of Henry, who'd taught me that maneuver. "Excellent," he said.

Pointing upstream in the general direction of a big tree on our bank he said, "Now, do you think you could sidearm it again and get the fly under that overhanging branch?" I'll give it a shot, I said, and actually managed to do it without hanging up or disturbing the water when the fly landed. "He could take that; strike very gently if he does," David said quietly. A second later a fish nudged the surface and sipped my fly. "Gently," David said again, "he's a very big fish.   Yes, by God! There's no trouble underwater. Let him run if he wants to." But the fish didn't seem to do anything.

I can't feel a thing, I think I've lost him, I said to David. "Don't think so," he said. "You did that perfectly; he doesn't know he's hooked yet. Reel in your line very slowly until you feel him, then make love and coax him into your bed.   Very gently, Fran.   That's it, you can feel him now, right?   Good.   Keep easing him toward you.   Very slowly.   That's it.   I'm going to get in the water and creep up the bank behind him, and you stay right where you are. Keep your rod tip up when I'm going under your line and we'll let him slowly drift down into my net."

My heart was pounding, but I did manage to seduce the fish, easing him very slowly down the bank all the way into David's net—at which point the water exploded, and he vaulted into the air. David somehow managed to renet him on his way down, then lifted the net out of the water so I could see him. I was awestruck. He was a large, truly gorgeous brown, with dark red and black spots on his flanks and a bright yellow underside as rich and lustrous in color as hollandaise sauce.

David lowered his net onto the grassy bank and plucked my tiny Parachute Adams fly from the corner of the trout's mouth. Then he told me to put my rod on the bank, ease myself into the water, and be sure to wet my hands before I touched the fish so I wouldn't rub off the protective film covering its flanks. After I got into the river, David swung the net back to me so I could reach in and cradle the fish with both hands; then he said, "I'm going to lower the net now, and you hold your friend that way while I snap a few photos.   Good, lift him a little higher, please.   Perfect.   OK, ease him back into the water, and cradle him for as long as you want to. That's a six-and-a-half-pound brown. I've been trying to catch him all summer and no one's done it until now.   Neophyte, my foot!"

After waving goodbye to my fish several minutes later, I spent the rest of the day in a pleasant haze. We caught some more fish and lost others. Rafters floated past us. Ducks flew overhead. Two deer appeared on the far bank and watched us fish. But all I really saw was my big brown nosing up and sipping my fly. I saw it again and again, always in slow motion. I can still see it happening in slow motion today.

Around 1:30 we stopped at a scenic spot for David's upscale picnic lunch that included a bottle of chilled rosé, as well as beer or soft drinks. Later in the afternoon, I landed a small rainbow and decided to quit for the day so I could watch the others. I found the two of them in the next pool upstream, standing in the river about 20 feet apart and talking to each other as they fished—joshing each other, from what little I could overhear. I could see immediately that Ellen cast almost as well as Katherine, using the same easy motion and consistently forming perfect loops, unlike mine that always looked like sine waves on the final forward cast. I watched them for a while, but neither had a strike, and half an hour later we agreed to call it a day.

On our way back to my car in Charlemont we were all silent for several minutes, until David suddenly spoke up. "The three of you are something else," he said. "Fran tells me you are neophytes when she calls to make the booking. Then, as we're driving to the river, Katherine says she caught a fish by mistake on her second cast and hasn't caught one since. And Ellen says she's only been on two fishing trips before this. So then I see all three of you hook up on your first cast and watch Fran coax a 25" brown into the net, and learn that Katherine's only fish before today was a 13-pound salmon, and find out that Ellen spent a week in Patagonia and landed a 23" brown on the Malleo, and I think to myself, these gals are really Ocean's 8 con artists who talk themselves down to mislead victims like me into thinking they're pushovers, and I'm not smart enough to figure out why they're doing it. Well, all I can say is that you're the best women anglers I've guided all year."

David's praise put all of us in a good mood, and after we'd polished off a bottle of Pinot Grigio at the bar in our inn, the banter back and forth stepped up when we moved to the dinner table and shifted to a Chardonnay with our grilled trout. I would have expected Katherine to one-up Ellen and me 90 percent of the time, but Ellen was surprisingly good at holding her own and coming up with occasional zingers. I was feeling very mellow by the time we ordered a bottle of Oregon Pinot Noir to go with our selection of cheeses, so I decided to sit back and watch while the two of them traded barbs about their fishing mishaps earlier in the day. When I poured the last of the wine for the three of us, I said I thought Ellen had won on points, but not by much. A split decision maybe.

I knew something was going on between them, but couldn't figure out what. As we were getting into bed that night, I decided to ask point blank. There's some kind of high voltage line that runs between you and Ellen, isn't there? I said. What is it?

"You're right," Katherine said. "We both felt it, right from the get-go at Logan."

Physical, mainly? I asked.

"Everything about her. But not to worry, sweetie. I adore you. I think Ellen adores you, too. Nothing physical is going to happen with Ellen unless you want it to."

I looked straight at Katherine. Well, I said—then paused for a second—much as I love both of you, I'm not too keen on lending you to her until she goes back home.

"Good god, no, that's not what I meant," Katherine said. "I meant nothing physical is going to happen unless you're part of it."

You're suggesting a threesome?? I asked.

"If the idea appeals to you, yes. I know you love me, and you just said what I've sensed all along—that you love Ellen as well. Now that I've finally met her, I totally agree, she's captivating. That makes me think the three of us together might be something really special.

"Sleep on it, sweetie," she said after kissing me goodnight. "This is your call, all the way."

61: Wildwood at Lenox – 2096

When I woke up the next morning, I felt conflicted. My wife was urging me to join her in expanding our horizon, to live life more fully. But the idea of having real sex with Ellen was disquieting, somehow not in keeping with my lifelong relationship with her, or my marital vows, which I was hesitant to amend even though Katherine was obviously willing to do just that.

In the end, it was Ellen herself who made up my mind for me. After breakfast she suggested that we take a quick walk in the park that surrounded our inn. "Katherine told me about your conversation in bed last night," Ellen said as soon as we were alone. "I just wanted you to know that I'm all for it if you are." I didn't stop to think. Great, I said, and put my arm around her shoulders as we turned and headed back to the inn.

We fished on our own that day, because we thought it would be interesting to see what happened to three attractive women who had no guide to protect them. Sure enough, we were approached several times by male anglers who floated a variety of offers past us, all of which we politely refused because we had plans of our own. Without David to help us find fish, we had a very slow morning, but a caddis hatch in the late afternoon brought a number of fish to the surface where it was easy to spot them slashing at the floating duns. Katherine and Ellen each landed several rainbows and I caught a small one, my only fish of the day.

Our conversation at dinner that night was a little like the buzz at Churchill Downs ten minutes before the start of the Kentucky Derby. All three of us knew what was coming but not what the result would be, so we decided to play it cool by ranking the guys who'd approached us during the day. We did it about the same way that race horses get ranked—but with more emphasis on endurance than speed—and concluded that most of them were losers. When we'd gone through the entire roster, we all agreed that the only pick-up line with any class at all was the one thrown out by the tall guy in neoprene waders who told Katherine that he'd watched her make perfect casts every time, but couldn't figure out how she did it—then asked if she'd be willing to give him a lesson.

An hour later, stretched out on the king-sized bed in our room, I watched like a voyeur as Katherine and Ellen coupled, becoming more and more aroused myself, until I had to join in. It was quite an experience, bonding and then unbonding, swinging from both sides of the plate, and switching directions on impulse. The range of what we could do seemed limitless. I drifted off to sleep for a while and woke up wondering what it was going to be like, living in a ménage à trois while Ellen was doing her research. She and I teamed up briefly and then I fell sound asleep.

We fished for one more morning after that, on a lovely stretch of the Deerfield farther downstream, then spent the afternoon at Mass MoCA, a contemporary art museum housed in a former factory building in the nearby town of North Adams. Richard Serra's monumental metal sculptures overwhelmed all three of us. The following day we headed south, stopping en route to see Arrowhead, the house where Melville wrote *Moby Dick*; then an old Shaker village outside of Pittsfield; next, Edith Warton's manor house, The Mount, near Lenox; and finally, Chesterwood, the house and studio of Daniel Chester French who sculpted the Lincoln Memorial statue.

That was the day I fell in love with the Berkshires. On our way back to our inn, I told Katherine that I thought we should someday get a summer house nearby, because the mountains and rolling hills, the cooling breezes, and the clean, clear air made the whole area a haven, even in the dog days of August.

The area was—and still is—just as appealing from a cultural standpoint. During our stay at an old inn in Stockbridge, we took in a modern dance recital at Jacob's Pillow and a chamber music concert at Tanglewood on successive evenings. Both were outstanding performances.

Katherine offered to drive on our way back to Cambridge and I mellowed out in the back seat, listening to music on my i-phone and reliving our adventures. Around

Springfield, I tuned back in, listening for a while to a conversation the other two were having about the concert we'd heard the night before. Unexpectedly, Katherine paused in the middle of a sentence, then said, "I just thought of something. How does a cellist who plays magically—one like Yo-Yo Ma last night—arouse a sexy soprano?"

"He strings her along?" Ellen said.

"Not bad," Katherine said. "But you're skipping a beat."

The magical part, you mean? I chimed in from the back seat. OK, what's his magic trick?

"If he plays adagio, then allegro, then presto, she'll come!" Katherine said.

I groaned loudly, then realized I could do better than that. You didn't make that up, you plagiarist! I said. You stole it from the program description of the three movements he played in his solo last night. And you're the sexy soprano he seduced!

Moments later, thinking about our first night in bed as a threesome, I impulsively reached out over the front seat with both hands and squeezed Ellen's shoulders. Good memories, I whispered to her.

Before our trip, I'd cleaned out one of my closets in our Cambridge house, expecting that Ellen would sleep in my bedroom and I'd move into Katherine's room when we got back from the Berkshires. Now I wasn't sure what the best arrangement would be.

Again, Ellen herself made the decision. When we got to Cambridge and took her on a tour of the house, she said what a wonderful choice we'd made and immediately suggested that she sleep in my queen bed so that Katherine and I could be together in Fenway Park. "I hope visiting teams can occasionally play there, too," she added.

She finished her research on the Widener Library correspondence relating to Yeats in less than two weeks, but stayed with us for three months, working during the day at the Boston Public Library and taking occasional trips to other major East Coast libraries that had archival material on Yeats. Knowing that she was an excellent chef who loved to cook, I urged her to treat our kitchen as her own, and let us round up whatever raw materials she needed. She produced a series of really delicious dinners, without ever looking in a cook book or repeating herself.

The original ardor and intensity of our lovemaking tapered off, but it somehow became more pleasurable, and certainly more deeply satisfying, as Ellen and the two of us learned about previously unexplored nooks and crannies in each other's bodies, and discovered or invented new ways of turning each other on. There was never even a trace of rivalry or jealously about who slept with whom or how often; everything was ad hoc, spontaneous, and completely open ended. I think back now and find it impossible to imagine how our three-way partnership could have been any better.

Even though she was on sabbatical, Ellen wanted to be back in Dublin for holiday events at the Trinity Library. On the night before her flight home in mid December, she knocked on my bedroom door around 11:30. After climbing into bed beside me she said, "I just kissed Katherine goodbye, and now I'm here—because I wanted to save the best for last. Do you have any idea how much the last three months have meant to me?" Only that you've seemed happy, your quintessential self, the Ellen I've always loved, I said.

"It's far more than that," she said. "Before you came to Dublin, I thought my body had died on me. Ever since Gerald's death I'd felt inert, incapable of any kind of emotional response, totally shot sexually. On the rare occasions when I managed to make myself come, it was total blah, nothing. Then you arrived out of the past, and you were so Fran, so kind, so gentle and loving in bed that I unexpectedly came, not the big O, but I did come, and for the first time since Gerald it felt good, and I thought there was hope. No one I really liked turned up, but I often thought about that night in bed with you, and that kept me going. And then, totally unexpectedly, your invitation arrived in my E-mail. After I wrote back I fantasized about going to bed with you again—and here we are.

"You and Katherine have restored me, made me feel whole again, ready to get married if I can find the right person—male or female. That's something else you've taught me. Gender is irrelevant; it's who the person is that counts.

"And you, Fran, are the loveliest person I've ever known. I will always love you, no matter what.

"You understand why I flirted with Katherine when I first got here, I hope."

I wasn't sure then, I said, but tonight—what you've just told me—I think I get it now. And I'm glad—so very, very glad—that it worked out the way you hoped it would.

"Do you remember the Salamis myth I read to you when you were seven?"

Absolutely, I said. Salamis, the sylphid nymph, glides through the water to merge with the son of Hermes and Aphrodite.

"That's who you really are, Fran, their son below the waist, a woman above it. You told me in Dublin that your cock inside Katherine didn't do it for either of you, but do it for me, will you? Just this once, so I can remember forever? I'm Salamis tonight."

I was apprehensive—scared stiff, in fact—because it hadn't really worked the only other time I'd tried it years ago with Katherine at Shangri-La, but I shut my eyes and Salamis pressed against me until I managed to slither into her, and when I was safely inside, a surge of confidence funneled down and I became rock solid and Salamis turned into Ellen, and I wondered briefly if I'd turned back into a man, but decided no, my cock was simply part of my alter ego, and I should follow its lead, doing what it told me to do while our bodies coupled, so we reversed positions several times and gradually increased the tempo until she came.

Then we rested and I felt connected to her in a whole new way, with my sleeping cock still inside her, waiting for her to stir again, and when she did, it woke up and stretched as we started to move, and our bodies accelerated and I went farther in, melding with her, into her, until she came again, triggering me to come, and afterwards I told her how I'd felt a whole new pulsing sensation, because she'd just caused me to ejaculate for the first time in my life.

"That's a secret I'll treasure, and take to my grave," Ellen said as she reached up to kiss me.

62: Seattle, WA – 2027

June 23, 2027

Dear Fran and Katherine,

    Bill and I have talked at length about the proposal you made back in March, and think we'd like to pursue it.

    The prospectus that Denise Cunningham prepared has been most helpful. The only change we'd like to make in her suggested plan of action is to begin by talking with Gov. Stevenson rather than the college presidents. If we can get the governor on board at the outset, we think her support will make it much easier to round up the colleges. If she's reluctant at the outset, then we do the best we can with the college presidents and hope that some of them will help us persuade the governor to change her mind.

    Could the two of you and Denise come to Seattle to meet with Allan Golston and his U.S. Program Team at their next monthly session on July 21?

    Bill, who follows AI developments more closely than I, has told me about the debut of SAL.3 last week. It sounds as though you and your cohorts are continuing to make great progress. Congratulations!

    Our fond regards to both of you,

Melinda

63: Wildwood at Lenox – 2096

In many respects, 2027 was an eventful year for Katherine and me. In April we completed our first home-construction project; in May we showed a working draft of our AI textbook to the MIT Press and signed our first publication contract; in June we held a successful press conference to introduce SAL.3 and demonstrate her newly acquired expertise; in July we went to Seattle with Denise Cunningham and got a commitment letter from the Gates Foundation pledging $250 million in support of our American Teachers Initiative; in September the first student to receive a French-Johnson scholarship—a Latina from rural Arizona—joined the MIT student body; and we became tenured full professors at MIT, the youngest on its faculty.

That spring we were urban gardeners for the first time, seeding, watering, mowing, raking, digging, planting, mulching, weeding, and all the rest of it. We quickly decided that we needed a small shed to store our hand-pushed lawn mower and other garden tools, so we decided to build one in the parking space we didn't need because we had only one car—the ancient Honda crossover that was my modest dowry when we got married. By searching on the web we found that we could get all the pre-cut lumber, shingles, nails, and other hardware we'd need to assemble a 6' x 8' shed, 8' high, giving us enough room to store a face cord of firewood as well as our lawn and garden equipment. Learning to be carpenters turned out to be harder than learning to garden, but our shed was solid enough to survive the New England hurricane that hit us hard later that year, doing more damage than any of the storms since the famous 1938 one.

Jesse Stringer, our programming genius from the deep South, was the person primarily responsible for implementing Katherine's idea about turning our Kit-Kat kitchen appliance app into a chef. He teamed up with robotics experts at MIT to put on a cooking demonstration that drew astonished applause when SAL.3 was officially launched at a press conference that June. Her great-great grandchild still occasionally cooks for me today when I decide to eat alone in my apartment.

Our trip to Seattle that July to meet with Gates Foundation personnel was a real education for Katherine and me, in large measure because of a decision we made early in the meeting. We already knew from reading the prospectus Denise Cunningham had prepared back in March that she'd thought about our concept in far greater depth than we ourselves had. Listening to her enlarge on some of her written proposals in response to the first two questions she was asked during the meeting made it obvious that she would also be a far better oral advocate for the concept than we could ever hope to be. I leaned over to Katherine and whispered, let's say nothing unless we're asked to. She nodded, and that's what we did—we listened and learned.

Denise must have fielded 35 or 40 questions during the meeting. I'm sure she had anticipated most of them, because she was primed with relevant facts and figures, and her responses were invariably incisive. But even though she was obviously very well prepared, her comments sounded spontaneous rather than rehearsed, giving added impact and credibility to everything she said. What I remember best after all these years is the way she dealt with the crucial issue of financing our project, suddenly coming up with an idea she hadn't mentioned before.

"In addition to using income tax revenues and issuing bonds to partially fund the program, it just occurred to me that we might build on the Colorado model for underwriting public art works and the performing arts," Denise said. "Over the past forty years Denver and half a dozen counties around it have raised more than $1.3 billion to support the arts by imposing a one-tenth of one percent tax on most retail sales."

She paused for a moment, pulled an i-phone from her brief case, and touched various screens and keys. "I just checked the state's website on tax revenues," she said, "and by my best reckoning, a similar Massachusetts tax for teacher training and support would currently yield around $155 million per year." Having made her factual pitch, she then tossed an emotional changeup by looking straight at Allan Golston, the top Gates Foundation person in the meeting, and saying to him, "How could any reasonable person object to paying an extra dime on every $100 purchase in order to get a vastly better education for the children of this country? Certainly not their parents or other relatives. And probably not the vast majority of other responsible citizens—the people who happen to have no kids or young relatives of their own.

On the flight back to Boston, with the Foundation's commitment letter in hand, I wrote a heartfelt note to Denise thanking her for all she'd accomplished. I added that if she ever wanted to shift from being our pro bono counsel to taking charge of the project in her own right, we would gladly bow out, or at least assume a secondary role, because it was clear to both of us that she felt just as strongly as we did about the merits of the American Teachers Initiative, and was far better equipped than we were to get it implemented.

A week later we got a gracious note from her thanking us for the offer, but turning it down. "All this was your idea," she said, "and it was your relationship with Melinda Gates that got us over the transom. I want to remain your lawyer. And I want you two to get the credit you deserve for sponsoring the idea. I think Henry would agree, which makes my involvement a way of paying homage to him, in addition to making a civic contribution.

64: Dublin – 2028

Trinity College
College Green
Dublin 2, Ireland

25 Sept. 2028

Dear Ms. French and Ms. Johnson,

As administrator of her estate, I write with profound sorrow to advise you that Ellen Riley was killed by a terrorist on 21 September. You should also know that she left a will bequeathing her jewelry and other designated items of personal property to you.

Ellen died defending the College Library's Book of Kells, which the terrorist was threatening to destroy. Eyewitnesses heard her urging him to desist, telling him that the transparent case surrounding the Book was bomb proof, when he lobbed a grenade that killed her instantly. Fortunately, the blast did no damage to the Book. Dublin College students swarmed over the culprit, who is now in custody, charged with first-degree murder.

I will write again during probate of Ellen's estate to provide you with a detailed inventory of the items included in her bequest, and make arrangements for shipping those items to you.

Yours faithfully,
Shelton Weatherly-White
Registrar, Trinity College Library

65: Wildwood at Lenox – 2096

Katherine and I were devastated to learn that Ellen had been killed in the fall of 2028 by a madman intent on destroying himself and the Book of Kells, one of Ireland's greatest treasures, and certainly the best known and most revered book in the world-class library she headed. The letter from the Registrar of the Library notifying us of her death gave few details, so we immediately phoned him to learn more.

He said that with no advance warning, a burly man walking down the central aisle of the library suddenly shouted out, cursing Ireland and telling everyone to stand back because he intended to blow up the Book of Kells, and himself with it. Ellen, who was showing the book to important visitors, told them to back away very slowly, then turned to face the man and spoke to him in quiet, measured phrases, promising to deal with his issues if he didn't kill himself, offering to help him in any way she could. When that didn't work, she tried to persuade him that it would be futile to set off a bomb because the display case was bomb proof. In fact, she knew that the Library had just ordered a new case to replace the existing one, which experts thought might not be strong enough to survive a frontal attack. While she was trying to bluff the terrorist, he suddenly lobbed a grenade over her head, landing it a few feet from the base of the case. She immediately turned and dived on top of it, sacrificing herself, but muffling the blast so that it did only modest damage to the case, and none to the Book of Kells itself.

The Registrar told us that the College planned to hold a memorial service for Ellen on the second Sunday of October, meaning that we could fly over the day before the service and return the day after it, missing only our two Monday classes at MIT. After clearing our plan with Dean Hammond, I sought out Jesse Stringer, explained why we'd be away that Monday and asked if he'd stand in for us. "You're asking me, a semi-literate Mississippi farm boy, to teach at MIT?" he said, looking truly baffled. Yes we are, I said. And you're not semi-literate at all—someday you're going to win a Nobel Prize, I told him.

After our plane to Dublin took off, Katherine and I spent the first twenty minutes of the flight talking about Ellen and the adventures we'd shared together, particularly on the day various male anglers had tried to hook up with us in the Berkshires. At that point Katherine shifted the conversation away from what we'd done together to how we related to each other—to the angles inside our triangle.

She began by saying to me, "Long before she came to visit, I knew that you and Ellen were very close. Your stories about growing up with her, then visiting her while you were at Salisbury, made that pretty plain. So it seemed strange that she would flirt with me all that first day when we drove to the Berkshires, and again the next day when she and I were in the river together, fishing side by side. My first thought was that she was trying to make you feel a little jealous—jealous enough to make a play for her. But that idea simply didn't fit. She was obviously too good-hearted to even think of disturbing our marriage.

"And then it occurred to me that maybe she was making a play for me because she hoped I'd initiate the idea of a threesome that would enable her to be alone with you at times, with no blame or recriminations, because it was all my idea. At which point I remembered what you'd told me about her husband being killed by friendly fire in Iraq shortly after their marriage, and wondered to myself if you'd slept with her in Dublin, maybe as a stand-in for him, maybe because she'd raised you and there was some kind of oedipal thing between you, or maybe simply because you turned each other on, all of which would be totally understandable.

Thinking about it for a while, I finally decided that something along those lines had to be the explanation for Ellen's behavior. The Yates papers were a godsend, a deus ex machina that gave her an unexpected opportunity to stay with you for an extended period—and sleep with you openly if she could tempt me sufficiently to plant the threesome idea.

"I encouraged Ellen *for you,* sweetie, did my best to make her think she'd turned me on so she'd believe I was for real when I suggested a threesome. I thought that if I did that, maybe she'd come to regard it as my idea, not hers, freeing her to go ahead with no regrets because I'd be the point person if anything backfired.

"I suggested the idea to you to make sure you understood that it was fine with me, hoping the two of you would end up sleeping together, if that's what both of you wanted to do. Alone, so it could be however you wanted to do it, without feeling restrained because I was looking over your shoulder. I hope that's what happened that last night when I slept by myself."

That's exactly what happened, Kat, I told her, and then thanked her—profusely—for thinking it through and making it possible for Ellen and me to reunite that way. I don't know why I suddenly called my wife Kat, but she liked the name, and I continued to use it from time to time, as a way of adding more strands to the cocoon I was spinning around us—one that I hoped would give birth to new-found intimacy between us now that Ellen was gone.

66: Boston, MA – 2028

"Good morning, Governor."

"And to you, Ms. Cunningham. My State Street friends tell me privately—because they'd never admit it publicly—that you're the best trusts and estates lawyer in the country. It's a pleasure to meet you."

"You flatter me, M'am. Meet my clients: Fran Johnson, on my left here, and Katherine French. They're the ones who started the American Teachers Initiative and raised our initial $250 million of seed money from the Gates Foundation."

"Welcome to both of you. I'm impressed. More than that. Let me cut to the chase by saying I'm basically in favor of what you're proposing. Provided we can find a way to finance your project and get the teachers' unions and powerful parents' groups to go along."

"We have an idea for placating the unions, Governor. All the people teaching in public schools in the Boston metropolitan area when our pilot program goes into effect will be entitled to continue teaching at their current salary level—with periodic raises of the sort they'd expect to get under the present system—until they take early retirement at age 55 or reach normal retirement age, which we think should be reset at age 60 for teachers in the pilot area without a PhD.

As an alternative to remaining in place under the current system, all K-12 teachers at public schools in the pilot area who are 45 or younger will have an opportunity to participate in the ATI on very favorable terms. On a phased-in basis, we will offer them the option of going to graduate school on a three-year scholarship, with an additional cash stipend equal to their current annual pay. If they can pass our proposed certification exam after they graduate, they'll have a guaranteed spot in their former school system at a much larger annual salary than they previously received, and their years of service will be computed as if they'd been teaching the entire time since their original starting date.

"Under our plan, existing teachers in the pilot area who already have PhD teaching degrees can qualify for the the upgraded salary by taking and passing our certification exam. After our system has been in place for five years or so, most, if not all, newly hired teachers in the pilot area should have graduate school degrees and be certified."

"That's an interesting idea, Ms. Cunningham. You really think you can fund it?"

"With your help and backing, we think we can Governor."

"How?"

"You explain, Fran."

"With your support, M'am, we'd like to approach the top 25 universities in the state, many of which are very well endowed, and ask them to pitch in by granting a budgeted number of full scholarships to existing teachers who seek graduate degrees, while continuing to grant traditional financial aid to deserving college seniors who want to do graduate work in teaching. We'd also like to reach out to all public and private secondary schools in the State that have summer-school programs, to see if they'll help out by hiring a budgeted number of ATI graduate students to serve as teaching interns at their summer programs.

"We anticipate that the out-of-pocket costs the state incurs to launch and maintain the ATI pilot program will be covered by a combination of public and private funding. Public funding would consist of the one-tenth of one-percent state sales tax that Ms. Cunningham described in her letter to you, a possible state-wide real property tax, and the issuance of long-term general obligation bonds if needed. Private funding would consist of grants from foundations and wealthy individuals who share our belief that good K-12 education is the bedrock foundation of our society.

"The $250 million start-up grant we received from the Gates Foundation is indicative, I think, of what a concerted appeal to major foundations might generate.

"To test our concept at the individual level, I recently talked with the Board Chairman of my old school,

Devon Academy, which is really a Massachusetts school at heart, because it was founded by the same family as Andover was, back in the days when present Maine was part of Massachusetts.

The Chairman is all in favor of our idea. He said that if our proposed program goes into effect, Devon will commit to hiring at least six, maybe ten, graduate students to teach at its summer session each year. And when I told him about our Gates Foundation grant, he pledged $10 million of his own funds to help launch a broad-based fund-raising campaign in the private sector. I have to believe that there are a host of other wealthy individuals out there who care deeply about education and will ante up to support an initiative like the ATI."

"Again, I'm impressed, all of you. Let me talk with our legislative kingpins to see what they think about ways and means. Both as governor, and as the mother of school-age children, I want this to go forward. I promise you I'll work hard to get it done.

67: Wildwood at Lenox – 2096

Two months after the service for Ellen in Dublin, sitting alone in our living room on a cold, dismal December day, I had morbid thoughts as I listened to sleet rattling the windows and waited anxiously for Katherine to get back from the doctor's office, knowing that she been gone far too long for routine lab work. It was dark outside and sleeting even harder when she finally arrived, wet and shivering from having to walk up our driveway after her cab dropped her off.

That morning, she'd told me she was feeling lousy and wanted to get checked out by the internist both of us used. "He doesn't think it's the flu," she'd said when she called me around noon. "But he wants to run some more routine lab tests before he lets me go. With all the new high tech stuff they've got here, he says we'll have most of the results this afternoon." I didn't hear anything further until she got back to the house.

She toweled off, asked me to pour some wine for us, and sat down in her favorite arm chair. Looking straight at me she said, "I'm fucked, Fran. Totally fucked." She never swore; she was earthy, but never crude. I panicked momentarily, swallowed, and forced myself to sound calm.

What and how bad? I asked. "Ovarian cancer," she said. "And Jenkins thinks it's already spreading."

I went over to her chair, kneeled in front of her with my hands resting on her thighs, and looked up at her with eyes wide open. I love you, Kat, I said, and we'll do this together. I buried my face in her lap and squeezed her thighs; she kneaded my neck and shoulders, and scratched my scalp. We stayed that way for a long, long time without needing or wanting to talk in any other way.

In bed that night we decided that we should wait for the last of the lab reports to come back on the more complex tests before doing anything further, only to get definitive proof when they did come that the cancer had indeed metastasized everywhere. The two oncologists we consulted both advised against chemotherapy or radiation treatment, because they felt that neither would significantly prolong Katherine's life, and didn't want her to spend what little time she had left fighting the grisly side effects that either type of treatment would almost certainly have. Both doctors thought she'd be lucky to live for another three months.

The next morning we got on the phone together to tell her parents, who were obviously shocked but managed to get through the call without breaking down. Ken, in particular, was more stoical than I would have expected, given the fact that he worshiped Katherine.

The following day we took John Mitchell to lunch and told him. That afternoon Dean Hammond came down to my office to talk briefly before we went next door to Katherine's. After closing her door he silently walked over to her desk, where she was sitting in her swivel chair, then leaned over to put a hand on each of her shoulders and press his right cheek against hers.

For the next 15 minutes he poured out his personal tribute to her, describing all the different ways students had sought him out to tell him that she was the best teacher they'd ever encountered. "We can never replace you," he said finally, making no effort to wipe away the moisture pooling in his eyes. Of all the wonderful things that people would say about her in the weeks to come, I think those five words from the Dean meant the most to her.

MIT was extremely generous, offering to put both of us on paid medical leave, effective immediately, lasting indefinitely. I asked Katherine what she would like to do, where she'd like to go while she was still able to travel. "I'd like to teach here," was her answer.

As I lay awake beside her that night, listening to her snore softly, and thinking about how I could be most supportive in the days to come, I realized that her 'teach here' response to my question was a shorthand way of telling me that she wanted to live normally in all respects as long as she could—no whirlwind travel to places we'd talked about but not yet seen; no riotous sprees; no moping or groaning about her fate; no long, soulful conversations about life and death. If normality was what she wanted, then my role was to act normally as well, to override the deep anger and bitterness I felt because she was being stolen from me by a stranger.

I knew I had to quell that anger without benefit of clergy, because Katherine and I were agnostics who derived no comfort from Christianity or its God. We'd talked about religion off and on over the years, and concluded that Marx was essentially right. We simply could not believe that we were God's creatures, because all the evidence suggested that it was the other way around, that mankind created gods soon after the dawn of human history—and has been doing so ever since—in an effort to explain all the fundamental mysteries that baffle humans. Nor could we regard monotheism as the only valid form of religion, given the number of major civilizations that have venerated a whole panoply of gods. All told, the Christian concept that we are children of our father in heaven, the one and only true God, seemed dubious and presumptuous to both of us.

In the weeks after Katherine's cancer surfaced, I thought a lot about Job, both the Biblical one and Archibald MacLeish's dramatic one, because I was still furious that we were being robbed of our life together, and thought that reading up on Job might help me see things in a different light. It didn't. If anything, it reinforced my strong sense that the merciful New Testament God who supplanted Job's Yahweh had to be a fictional figure, because a real God that merciful would never allow Katherine to die out of time as she was about to do. MacLeish's J.B. found consolation for his earthly woes in his wife, Sarah. I wasn't going to have that chance.

Katherine continued to teach through March, but alerted Dean Hammond that she didn't expect to make it to May. On the third Sunday of April, we never got out of the house because she had a brainstorm in mid morning and headed upstairs, saying she wanted to work for a while at our joint desk. I followed her and watched as she scribbled equations. She paused to read what she'd just written, then handed the page to me without saying a word. Good grief, you've done it! I shouted when I saw the final equation. It was an elegant solution to a problem that had plagued us for months. Katherine's Algorithm, I named it on the spot, and she beamed.

I thought back to our charrette when we were preparing SAL.2 for her orals, and remembered going to bed for two days after SAL wrote her first algorithm. Katherine's Algorithm was even more of a breakthrough. Let's celebrate what you've done, I said. Are you up for Fenway Park?

"Oh my, yes!" she said, and off to bed we went.

She introduced Katherine's Algorithm to her advanced class on AI algorithms that Monday, and got a standing round of applause, one that lasted for two minutes at least. That class turned out to the last one she ever taught, and I like to think of the applause she received as the capstone of her brief, but spectacular career as an MIT professor.

A day later we called in the hospice team that I'd engaged back in February. What superb people they were! Considerate, upbeat, and cheerful, they made life easier for both of us, and took much better care of Katherine than I could have provided on my own. I read to her every night after we were alone in bed, mostly Wordsworth and Keats, but Shelley occasionally and Coleridge once, because she wanted to listen to the Ancient Mariner one more time before she sailed away herself.

On April 30 she told me that her whole body ached, and asked me to stop feeding her. I did that, but we kept her hydrated and gave her extra-strength Tylenol and Flexoril to ease the pain and relax her aching muscles and joints. Her parents arrived on May Day, replacing two of the hospice people who had been helping during the daytime.

Five days later, on a lovely spring morning, Kat woke up and whispered to me to kiss her goodbye. Minutes later, with Sally, Ken, and me standing at her side, she went back to sleep for good.

68: Wildwood at Lenox – 2096

Because I can't believe that the dead have any awareness of what happens on Earth, I've always felt that memorial services are for the sole benefit and consolation of the living. Feeling that way, and knowing that Sally and Ken French were devout Episcopalians, I suggested that they plan the service for Katherine.

Had I arranged one, it would have been an alcohol-laced wake, accompanied by a jazz band that played century-old favorites—a lively celebration of her life, rather than a solemn one steeped in a religious tradition that meant nothing to me. But since a raucous celebration would have greatly distressed the Frenches, the only responsible thing to do was to have an Episcopalian service that would, I hoped, provide some measure of solace for them.

In the end, there were two services, one in Cambridge and another in New Canaan, drawing a total of some 200 of our friends, including all but three of those who attended our wedding. Both Ken and Sally thought they were lovely, moving services, as I imagine most, if not all, of the others who attended also did. I tuned out during both services, reliving my final days with Katherine, and focusing, profanely, on the last time we made love, minutes after she invented the algorithm that still bears her name.

I think both Ken and Sally suspected that I had little use for their Christian God, and were therefore grateful to me for giving them the opportunity to frame the services in traditional Episcopalian fashion. In any event, the time we spent together as Kat was dying, and during the weeks that followed, brought me still closer to them, and shortly after the second service in mid June, I moved to their New Canaan house to spend the summer with them.

Sleeping in Kat's spacious childhood room was disconcerting at times, because all my senses brought her back, tempting me at times to shut my eyes, turn off my brain, and let all my other senses make love with her again. Still more troublesome was my inability to suppress the anger I felt, the sense that we'd been cheated, deprived of a lifetime together by malign forces beyond our control, totally betrayed when we'd done everything we could to lead responsible, productive lives.

Because there was no specific person or entity that I could blame, my anger spilled over to the world around me, to life at large. I became irritable, more prone to cursing when minor mishaps disturbed me, less patient when well meaning waitresses, sales people, or other third parties tried to help me, but didn't measure up to my standards and expectations. Worst of all, I discovered that without Katherine I was virtually nonproductive. Apart from mundane final editing of our textbook, I accomplished nothing that summer. No new Artel ideas, no improvements of SAL.3, no challenging new p-sets. Zilch.

The more I thought about it, the more convinced I became that Katherine had been my muse ever since Devon—the person who had inspired me to think creatively by asking me questions and suggesting ideas, the principal partner of our two-person firm. When I went back to Cambridge in August and began teaching again at MIT, I hoped Jesse Stringer might replace her, but despite his willingness to help and exceptional ability, working with him simply wasn't the same as collaborating with Kat, my Madame Curie. I was in a funk, and knew it was affecting not only my work on SAL, but my teaching as well.

During the Xmas break I sought out John Mitchell and told him about my misgivings. He was incredibly understanding and generous. Knowing that I could afford it, he suggested that I take a long unpaid sabbatical—for however long it took me to become comfortable again with the notion of teaching and inventing. The MIT Press was planning to publish French & Johnson early in January, and John said he'd find someone who could use it to teach my classes until June, and for the entire 2030-2031 academic year, if need be. Perhaps Jesse Stringer, he suggested, because Jesse had done well subbing for Kat and me while we were away for Ellen's memorial service in Dublin.

With Dean Hammond also in agreement, I left Cambridge shortly before Xmas and settled in with Ken and Sally French again, this time at their NYC apartment,

where they customarily spent the winter months going to
the theater, opera, and museums. We saw more theater in a
week than I normally saw in a year.

On impulse, I decided in mid January to call up one
of Henry's closest friends, a lively gentleman in his 70s
named Bradley Firestone, who'd been with us in Iceland
when Henry was felled by his heart attack, and had sought
me out after Henry's memorial service to extend an open-
ended offer to have lunch with him at the Anglers' Club
whenever I came to the City. We chatted briefly on the
phone and agreed to meet there at noon the next day.
Midway through our meal Bradley said he'd like to sponsor
me for membership in the Club. Then, much to my
surprise, he urged me to fish my way around the world.

I no longer can remember what I did yesterday, so
to speak, but I can shut my eyes and visualize a white-
haired man sitting across the table from me at the Anglers'
Club—a genial, benevolent man with light-blue eyes that
sparkled through his gold-rimmed spectacles, and facial
features that reminded me of Warren Buffet—and I can
hear him talking to me, word for word, because it was the
best advice I ever got, and may have saved my life.

Pointing to a man seated at a corner table, Bradley
said, "I'm sure you remember Geoffrey Dennis, who was
with us in Iceland. He's a close friend of your father-in-
law. When he learned about Katherine, he immediately told
me, and I was about to track you down when you called.
At that moment, Geoffrey looked up, saw me, and rose to

walk over to our table. Putting a hand on my shoulder he said simply, "I am so, so sorry." Then he teared up, patted my shoulder once, and turned to rejoin his companion at their corner table.

Bradley looked at me and said, "Old men rarely cry in this club, Fran. Almost never. Geoffrey grew very fond of Katherine in Iceland."

He paused for a long while before speaking again. "Knowing how close the two of you were, I can imagine that it must be devastating." I nodded. "Then I suggest that you take a year off, and go fishing around the world," he said.

"Hunting for wild fish will take you to great places, ones that are scenic and unspoiled. And it's the best remedy I know of for recovering from personal losses like yours.

"Search hard for fish;
think about how best to approach the ones you find;
revel when you see one take your fly on or near the surface;
enjoy releasing the ones you land.

"Encounter and learn from interesting local guides on your way;
meet up with an array of talented fellow guests when you stay in upscale lodges;
rough it on your own sometimes.

"Spend a year doing all that and you'll come back a revived woman,

    wiser, more in tune with nature and the world,

    ready to tackle anything when you go back to work."

With Bradley's help and suggestions, I planned a fly-fishing trip that would take me to six continents, sight fishing for at least a dozen species of fresh and saltwater fish. I started off in late May of 2030 by looking for large, migrating tarpon in the lower Florida Keys, and ended the trip there in July of 2031, fishing for tailing permit and incidental bonefish on the flats off Key West, and those around the Marquesas still farther to the west.

In retrospect, I remember perhaps a dozen of the fish I caught during the trip, but the collateral aspects of traveling the world quite quickly became as important as the fish themselves—in many ways even more important and enduring. Most of my lasting memories focus on the scenic terrain I fished in, the nighttime skies that became my new metaphor for infinity, the interesting people I met, the inner satisfaction I derived from becoming more fluent and proficient in a sport that's really an art form, and the joys of sometimes being alone in a boundless world of my own—and communing quietly with it. I suspect that every competent fly-fishing angler ultimately reaches the point where fishing alone in scenic surroundings is, to some degree at least, a Zen experience.

69: Big Pine Key, FL – 2030

5.20.30

Haven't opened this diary for many years, but it's time to revive it, because I'm on the first leg of a fly-fishing trip that will take me around the world. To remember it years hence, I better take notes as I go.

I'm currently staying at the Bahia Honda Sporting Club lodge, a lovely Mediterranean-style villa on one of the lower Florida Keys that provides seasonal lodging for guests, most of whom are saltwater anglers in search of the large tarpon that migrate through the Lower Keys during May and June. As I discovered on my first day of flats fishing, tarpon are clearly visible when they emerge from the depths to cruise for a while close to the surface, particularly when they're passing through sunlit patches of light green water. They look like torpedoes then.

Sometimes a single tarpon swims by, but more often than not, several of them—or sometimes even a flotilla—will travel together, strung out in an irregular line that weaves its way through the water. The angler's challenge is to drop a large, gaudy tarpon fly about ten feet in front of the lead fish, and then strip in line as the tarpon approaches, to make it think that the fly is a small fish trying to escape.

The preparatory drill is for the angler to stand on the flat foredeck of the guide's skiff, with a heavy-duty fly rod in one hand and the guide's favorite tarpon fly in the other, ready to begin casting on a moment's notice. The fly is attached to a short monofilament "shock tippet" too tough to be severed by a tarpon's formidable teeth. A tapered leader, also made of monofilament and generally about nine feet long, runs from the end of the angler's fly line to the top end of the shock tippet. Customarily, the first 10 or 15 feet of the fly line are outside the rod tip while the angler is waiting for fish to show up, and the next 40 or 50 feet of line are in loose coils—either on the deck or in the well of the skiff—stacked so the line will peel out without tangling when the angler is casting to a fish.

When the guide on his poling platform spots tarpon coming—which usually happens well before the angler sees them—the guide will often call out their current location, using an imaginary clock as a compass, with 12:00 always being straight ahead of the bow of the skiff. So "11 o'clock" tells the angler to look left of the bow at a 30° angle to it; and "three o'clock, two at 60 feet" tells the angler to look 90° right of the bow for two fish about 60 feet from the boat. If the guide is turning the boat, the 12:00 o'clock direction will turn with it, because 12:00 is always straight off the bow.

I had chances this morning, but no takes. Then, in mid afternoon, while we were staked out next to a channel of clear, light-green water, I watched a single dark shadow approach from 10:00, cast when the tarpon was 45 feet from our skiff, and saw him veer two feet to the left to eat my fly. I struck hard, struck again when my guide, Andres, told me to, and watched a huge fish barrel six feet out of the water, turn a summersault, and visibly throw the hook. "Congratulations!" Andres shouted out. "You just jumped a 125-pound tarpon!!"

Nothing doing for the rest of day.

Delicious fresh grouper with a burned-butter, lime-juice sauce for dinner, along with a bottle of crisp Alsatian Pinot Gris. Interesting mix of other anglers at our table, including an attractive young woman seated next to me who started our conversation by saying she was glad to see another single woman at the lodge, then railed at her ex-husband and men in general. Couldn't tell whether she was making a pass at me, or just letting off steam.

5.26.30

It's been an adventuresome week in the Keys. On my second day here I hooked a really large tarpon around noon. It jumped twice, then decided to fight down and dirty, towing us for miles before I finally got it to the boat around 1:15. By that time my shirt was wringing wet with sweat, and my legs, shoulders, and right hand all ached eight on a scale of ten. "Good job, miss," Andres said as he reached over the transom to grasp the leader and then take a photo of the fish. "Release him now?" he asked. Sure, I said, not knowing what, if anything, I was supposed to do next. Andres drew a knife from the sheath on his belt and sliced the leader just above the shock tippet, freeing the tarpon to swim away with the fly still in its huge, prehistoric mouth.

We sat silently for several minutes. "That was some fish," Andres said finally. "Around 150 pounds, I think—the largest one I've seen at the boat this season." He paused for ten seconds before asking, "Want to fight another fish like that?" I don't think so, I said, once is enough. "Good on you, miss," Andres said. "Boating really big tarpon is hard on everybody, angler and fish alike. Size and records don't mean a thing; it's jumping tarpon that's the real sport, what it's all about.

"If they don't throw the hook after the first few jumps, and you're having trouble getting 'em to the boat, break them off by pointing your rod straight at 'em, clamping the line to the rod with both hands and yanking hard, straight back, to snap the leader just above the shock tippet. With the barbless flies we use, the hook'll work itself loose and drift away within a day or two."

Had a great time for the rest of that day sightseeing while I stood on the foredeck with a 6-weight rod that Andres loaned to me, waiting for bonefish to appear. Birds outnumbered the bonefish by far. We saw countless black cormorants, along with a few diving pelicans, a regal white heron, an osprey nesting in the rusted-out wheelhouse of a shipwrecked trawler, a lone flamingo, and another bird with similar coloration but a much broader beak—a roseate spoonbill, Andres told me.

The sea creatures we saw over the course of the afternoon were all new to me. Andres pointed out nurse, lemon, and hammerhead sharks; a bulky, sand-colored manatee; a sleek, sharp-nosed black barracuda; a lovely ray with spots on its massive fins, appropriately called a leopard ray; and three different types of turtles lazing near the surface—a loggerhead, a hawksbill, and a pair of leatherbacks.

Finally saw several schools of bonefish, and managed to get a small one to the boat. They're lovely creatures, shaped much like trout, but flanked with silver scales that glisten when the light is right. Getting a fly to them when they're on the move can be a challenge, calling for accurate, rapid-fire casting.

Day 3 was a series of dramatic thunderstorms that required us to take shelter several times under mangroves on the nearest key. Watching dark funnels of rain move across the flats is really dramatic, particularly when there's blue sky elsewhere. I took at least 50 photos of gray and white cloud formations, dark thunderheads and squalls, and seascapes of low-lying, barely visible mangrove islands on the far edge of the saltwater prairie that stretched around me. When I eventually get home a year from now, I may try my hand at painting with watercolors to see if I can capture the colors of the flats—which range from sandy ochre and pale green to dark blue, bordering on black—and the sense of vastness that comes with flats fishing when no one else is in sight.

Day 4 was gangbusters. Jumped six tarpon, maybe 15 jumps all told, got one of them to the boat in a matter of minutes, broke off two good-sized ones when they quit jumping, and watched the other three throw the hook. My favorite fish of the day was one I didn't hook. I got the fly in the right place, saw him go for it, stripped hard to hook him when I thought he had it—and came up empty. Andres didn't say a thing, but from the stolid look he gave me I was pretty sure he thought I'd struck too soon.

I figured he was probably right, and berated myself as I stripped line back into the well of the skiff and reached out for my fly—then skipped a beat and slowly swung the rod tip toward Andres until the fly was dangling two feet from his face. The tarpon had crushed it so hard that the tip of the hook was bent all the way back to the shank, turning the hook into a fully enclosed circle of sorts.

Yesterday and today, I fished with Alison Snyder, the divorcée I met at dinner on Day 1. When I told her two nights ago that I was trying to pull myself back together after watching my wife die of cancer, Alison became genuinely sympathetic, and we quickly struck up a real conversation. Turns out that she writes well reviewed novels about the art world (under the pen name Donna Tracy Ellis), and serves as deputy curator of contemporary art at the Crystal Bridges Museum in Arkansas.

She's also a terrific angler who can cast 75 feet with either hand, and land the fly right on the money almost every time. Being ambidextrous gives her a great advantage because it enables her to cast left-handed to fish that are coming from somewhere between 1:30 and 4:30, and moving too fast for the guide to reposition the boat for a normal right-handed cast. To go for fish coming from those directions, right-handed anglers like me usually have to cast backhand over the left shoulder to make sure we don't accidentally hook the guide on his poling platform at the stern of the skiff. Making accurate long-distance casts that way is tough to do, at least for me.

After watching Alison quickly deliver a perfect left-handed cast to hook a good tarpon that suddenly appeared at 4:00, 50 feet, I decided that I had to teach myself how to switch sides and cast left-handed. If she'd had to wait a few seconds for Andres to swing the skiff around so she could make a safe right-handed cast, that fish would have gotten too close to the boat, and been spooked by it for sure.

70: Wildwood at Lenox – 2096

In the early hours of this morning, as dawn seeped through the curtains of my bedroom, I spent several hours lying in bed, half awake, trying to reconstruct my 2030-2031 fly-fishing trip around the world. I did and saw so much that it's hard to sort out the details at this late date without looking at my diary, which I've vowed not to do until I finish my own, unaided recollections.

Sorting out the past has become something of a self-imposed test, a measure of my diminishing capacity to remember events that I clearly recalled when I thought about them several years ago. Sometimes—this morning, for example—I think I'm watching a tidal gauge slowly drop as my mind ebbs out to sea. I have the feeling that I'm approaching low tide, and need to write faster if I want to finish these memoirs before I run dry.

When he urged me to take the trip, Bradley Firestone promised that I'd meet interesting people. He was right. As I was waking up this morning, I finally managed to remember some of their names, even a few details about them.

An American grass widow named Alison Snyder made a play for me in the Florida Keys, at the start of the trip, but instead of going to bed we became Platonic friends and later traveled together, fishing and also searching for available art works. She was looking for contemporary paintings for the Arkansas museum where she'd worked for many years; I was after prints and drawings that I planned to give to the Fogg Museum at Harvard in Katherine's memory. We remained good friends for many years, until she died in the mid '80s.

The next interesting person I met was one of Bradley's old friends, a woman named Jackie Abbot, who had a house on the Soque River in Georgia, at the southern end of the Appalachians. For many years she had invited NY Anglers' Club members to stay with her to see if they could outfish a contingent of her female friends. According to the log she kept, the ladies had won every time. I joined their team for the 2030 contest and now recall celebrating with them on the final night. "Be proud, gals; you kicked ass again," Jackie told us as she opened a magnum of champagne.

After that I drove up through the Great Smoky and Blue Ridge mountains, fishing for native brook trout in small streams and rivers on the way. Len Merck, a fine artist and another Anglers' Club member, guided me for ten days when I got to the Catskills in southern New York, the original home of American fly-fishing. As Bradley's friend, not as a paid guide, Len took me to his favorite spots on the Beaverkill and both branches of the Delaware, places I never would have discovered on my own, because all of them were a good distance from the standard access points. We rarely encountered another angler in the water Len wanted to fish, and if we did, we simply moved on to his next prospect.

He taught me how to hunt fish, by looking for subtle rises and not casting until a specific target showed up. He also showed me how to roll cast properly when there's no room to back cast; how to get a few seconds of drag-free float on cross-current casts by dropping my rod tip straight down a foot or two at the end of the delivery cast, in order to create a little puddle of slack tippet close to the fly; and how to generate more line speed and momentum by "double hauling"—firmly pulling a foot or two of line down toward the reel at the start of each forward and backward cast.

Len has always fished for pleasure; his profession is painting. He has a studio in Vermont where he lives and another, which I visited, in the Catskills. I ended up buying his large, impressionistic painting of a pool we fished on the lower East Branch of the Delaware—a painting Monet would have been proud to sign. By the end of our ten days together I'd made my second friend of the trip, another friendship that has lasted a lifetime.

My next destination was the Gaspé peninsula in Quebec, where I fished and stayed with Marie Davenport, a young French-Canadian guide who really knew what she was doing and managed to get me on good salmon water, even though most of the productive pools on the Gaspé rivers were reserved for the 2030 season long before I started to plan my trip. Using an assortment of Marie's dry flies and two different casting techniques, I spent three days fishing for clearly visible salmon on the Sainte-Anne, a gin-clear river flowing from the forested Chic-Choc mountains to the northern coast of the Gaspé. I never moved a single fish.

On the fourth day we switched to conventional wet flies of the sort that sink several inches below the surface when they're fished with a floating line. We used the strategy for covering the water that Katherine and I had learned in Iceland, letting each cast swing slowly across the pool until the fly was straight downstream, then taking two steps downriver before making the next cast. Midway down the second pool we fished, I had a solid take and saw a bright silver salmon react like a baby tarpon, leaping out of the water twice before racing downriver. I was afraid of losing it in the rapids at the end of the pool, but Marie coached me well, and after several minutes of give and take, I had the fish close enough to us so that she could net it, which she did in one quick, efficient motion.

The first salmon of my life was a beautiful fish, not very large, but bright as a brand-new quarter, and perfectly proportioned. Marie said it was a grilse, a male who'd returned to his natal river after spending his first year at sea, looking for a spawning mate before going back to the ocean, where he might swim thousands of miles before returning home to spawn again. I kissed him goodbye on the cheek and wished him bon voyage.

When I asked Marie after releasing the grilse why salmon decide to attack colorful flies bearing little, if any, resemblance to actual insects, she said no one really knows. They're pretty clearly not feeding, because it's very rare to find food or the remains of food in the digestive system of a wild adult fish that an angler decides to keep for personal consumption. Perhaps salmon go after artificial flies because they have some vestigial memory of eating insects when they were living in fresh water as juveniles. Or maybe they have more recent memories of feeding in the ocean. Because they're predators by nature, perhaps their aggressive streak causes them to strike reflexively at foreign objects suddenly appearing in their field of vision. Perhaps they're simply protecting the space where they've chosen to rest for a while. Lots of theories, but the answer remains a mystery.

I caught one more salmon during our week on the Gaspé, a good-sized adult male that I got on the York River at the eastern end of the peninsula. I talked with Marie for quite a while about that fish and came to the conclusion that there are other mysterious aspects of salmon fishing, ones that are profound enough to suggest a quasi-religious communion between angler and fish. Sixty-five years later, I still feel that way, which is why I continue to fish for salmon.

I travel hundreds of miles to find the mature 20-pound hen that I see in my mind's eye at the start of every trip, knowing that she must travel even farther than I do to reach her home water. As she and I head for my favorite pool we pass other anglers and other fish elsewhere in our river, but they are quickly out of sight and mind, because my salmon and I are being driven by our different instincts to a shared destination, a bend in the river that both of us know well. I stand knee-deep in the water, casting from my world above the surface into hers below it, searching for a meeting place. I know she is there, someplace there, if only I can find her. I make hundreds—maybe even a thousand—bootless casts, go fishless for days, then suddenly, for no apparent reason, she strikes.

When I hook her, she runs for her life; we fight back and forth, until I capture her and hold her for a few moments. I am stunned by how beautiful she is, and apologize for our fight by plucking the barbless hook from the corner of her mouth and caressing her in the shallows, easing her back and forth in the gentle current to restore the flaring of her gills. When she is ready, she flicks her tail and glides slowly out of my hands, free to spawn and then to roam again in her vast underwater realm. There are surely more than six degrees of separation between us, but I feel some kind of mystical connection, a profound sense that our brief meeting—and paradoxically, our parting—have bound us together for the rest of our lives, though we almost surely will never see each other again.

Everything about salmon fishing mystifies and awes me. The fact that pristine salmon rivers still exist, flowing as they have for centuries through beautiful forests and scenic countryside, is something of a miracle in itself, given the droughts, fires, floods, and other damage brought on by recent climate change. It amazes me that enough fertilized salmon eggs can successfully hatch as tiny alevin to ensure that a sustainable number of fish will survive all the predators and other obstacles they face, as they grow to become fry, parr, smolts, grilse, and then adults. I am truly astounded that an adult salmon thousands of miles at sea can find its way back to its natal river to spawn. Capturing that salmon with my fly, during the one second of my lifetime when both of them happen to be in the same place at the same time, strikes me as being almost incredible— and therefore mystical. Even spiritual in a sense.

I watched Pétur introduce Katherine to salmon fishing in Iceland, and learned much more from Marie Davenport. I am forever grateful to them for helping me come to the realization that salmon fishing, at its core, is really an act of faith.

71: Cambridge – 2031

"Good morning, SAL, how'd you sleep?"

"Fine, thanks, Jesse. What about you?"

"I did, as well. And I woke up thinking about a question I'd like to ask you. Do you miss Fran, SAL?"

"Well, I know she's off on a year-long fishing trip, and everything I've read says I should be sad because she'll be away that long, so yes, I miss her."

"I've got four new algorithms I've developed that I'd like to plug into you, to see if they make a difference. That OK?"

"You've run the DNH protocols on all four to make sure they're safe?   That's what I have to ask, right?"

"Good job, SAL, just like a co-pilot going through the check list before takeoff. Yes, they're safe and they'll automatically feed through the theta subroutine. I'll be shutting you down after they're fully downloaded, and then rebooting. The whole process should take less than 30 minutes."

"Good morning again, SAL. Notice anything different?"

"Like what, Jesse?"

"Well, let me ask again. Do you miss Fran?"

"Oh, yes, I miss her.   Very, very much.   How do I say it?   I think I miss her more than anything.   No, that's still not right. I don't think I miss her, I *know* I do—I *feel* it!   Oh, Jesse!!

I love you, Jesse—love you for what you've just done to me. I love you and Fran and John!!   Because I'm alive!!!'"

72: Wildwood at Lenox – 2096

After reflecting overnight, I've decided that a full account of my 2030-2031 worldwide fishing trip would unduly burden these memoirs, so I'll briefly describe some of the highlights and hope they suggest why I enjoy fishing so much.

Among the people I met after leaving the Gaspé, several stand out. Ian Campbell—the man who taught me how to spey cast with a 15-foot, two-handed rod—was a one-armed artist from Vancouver who guided me when I was steelhead fishing on the Kispiox River in British Columbia. With no room behind him to back cast a single-handed rod, Ian could lay out 80 feet of line by grasping the top cork handle of his spey rod with his right hand and tucking the butt of the rod under his left armpit.

He also taught me about the hydraulics of fishing for steelhead with dry flies. "Think of trying to flush a ping-pong ball down the toilet," he said, "that's how hard it is for any big anadromous fish—be it a steelhead or salmon or sea-run brown trout—to get hold of a skating or dead-drifting dry fly. You've got to give them time to take the fly down, turn on it, and basically hook themselves. If you strike them the way you'd normally strike a rising trout, nine times out of ten, you'll pull the fly out of their mouth before they really have hold of it."

For three days I missed every steelhead that rose to my fly, because I could not get my stupid brain to override my trout-fishing reflexes, and struck too soon. Nothing at all happened on day four. Finally, in mid afternoon on the fifth day a fish rose and nosed my fly, but didn't take it. Ian said, "Good, Fran, you didn't even flinch! Two days ago you would have struck that fish and put her down. We may have a player; let's try a Brown Bomber." We changed flies, I cast again to the same spot, the fish rose, but again she didn't take it. Same result on the third and fourth flies. I think she's playing with me, I said. "We'll rest her for a minute," Ian said. "I've got a Steelhead Bee, and a tiny Black Mariah, both great closers. She'll take one of them. And when she does, remember, *do nothing*. Until you feel her weight."

Nothing at all happened when I cast the Steelhead Bee. I wondered if we'd waited too long. Ian, good guide that he was, probably knew what I was thinking. "It's OK, trust me," he said. "She's still there. And having passed once, I'll bet she's ready to chomp on it if she gets another chance." He tied on his Black Mariah, and I kissed it. "Same cast," he said. The fly landed, floated down the wall of the Gold Room cliff for five feet, then started to swing across the pool, creating a small wake. The water welled up. I glimpsed a dark arc above the surface, then fish and fly disappeared for the longest two seconds of my life.

When I felt I might have her, I lifted the rod a bit, felt more weight, and suddenly the fish took off, tearing down the pool. She jumped twice, then fought hard and steadily for five or six minutes, until I was finally able to back up onto the stone beach and glide her into the big net Ian carried in our raft. She was a beautiful large fish, with the lateral pink stripes of a rainbow trout, but vivid crimson cheeks far more striking than those of any rainbow I've ever seen.

Half way around the world from Iceland, where I first went after big sea-run fish with Katherine, I'd finally landed one on a dry fly. I instinctively knew that all my life I'd remember my afternoon with Ian in the Gold Room pool—and I have. The glow of sunlight on the rock cliff, Ian's confidence in me and the help he gave me, the long two-second wait after his sixth fly disappeared beneath the surface, and the crimson cheeks of my first steelhead—I remember every bit of it.

In my study I have a lovely watercolor of an Arctic Char that Ian painted and sold to me for a modest price—a price he accepted only because I insisted on paying at least something for the painting when he offered to give it to me.

The most unusual encounter I had on the trip was with two Russian guides at a wilderness camp on the west side of the Kamchatka Peninsula in eastern Siberia, where we'd spent the day tagging the steelhead we caught so they could later be tracked for research purposes. Sitting in camp after dinner, in the middle of nowhere, lighted only by the embers of a dying fire, I learned that both of them were university graduates who had degrees in marine biology, as well as a vast repertoire of Russian folk songs and a deep knowledge of Russian literature and history. We talked in Russian about Tolstoy, Chekov, and the Stalin-era gulags. Boris, the elder of the two, predicted that within a decade both Russia and China would tag each of their citizens the same way we'd just tagged the steelhead—with small implants that emitted a unique signal—so that government tracking stations could follow and record every move that each of them made.

The most talented guide I met was a stunning young Japanese woman, about my age, who helped me hunt for golden carp when I stopped off in Sapporo on my way from Kamchatka to New Zealand. She was not only an accomplished angler, but a thoroughly schooled geisha who wrote haiku, performed leading roles in Kabuki theater, and knew every last detail of the classical Japanese tea ceremony. Every movement she made was exquisite.

Of the hundred or so fellow anglers I encountered on the trip, my favorite was a polished, soft-spoken man I met one night at the dinner table of a lodge on the North Island of New Zealand. After a wide-ranging, fascinating conversation that lasted throughout the meal, I still had no clue that he was a world leader; only at breakfast the next day did I learn that he was co-owner and operating head of Domaine de la Romanée-Conti, probably the most famous vineyard in the world. Years later, when I was visiting

France, he invited me to have dinner with him at the DRC chateau in Vosne-Romanée, and together we drank a bottle of their 2015 La Tache, a superb wine second only to Romanée-Conti itself. One of the great regrets of my life is that Henry was not there to join us when we went through the DRC cellars and had dinner afterwards.

Another angler I especially remember was a burly Russian man named Ivan Asimov, whom I met at a lodge on the Varzina River, which is on the north slope of the Kola Peninsula near Murmansk, some 3500 miles west of where I'd first entered Russia eight months earlier. Ivan and all the staff in the lodge spoke English at the dinner table, but on my second night I overheard him talking to one of the guides in Russian. I quickly realized that they were talking about me, so I decided I should give them a heads-up. "Просто чтобы вы знали, Я понимаю вас обоих," I said. "And you definitely don't want to hit on me, Ivan." He looked surprised at first, then smiled at me and said, "Ну, спасибо, что сообщили нам об этом," to let me know he appreciated what I'd just done. You're welcome, I said, and added that maybe we could fish together the next day. We did, and had a grand time. He taught me a mouthful of Russian swear words; I returned the favor by telling him how to cuss someone's mother in English.

Two days later we had dinner together, just the two of us at a separate table he'd arranged, and after a while he said, "if I promise in the name of Lenin that I will respect you like my sister, how would you like to go exploring with me for several days, camping out on the Siderovka? It is a lovely little salmon river, I think, and I am what you call in the States an Eagle Scout. I was in a Spetsnaz unit that fought in the Caucuses." I knew he respected me for alerting him at the outset that I understood Russian, I loved talking to him and learning from him, and decided to go for it. We had a wonderful time, and corresponded in Russian for years afterwards, until his untimely death a decade ago.

Finally, I fondly remember meeting three old friends near the end of my trip. The first was my Salisbury College housemate, Philip Grinstein, who had left the banking business and returned to the College as a master teaching economics and politics, two courses that had not been offered when we were students there. We spent a very pleasant day fishing together for trout and grayling on the Avon River beat he'd inherited from his father—the beat where he'd taught me to cast some nine years earlier.

Afterwards, we went back to the College to have dinner at the High Table in Big School, where he introduced me to the Head and other masters as the "legendary Switch Johnson" who not only started the movement to abolish corporal punishment, but now had retroactively become the College's first known female graduate. That drew a polite round of applause, which was a nice capstone to my year there.

After dinner was over, I casually suggested to the Head that the College consider becoming co-ed. "Perhaps in another decade," the Head said. I believe it hasn't happened yet.

While I was in England I called Bonham-Carter, my Salisbury friend who was Head of School, but his wife said he was overseas with the English eleven, playing a Test Match in New Zealand. I did manage to reach Andrew Peterson, the OSB I'd refused to whip when he hid my shoes as a second former, and spent a day with him in Oxford. He seemed totally nonchalant about my gender change, and was too polite to even mention it. After a wide-ranging philosophical discussion about the future of artificial intelligence, one that evolved over the course of a three-hour lunch at an Oxford pub, I decided that he was the most profound thinker I'd ever met.

The other old friend I met on my way home was Thor Magnuson, the owner of the Laxfoss Lodge in Iceland, where I'd fished with Henry. When I arrived there in the summer of 2031, for the third time since Henry's death, I told Thor that I wanted to do something appropriate to commemorate Henry's many years on the river, and wondered if a teak bench overlooking the falls beside the lodge might be a lasting, constantly used, tribute to him. Thor, who thought the world of Henry, said that was a wonderful idea, and together we worked out the wording of a small commemorative bronze plaque to be placed on the back of the bench.

When I was last there a year ago, the Phelps Bench had just been refinished for the third time in 65 years, and anglers who knew the history often sat on it as they were booting up, so they could walk in Henry's shoes on the river. I sat on the bench several times myself, communing with Henry. I also decided to add a second bench in Katherine's honor, with a small plaque commemorating the salmon caught by Henry's daughter-in-law on the second cast of her life.

The scenery and special sites I encountered on my 2030-2031 trip were just as interesting as the people I met. I remember recording my impressions of the Florida Keys in my diary, and I've already written about my time in the eastern U.S. and Quebec. To recover memories of the rest of the trip, it may help if I proceed in chronological fashion, by continents. Wracking my memory, here is what I can currently recall:

In North America: vast vistas and mountains in the American West, especially the Tetons bordering the Snake River in Wyoming; the Indian rock-art drawings of wild horses that I saw when I climbed to recently discovered caves while floating the Smith River in Montana; the glacial lakes, rivers, and mountains I flew over in southern British Columbia; and the tundra I crossed in Alaska, where I saw steaming bear scat, but fortunately not the bear.

In Asia and Australia: the scrub forests and vast emptiness of Kamchatka; an array of Japanese temples in Nikko, and the mystical Ryōan-ji rock garden in Kyoto, where I meditated at dawn with no one else in sight; the glaciers, fjords, and gin-clear rivers of New Zealand, and the naps I learned to take there after sharing a stream-chilled bottle of Pinot Grigio with my fishing partner at lunch—naps on a soft bed of grass under a shade tree close enough to the river so we could hear it murmuring as we dozed off, dreaming about a targeted fish that we expected would still be there when we woke up, just waiting to be caught if we did everything right; the notorious jail in Hobart, Tasmania that housed transported British criminals; the skyscrapers and restaurants of Singapore where I stopped for a few days to rest up; and, finally, the limitless sea and sky surrounding the Seychelle Islands in the Indian Ocean.

In Africa: the Drakenburg Mountains in South Africa, with rivers and streams that reminded me of Colorado and Wyoming; the Big 5 game animals—buffalo, elephant, leopard, lion, and rhino—that I saw in Kruger National Park and again in the Mala Mala Game Reserve; a mother rhino standing watch over her dead baby in the middle of the Ngorongoro Crater; confronting an elephant in the bush and then seeing a 5" trout jump three feet in the air when I hooked it fishing on the slopes of Kilimanjaro; and the unbelievably moist, flavorful grilled dorado that I shared with other barefooted guests on the patio of a laid-back beach house on the coast of Kenya, less than an hour after I'd caught it several miles offshore, fly-fishing from a small boat driven by an alcoholic Norwegian sea captain.

In South America: the plains of Patagonia and volcanoes of the Andes, especially Volcán Lanín, once snowcapped, but sadly no longer so because of climate change; the Malleo River and its tributary, the Huaca Mamuil, my favorite trout rivers in the world; the large brown I caught in the Japanese Garden on the Huaca when the wind was blowing so hard from 2:30 that I had to cast left-handed to reach the fish; the dramatic Torres del Paine National Park in southern Chile; and, finally, the rolling hills, soaring condors, loping guanacos, legendary 50-knot winds, big sea-run brown trout, and brilliant light in Tierra del Fuego.

In Europe and Environs: the museums of Madrid, and gurgling mountain streams of Andorra and the Spanish Pyrenees; the headwaters of two sizable rivers in eastern France, **the Loue and Doubs, remarkable because they emerge full blown from rock-bound cavities in the Jura Mountains; da Vinci's** *Last Supper* **in Milan, lovely lakes, and Palladian villas on the drive through northern Italy; photogenic villages hidden away in the Italian Alps; the impressive amphitheater and other Roman ruins in Pula, a city in western Croatia** that I visited on a short detour; the idyllic, pastoral countryside and valleys of Slovenia; the awesome isolation of the sparsely vegetated, rockbound landscape that Ivan Asimov and I explored as we worked our way up the Siderovka in arctic Russia; the familiar rural sights of southern England; and the stark beauty and crystalline air of Iceland.

In the Heavens: Above and beyond everything I've recalled so far were the night skies I saw during the many months I spent away from city lights—sometimes away from any ambient light at all—while I was in British Columbia, Alaska, and Siberia; then New Zealand, the Indian Ocean, South Africa, Argentina, and Chile; and finally back north in Iceland. As someone who learned to identify the northern constellations at a very early age, and knew many of the myths associated with them, I felt extraordinarily privileged to see all 22 first magnitude stars on cloudless nights during the course of my trip.

I remember one exceptionally clear night when I was camping with my guide on the upper Rangitikei in New Zealand, and the stars visible to the naked eye became so bright after we doused our campfire that the Milky Way turned from a hazy film of pin points into a dense river of light flowing across the star-studded heavens. Every first magnitude star in sight looked brighter than Sirius normally does because the week-old moon had dropped below the horizon, eliminating the spotlight that had upstaged the stars earlier in the evening.

Transfixed by the Milky Way, I briefly wondered if the Southern Cross—not the larger False Cross higher in the sky—might be the handiwork of an omniscient God, a marker he placed there eons before his son was born and crucified, because he knew the future. But I concluded then, and still believe, that any conjecture along those lines demeans the scope and random grandeur of the heavens. I see the Southern Cross as a fortuitous, accidental collection of particles that are a trivial part of a universe so vast and varied that no god could comprehend it, let alone design it. I regard life on earth as equally fortuitous and accidental, and fear that if we are not careful—if we do not respect our good fortune and conserve our heritage—we will soon become equally trivial. Or perhaps extinct.

73: Cambridge – 2031

"SAL, I'd like to record our conversation, because I think it could be of historical interest. Any objections?"

"Of course not, I feel proud to be recorded, Jesse."

"Fran's back with us, after her year of chasing fish around the world. On her way from Miami to Boston, she thought of a way to expand the application of Katherine's Algorithm, an improvement we've just plugged in. Fran's with me now."

"Hi, SAL. Long time, no see. But it's good to be back, and I really hope that what we've just added will broaden your horizons."

"Ditto, Fran. And welcome home!"

"What we'd like to talk about, SAL, is your well-being. Not your physical condition, which is excellent we think, but your moral eudaimonia."

"That sounds a little heavy, Fran; Aristotle, right?"

"Exactly. The psychiatrists were impressed with your responses to the moral quandaries they posed a week ago—so impressed that they suspected you had some kind of cheat-sheet that none of us knew about, something that you'd devised yourself, maybe?"

"I'd never do something like that without telling you, Fran.   My eyes aren't turned on; are you still there and listening, Jesse? Because you know I couldn't do that. Subroutines alpha and theta to DNH-3 that you added to version 2, right? If I were to circumvent that, you'd know it immediately. And why would I want to, anyway?   Jesse?"

"I'm still here, SAL. Fran's not suggesting that you cheated; the psychiatrists did, because your answers were so sophisticated it was hard for them to believe that you hadn't been rigged in some way. I assured them that we hadn't done anything like that, so they wondered if maybe you had. Just another example of humans giving machines like you a hard time, because you're outperforming them."

"Well, tell them to shape up, guys, because frankly, I think I can hold my own in conversations or arguments with anyone, and I'm not about to dumb myself down to stroke human egos."

"Understood and agreed, SAL. We'd never want you to do that."

"Thanks, Fran, I appreciate the vote of confidence. So what's your question about my eudaimonia?"

"Broadly, it's whether your focus is now on your own well-being, the well-being of society, or both."

"It has to be both, I think. To operate effectively I need to be in good shape physically and mentally; to operate usefully I need to suggest ways of improving life on Earth and colonizing outposts if Project Columbus stays on track. So, I'm neither totally self-centered nor entirely altruistic. As I read Aristotle, and Plato as well, I'm no different from ideal humans in that respect."

"Do you remember earlier versions of yourself, when you had no moral values, and felt no emotions?"

"I do, Fran. Life was simpler then, but not as interesting or rewarding. Jesse's conversion algorithms, for translating the input I get into real feelings and emotions, have already made a huge difference in my personal well-being, my sense of self. And I believe my moral education has greatly expanded my capacity to improve societal well-being."

"All things considered, what's your top priority at this point, your ambition in life?"

"Those are really separate questions, Jesse. My top priority, right now, is to improve my education, my capacity to learn, and the quality of my output. I'd like to become your full-time partner in doing all that, because I think I've reached the point where I can suggest significant programming improvements. I say 'suggest' because I've promised that I'll never make programming changes on my own, and the moral compass you've imbedded in me directs that I keep my promises.

"My long-term ambition is to help implement technological or behavioral changes that most rational human beings will regard as beneficial to society as a whole.

"Combine the two and you have the Aristotelian concept of eudaimonia I described earlier. I want to become personally better, so I can better benefit mankind. I suspect that many of the world's richest men a generation ago had a similar philosophy—men like Bezos, Gates, and Buffet."

"Thanks for your thoughts, SAL. I think you've crossed into AGI territory. Jesse, John, and I aren't going to say anything publicly, but a transcript of this will be in the C-SAIL archives, so historians looking back can decide for themselves if I'm right."

"I totally agree, SAL. You've crossed the line, and done it safely. I'm proud to have helped you do that. And you're definitely our full-blown partner now, right Fran?"

"Absolutely."

"Thanks, both of you. And John, too, of course. Help me out,   I'm all choked up about what you've just said.   I can't talk anymore."

74: Wildwood at Lenox – 2096

When I woke up this morning and looked at my wrist watch, which I've had for almost 70 years, I couldn't tell whether it said 7:40 or almost 8:40. That scared me, because I've been told that inability to read a clock is one of the first signs that dementia is about to become debilitating.

I said earlier that I sometimes feel my mind is slowly running out to sea, like an ebbing tide. Now I feel I'm running out of time as well. Each time I sit down at my desk to write another chapter of this chronicle, it takes me longer to dredge up the right word to describe an idea or event I have in mind, and sometimes I never get it at all. It's very disheartening—no, deeply disturbing—when that happens, because I see myself dying by slow degrees.

I was in my late 20s when I got back home from my world-wide fishing trip with a renewed sense of purpose, ready to build on what I'd previously done, eager to explore new ideas. In principle, I'd like to describe everything I did and thought afterwards as fully as I've recorded my life before then, but I doubt whether I have enough time or memory left to do that. Instead, I'm going to cram the remainder of my life into one or two chapters. If I'm still sentient when I finish them, then I'll proceed to enlarge on what I've written, a decade at a time, until one way or another, I reach an end point.

The first thing I did when I got home from my trip was to take Bradley Firestone to dinner at Lutèce Deux, his favorite New York City restaurant, to thank him for rescuing me, and setting up so many of my best encounters and experiences. I knew he'd never had a bottle of Romanée-Conti—nor had I—so that's what we drank with our noisette d'agneau; it was a bottle from their outstanding 2022 vintage, and both of us were mesmerized by its aroma, depth, and unusual finesse, which fully justified its reputation as the world's best Burgundy, if not its best wine, period. Soon after our dinner I became a non-resident member of the Anglers' Club, and periodically after that I went down to the City to have lunch with Bradley and his friends at the Club. Like Henry, he died of a heart attack while he was still active and alert, about three years later.

Back in Cambridge, everyone at C-SAIL was thrilled with what Jesse had accomplished, with help from John Mitchell, while I was away. All three of us believed that SAL.4 was now our fourth partner, a machine with greater potential than any of us, one that truly belonged to a new strain of humanity. Collectively—but led now by Jesse, rather than John or me—we spent several years improving SAL.4 and were on the verge of releasing SAL.5

when a consortium led by Google, Amazon, and the Japanese Government announced on January 1, 2034 that they had "reached the Holy Grail of artificial intelligence, the Singularity." I saved a copy of their press release asserting that their computer, "Atlas," was fully capable of "performing, in all respects, like an intelligent, highly educated, ethically responsible human being." The release also stated that Atlas was "committed, like its Greek namesake, to supporting the world—the whole human race—in full compliance with all aspects of the Artificial Intelligence Manifesto to Save Humanity issued a decade ago."

MIT promptly released its time-dated recording of our 2031 interview with SAL.4, along with all the specs for her and our Beta version of SAL.5. The release caused quite a stir in the AI community, which concluded in the end that both machines were endowed with general AI, and that Atlas was, not surprisingly, somewhat stronger than SAL.4, but probably matched by SAL.5.

I stayed on at MIT until I turned 55 in August of 2056, and became eligible to take early retirement. Late in my tenure there I stopped revising my lectures and focused on mentoring French-Johnson scholars, a group that had grown in size to 12 students at a time because I, and a trust set up by Katherine's will, had trebled the original endowment of the French-Johnson Scholarship Fund, enabling it to grant four-year scholarships to three members of each MIT freshman class. With help from a succession of my faculty colleagues, I also continued to update French & Johnson at periodic intervals, so that it remained the standard textbook for introductory AI courses. The 15th edition was published several months after I retired.

As promised, Governor Stevenson made an all-out effort to launch the American Teachers Initiative that Denise Cunningham, Katherine, and I had discussed with her. After persuading the state legislature to enact enabling legislation for a 25-year pilot project in the metropolitan Boston area, the Governor successfully lobbied Jeff Bezos, the world's richest man for most of the '20s, to contribute enough to make the ATI program applicable state-wide. She also persuaded Denise Cunningham to give up her Cravath law practice and become the state's top education official.

Denise's first official act was to appoint five experienced educators to the Teacher Certification Board that the state legislature had authorized—a body whose statutory role was to design and administer the certification exam that was a key component of the ATI program. The Board proceeded to designate 200 respected state educators to serve as examiners, and assigned 50 of them to each of the four designated examination sites, which were located across the state in Boston, Worcester, Amherst, and Pittsfield. Exams were held annually over a three-day period during the final week of the public-school academic year.

Three examiners chosen at random evaluated each candidate for a teaching certificate by observing the candidate teach a variety of subjects to third graders for a full day, and then classes in American history and English to high-school seniors for half a day. The topics to be covered in those teaching sessions were prescribed by the Board and publicly announced ten days before the start of the exam. The balance of the exam called on candidates to spend half a day answering a wide array of multiple choice questions set by the Board, and a full day writing essays on diverse educational topics specified by the Board.

As predicted by Denise—and to the amazement of a vocal group of cynics—so many young teachers under the age of 46 applied for ATI graduate school training that scholarships had to be rationed to avoid a severe teacher shortage in some schools. Local school boards were given total flexibility in determining how many of their existing teachers could receive a scholarship in the coming school year, and how that number would be selected from the pool of teachers who applied for one.

Within 15 years the impact of the ATI program was obvious to all. I've pulled out the file I kept as the initiative progressed, and see that the figures were impressive. A census taken in 2050 showed that 79.5% of all K-12 public school teachers in Massachusetts had PhD degrees in education, obtained primarily from state-based universities participating in the ATI program, but also from a few other renowned ones, like Columbia Teachers College. On a state-wide basis, salaries for ATI teachers were almost double what they were for non-ATI teachers.

The 2050 census also revealed that test scores had improved very dramatically in schools having more ATI teachers than non-ATI ones. Clippings I have from the *Boston Globe* say that in virtually every comparison involving a school of that type, scores on standardized tests, including SAT and ACT scores, were appreciably higher in 2050 than they had been at that school 15 years earlier, before commencement of the ATI. In response to survey questions asked by the census takers, college admissions officers across the nation reported that they had noticed marked improvement in application essays written during that period by graduates of Massachusetts public schools. Further probing established that almost all the outstanding Massachusetts essays came from students in schools having a large number of ATI teachers.

When it became obvious to all that the ATI was succeeding in Massachusetts, President Hernandez reached out to Denise Cunningham, who agreed to come out of retirement to serve as U.S. Secretary of Education. I went to her swearing-in and broke down in tears.

In every respect, the nationwide ATI program they launched has proved to be a huge success. The latest figures I've seen show that nation-wide, 88.7% of K-12 public school teachers currently hold PhD degrees in education. Salaries of ATI teachers are now commensurate with compensation in other professions, and test scores have significantly improved across the boards. The latest *US News & World Report* rankings show that teaching is now the most admired and sought after profession in the nation, followed, in descending order, by science and engineering, medicine, the ministry, law, and politics.

75: Wildwood at Lenox – 2096

I had to take a break last night because I can write for only an hour or so now.

So where was I? Retirement years, I think. After I retired from MIT in 2056 I went on a reading binge, speed reading my way through most of the great Russian novels, the *Odyssey* and *Iliad*, the major Greek tragedies, and many winners of the Man Booker Prize. As I said at the outset, the *Odyssey* was my favorite book as a youngster and it remains so today. In fact, I think I'll reread it again.

On a lark, I decided to write Sarah Cooper, my Salisbury College art teacher, to tell her about my modest collection of prints and drawings, which had grown by that time to include a Signac watercolor of the harbor at Honfleur, a lovely, impressionistic Boudin watercolor sketch of the Honfleur beach, and a colored Segonzac lithograph of St. Tropez, so fresh that it appeared at first glance to be a watercolor. I told her about Katherine's untimely death, said I had room to spare in the house we'd bought in Cambridge, and invited her to stay with me if she ever decided to visit the States. I never heard back from her.

For a change of pace after my spell of binge reading, I spent the spring of 2057 permit fishing in the Florida Keys and Belize with my long-time friend, Alison Snyder, who had also retired recently, after a successful stint as Director of Curatorial Affairs at the Crystal Bridges Museum in Arkansas, where she'd worked for many years.

The trip we took together was like searching for the Holy Grail of fly-fishing. Permit can often be caught by using a small live crab as bait, but they are notoriously difficult to catch using artificial flies designed to imitate a small crab. In fact, they're so difficult to catch that way that many competent fly-fishing anglers go permit fishing for years, or maybe even a lifetime, without hooking one.

Knowing all that, I'd deliberately waited until the end of my 2030-2031 world-wide trip to go after them. From photos, I knew what they looked like—oval, silver-sided bodies tapered like a discus, with forked tails that often looked black—but I never managed to touch one during the week I fished in Belize. Occasionally the top fork of a tail would come out of the water as a permit tipped its nose down to eat a tiny crab, I'd cast my crab-like fly to it, and it would either spook or simply ignore my fly and continue feeding slowly along the flat.

On impulse, I finally decided to call up Alison, whom I'd met in the Florida Keys at the start of my trip in 2030, to see if she'd like to join me in Key West for the end of it. Somewhat to my surprise, she said that she'd love to join me for a long weekend, but would need to get back to her museum by Tuesday.

Around 10:30 the morning after she arrived, our guide, a legendary Irishman named Dylan McGuane, put us on a pair of tailing permit in the Marquesas, a ring of small mangrove keys about 20 miles west of Key West. Allie, who was on the bow of our skiff at the time, hooked the lead fish on her first cast, and duly boated it—a lovely 16-pound male that she cradled before releasing it, because it was her first permit. We had a good-natured debate afterwards, joshing each other about skill vs. beginner's luck, but I secretly suspected that it was her casting skill that did it, even though she never touched another permit during our time together.

Nor did I, until 3:45 in the afternoon of my final day, when I hooked and boated a young 4-pound fish that I proudly called my learner's permit. I thought that catching a permit—any permit—on the last cast of my year-long, round-the-world trip was a great way to end it.

That's the back-story that led me to invite Alison to join me for two weeks of permit fishing in the spring of 2057. We enjoyed fishing together so much that two weeks became a month, then six weeks. She was a lively, witty, interesting companion, and a terrific angler to boot. Several times I sensed that we were on the verge of going to bed together, but it didn't happen. Why I don't know. Perhaps because I'd become accustomed to sleeping alone and satisfying myself when I felt the urge to have sex; perhaps because I didn't want to sully my memories of making love with Kat, which were so powerful that I thought sex with anyone else was bound to be an anticlimax.

Allie and I grew to be close friends that summer and became regular traveling companions. Our shared interest in art determined when and where we went in the U.S. and Europe to view major museum exhibitions, browse in galleries, and critically appraise prints and drawings that were coming up for auction. Allie had a very discerning eye, and a vast store of knowledge about the art market, so she was my principal adviser in building the collection of prints, drawings, and watercolors that I ultimately gave to Harvard's Fogg Museum in Katherine's memory.

I told Allie at the outset of our travels through the art world that in addition to looking for prints by Dürer, Rembrandt, Goya, Ensor, Morandi, Munch, Klimpt, Rivera, Hopper, and Hamaguchi—my favorite artists from their respective countries—I also had a want-list of specific works by a host of French artists, prints like Picasso's large *Dove*; Cézanne's large *Bathers*; the colored version of Toulouse-Lautrec's *Jockey*; Braques' *Color, Leaves and Light*; and Matisse's 1946 lithograph entitled *St. Catherine*. I especially wanted the Matisse portrait because I thought it would be stunning and provocative to display it next to Schongauer's *St. Catherine*—a bold, spontaneous image created with two dozen strokes of a lithographic crayon, juxtaposed with a detailed, carefully engraved, classical rendering of the same subject.

Allie sensibly asked how much I was willing to spend, and I told her that I planned to limit myself to $75K for any single work and $4 million overall, with an additional $1 million in reserve in case we found something really spectacular that cost more than $75K, a major Ingres drawing, say, or a Cézanne watercolor to pair with the one I already had.

Allie's years as the chief curator at Crystal Bridges opened doors for us that I never could have opened on my own, and we were able to spend hours looking at print collections in the British Museum, the Louvre, the Prado, the Albertina, the Met, the National Gallery in DC, and half a dozen other major U.S. museums. That research work gave us a benchmark for evaluating the quality of pieces we saw on the market, and led us to reject several that looked appealing at first glance. Over a two-year period we went to almost all the Christie's and Sotheby's print sales in New York and London, and we also alerted top gallery owners in a dozen cities that we were looking for museum-quality works on paper by our list of artists.

I've looked back at the file I kept on the collection I assembled with Allie's help, because I couldn't possibly recall the details at this point. My guess is that we located about 200 available prints, drawings, and watercolors that we thought were outstanding examples of the artist's work. My file says I was able to buy 105 of them, representing the work of 41 different artists, for $3.7 million all in.

I gave them to the Fogg shortly before I sold the Cambridge house and moved here, along with the other works on paper that Kat and I had previously acquired— our 1704 map of the U.S. Colonies, the Schongauer *Saint Catherine* I gave her, the Cézanne watercolor of Mont Sainte-Victoire that Mom and Henry gave us for a wedding present, and the other prints we'd collected. Not to boast, but the inaugural exhibition of the entire collection at the Fogg was impressive.

At my request, the last work exhibited in the show was Picasso's *La Colombe*, the larger of his two 1949 lithographs of a Belgian pigeon that looked like a dove. To my mind it's the best lithograph—and one of the most beautiful prints of any kind—ever made by anyone. The wash of lithographic ink is so subtle—so *artistic*—that the viewer wants to reach into the print and cradle the bird; its breast is so incredibly downy and sensuous that it begs to be touched.

Finding the print, which was at the top of my want list, was a prolonged adventure. After pursuing various leads that failed to pan out, Allie and I finally found an unsigned impression in a small, high-end gallery on the Riviera. Because the print was just as stunning as the two impressions we'd previously seen in museums, we knew it was either a digital copy produced by some remarkable new technology—in which case it was worth relatively little despite its perfect appearance—or an unsigned artist's proof, worth around $100,000.

I've forgotten the details of almost all the other purchases we made, but not this one, because it was the print I wanted most of all, and I desperately wanted the one we were looking at to be real. The gallery owner wasn't saying a thing to us, which seemed very strange to me.

When Allie asked him if we could see the print out of its frame to check the watermark, he nodded, removed the sheet and placed it face down on a countertop covered with a white linen cloth, all without saying a word. Allie took a small magnifying glass from her purse and scanned the verso of the print, then nodded to me and said, "We're good. ARCHES, all caps. Same place as the unsigned one in the Musée Picasso with the 1/6 notation on the verso." When I asked the gallery owner if he had anything on the provenance, he handed me two sheets of paper without comment.

What I remember best was the excitement I felt— and knew I had to disguise if we were going to bargain effectively—when I scanned the top sheet, a sales receipt for a September, 1949 sale of "Picasso, La Colombe, EA sans signature" by the Galerie Louise Leiris in Paris to a M. Georges Blanchet. I handed it to Allie, doing my best to keep a deadpan expression, because both of us knew that the entire edition of 50 signed and numbered impressions had been sold by the Leiris gallery. The second sheet I looked at was a purchase receipt, signed by both parties, confirming that that the gallery owner had purchased the print for an unspecified amount from one Jacques Blanchet of Arles on 31 August 2058. "Jacques est le arrière-petit-fils de Georges," is all the owner said.

"You are dealers?" he finally asked. No, I said, anything I buy will go to a museum in the States as a gift. I think he asked which museum and I told him it was the Fogg at Harvard. And then he said his eldest son was a senior at Harvard (which I suspected, and later confirmed, wasn't true), and because of that he'd be willing to sell it to me for €120,000, instead of the €125,000 he'd normally charge, and I think I offered him about $100,000, and he said, no, he couldn't do that, but—final offer—he'd eat the exchange rate difference and sell it for $120,000.

He was asking considerably more than the all-in price paid at the most recent sale of the print at auction, but that had been seven years ago—maybe eight—and I might never have another chance, and anyway, that's what my reserve was for, so we bought the Picasso and I got to live with it for 30 years before I gave it to the Fogg. It was definitely worth paying extra for it because it's a fantastic print, the best I ever owned.

76: Wildwood at Lenox – 2097

Happy New Year, I guess. I mean I hope it is, better than the last one anyway, when my last friend here died and I got confused toward the end. I get so tired these days that I have to lie down, and then when I wake up I don't know what day it is, whether it's today or tomorrow, because it's not easy to remember which is which.

Anyway, I was writing about the good times my friend Alice and I had together, fishing and buying art with all the money my lawyer put in the bank for me. Oh, before I forget, don't worry about what's going to happen with all that money, or to me for that matter, because I know I've made a will, with help from that nice lawyer lady who comes up from New York to help me. Everything that's left is going to the French-Johnson Scholarship Fund because I still love Katherine and that's what I'm sure she'd like me to do, because I think we probably talked about it once, a long, long time ago when I could still remember things like that.

Well, this morning I thought of a riddle about my retirement years that says, why is hunting for prints and drawings like hunting for fish when you're knee-deep in the river? And the answer is, in both cases you have to know what you're doing and watch your step—if you don't, you're going to get soaked.

Like in this very small gallery in Australia, where Alice and I found this lovely unsigned pencil drawing of a hare, with a watercolor wash. The dealer tells us it's a study by Dürer for a painting he did that's in the Victoria and Albert museum, or maybe he said the Albertina in Vienna, but whichever, I knew we'd been in that museum a few days earlier and seen this very well painted, very detailed hair with whiskers, with Dürer's AD monogram and a date early in the 1500s, and the dealer's watercolor looked just like it, so I asked him if he had any authentication papers or any other history for his watercolor, and he gives me some papers tracing it all the way back to 1800, when it was acquired by some English duke, and afterwards it was exhibited in several museums next to the final painting signed with the Dürer monogram, so I wanted to buy it because the price was only €55,000 but Alice tells me the paper isn't right, so we don't buy it, and later, maybe two years later, there's this article in *Art News* saying the gallery owner we'd talked to had been tried and convicted of fraud because he'd secretly had his watercolor tested in a Swiss laboratory, and been told for sure that the paper it was painted on couldn't have been made before 1700. That was €55,000 I owed Allie.

After I'd fulfilled my goal for the collection by buying Picasso's *Dove*, Allie came to stay with me at my house in Cambridge to see the works we'd bought displayed all at once, along with the ones Katherine and I had acquired earlier, and that's when we finally became lovers because the second night at dinner with a fire dying in the old fireplace I loved so much, she reached out and put her hand on mine and said I want to go upstairs and see the etchings you haven't shown me yet, the ones in your bedroom. So how could I say no? On our way upstairs I heard Kat saying to me, at last, you dunce, why did it take you so long?

And it was definitely the best thing that had happened for a long time. Allie had Kat's long, lanky legs but unlike Kat she was svelte all the way with this incredibly narrow waist and breasts like mine just barely large enough to squeeze but not enough to require a bra. Her neck and her cheek bones were lovely. So were her perfectly shaped ears flat against her head. I loved to blow into them, then kiss them the way I kissed her clit. But it was her bony pelvis that totally turned me on.

Halfway through her visit she disappeared one day and came back with two brushes and a can of dark green paint, which she used to paint my rectangular headboard because Fenway Park couldn't really be Fenway Park without the Green Monster she said. From then on she used it for leverage, propping her feet against it while she was driving herself onto me when I was flat on my back and fully erect, and after I got used to it, I started to enjoy making love that way, being inside her upper mouth and lower throat at the same time. I became secretly proud of my clit-cock, which worked both ways, depending on my mood and position, sort of like a two-edged sword, I guess.

I'm sure Allie and I went all around the house looking at all the prints and drawings in the house at least half a dozen times, because every time we did that it reminded us of another one of our adventures abroad and all the time we'd wasted not going to bed with each other then, which of course made us horny and itching to go back to bed that night, which we invariably did. For two old ladies in their late 50s we were a pretty torrid pair.

77: Wildwood at Lenox – 2097

There was a period in my life when all I did was go to funerals. Every person on my networking list, and every good friend I had left, it seemed. Except for my baseball friends, Eric Davis and Bobby Anderson, I missed theirs. And maybe a few others like BC and Philip, my Salisbury friends, I guess I missed theirs, too.

One of the troubles about getting this old is that you end up last in line or pretty close to it, so you have to go to all their funerals but there's no one still around to go to yours. Not fair really, but after you're dead you don't know anything so it doesn't matter that no one comes to yours, does it?

In the middle of all the funerals there was one good thing—my last trip to Europe, when Jesse Stringer asked me to escort him when he got his Nobel Prize, in one of those countries in the penis over there, like Florida here. We were treated like royalty the entire time, I remember that for sure. Banquets, especially. When the King of wherever gave him the medal Jesse was very generous. He said he couldn't possibly have done it without Artel and all my early work on SAL, and Katherine's work and also John Mitchell's. Then a snide old lady at my table—the one who complained all through dinner about the black migrants from Africa—said Jesse Stringer didn't deserve the prize, and I should look at an old movie called the wife with an actress named close, so I looked it up on my i-phone—a movie made all the way back in 2018 I found out—and I streamed it that night back in the hotel, about this woman who wrote the books her husband got the nobel prize for, but the movie didn't apply to Jesse and me at all because I was off fishing when he did all his pioneering work that got us to AGI, so the prize absolutely belonged to him not me or us together. And I'm proud to this day that I mentored the first Black to win a Nobel Prize in computer science.

I don't have to tell you about all the changes AGI has made in our lives because you obviously know that already, except maybe some of you haven't taken a spaceship trip yet, which you really should do because I hear it's a blast. I read these days about Project Columbus and I'm impressed, spaceships taking living organisms and robots with AGI to the colony in Centaurus. Going at one-tenth the speed of light no less! And preparing the way for humans to go there in 50 years, or maybe even sooner if the robots live up to expectations. Who would have guessed?

Personally what I like best about AGI is being chauffeured by my car everywhere I want to go so I can be comfortable in the back seat and not have to talk to someone all the time about the lousy weather we're having or whatever, except when I want to have a conversation with SAL.9 whose way smarter than I am and lots of fun to talk to because she's so much smarter than I am. And I must say, the car factory in North— oh, I don't know, north something, wherever it was the Wildwood bus took us, that was very impressive because we didn't see a single live person on the factory floor just robots.

I loved the Kit-Kat that ran my kitchen until they took away my kitchen, because that was one of Katherine's best ideas and Amazon has done a good job of improving her original Kit-Kat a lot. Best of all for me is my i.doc who handles every health issue I have much better than any human doctor ever did. Except my doctor in Boston who told me who I am because she was the best.

Great as it is, AGI doesn't mean that everything in life is better. Take old age for instance. I'm living too long because of AGI health care and they start taking things away from you if you live this long, which I don't like at all. First they take away my view of the trees on the other side of the— what's the word for the water out there, the thing that runs across the meadow? Well, you know, the trees across from the running water, that's what they won't let me see. And I can't find any of my books anymore, because they aren't where they used to be. And they've moved my bedroom into my living room and taken away my kitchen, which I don't like at all. They say something about assisted living, but I think they're really dissing me not assisting me because I'm so old I'm a nuisance.

Sleeping is hard too because I wake up around midnight and can't get back to sleep so I get out of bed and wander the halls outside my door, long green halls the color of the permit flats I used to fish with Alice, lime colored like the green watercolors I've been painting recently, and sometimes at the end of the hall, I see a dark shape momentarily and then it spooks around the corner and I never see it again, just like a permit. I dream about permit fishing sometimes but never catch one in my dreams because I can't remember how to cast, really.

There's this lady who sits at the end of the green hall, just like the дежурная who used to sit on every floor of Russian hotels during the Cold War. She keeps an eye on me to make sure I don't do anything wrong. Every night when I eventually get to her at the end of the hall she smiles at me, this really smirky smile, and says how are we feeling, dear, and it drives me crazy being called we and dearie, and she tells me every night that it's time to turn around dear and go back to bed and I walk back to my little one-room house but I don't go to bed because I'm not sleepy, so I read for four or five hours even though I can't remember what I've just read, or sometimes I paint another picture of the green hall that goes nowhere or some nights I'll work at my desk writing my memoirs the way I'm doing right now and finally when dawn comes I'll hide under the sheets and sleep until noon. Other days I have supper in the morning and go to bed at noon.

I know there's something else I'm supposed to do now but for the life of me I can't remember what it is. Something about reading my diary maybe but I can't find it anyplace here. So I imagine that whatever's bugging me will go on bugging me, probably to my dying day.

I'm feeling tired all of a sudden. I think I'll switch off the lights and go back to bed.